The Elusive Dietrich

Jared Cade is the Amazon number one bestselling author of *Agatha Christie and the Eleven Missing Days.* He is a former tour guide for a bespoke luxury travel company, escorting parties around Agatha Christie's home, Greenway, which is now open to the public courtesy of the National Trust. During an appearance on the British television quiz *The $64,000 Question,* he won the top prize on his specialist subject of Agatha Christie's novels. Jared Cade is the creator of the Lyle Revel and Hermione Bradbury mysteries. He is also a member of the Crime Writers' Association and the Society of Authors. Readers can connect with him on Facebook. His latest book *Secrets from the Agatha Christie Archives* was longlisted for the ALCS Gold Dagger for Non-Fiction Award.

Also by Jared Cade

Non-Fiction

Agatha Christie and the Eleven Missing Days

Secrets from the Agatha Christie Archives

The Lyle Revel and Hermione Bradbury Mysteries

Murder on London Underground

Murder in Pelham Wood

Deadly Fortune (coming August 2025)

Jared Cade

The Elusive Dietrich

SCARAB BOOKS

Published by Scarab Books

ISBN 978-1-0686729-0-3

Cover Design by GermanCreative

To the memory of Dame Vera Lynn
(1917–2020) and others, before and since,
who have led the way

'Flowers are the bright remembrances of youth; they waft us back, with their bland odorous breath, the joyous hours that only young life knows, 'ere we have learnt this fair earth hides graves.'

Marguerite Gardiner, Countess of
Blessington (1789–1849)

Prologue

Diana stood with the prisoners by the side of the quarry. The sky was wreathed in cobwebs of mist and the cold breath of the February morning seeped into her bones. She shivered uncontrollably and was filled with hatred and revulsion for her captors.

Captain Dietrich, the Gestapo officer in charge of the raid on the chateau, addressed the prisoners. 'You have all underestimated your enemy and resisted the will of the Führer. In a moment you will be given an opportunity to show your remorse.'

Diana was not afraid to die because she knew that without freedom there is no point in living. She was aware the German officers guarding her and the other prisoners would use their sten machine-pistols at the slightest provocation. Any prisoner trying to escape into the woods surrounding the clearing would be cut down within seconds by a hail of bullets.

Captain Dietrich went on, 'Some of you may be wondering why your employers are not here. Theodore and

Odette Mariette were executed last night for colluding with the French Resistance. When I give the command, you will walk in a single line to the edge of the quarry. At two-minute intervals, you will push the prisoner in front of you over the edge. If you disobey, you will be shot dead immediately.'

Diana's throat was swollen with grief. She was going to miss her friends so much. She knew the Mariettes' servants shared her horror and outrage at their murders and the fate that now awaited them. The Mariettes had sheltered Allied soldiers and airmen trapped behind enemy lines and given them forged papers to aid their escape from German-occupied France. Who had betrayed them to the Gestapo?

The horrific events of the previous night were burned indelibly in Diana's memory. After interrogating and killing Theodore and Odette Mariette in the cellar of their chateau, Captain Dietrich had eaten a meal prepared for him by one of his officers. His ice-blue gaze had flickered lasciviously between Diana and the painting of a nude woman on the dining-room wall.

'What's the name of the painting?' he asked.

Diana's heart missed a beat. *'Nu Dans Sa Chambre,'* she replied in a soft, subdued voice.

Captain Dietrich's smile widened. *'My commandant enjoys ransacking the homes of the rich. Some of the stolen artefacts end up in my possession. I'm going to steal the painting because the woman in it reminds me of you.'*

Without pausing for breath, he ordered two of his officers to interrogate Diana. She was taken to an empty room on the second floor of the chateau. For the next hour she denied being a member of the French Resistance or knowing anything about their activities. For some strange reason unknown to her, the two officers were unaware her codename in the Resistance was the Vixen and that she was currently the most wanted female enemy agent in France. They became angry and started arguing with each other.

'We're dealing with a half-witted peasant.'

One of the officers punched Diana in the stomach. The force of the blow sent her sprawling to the floor. The second officer kicked her in the side of the head. Her body was wracked with pain, but her instincts told her the only way to remain alive was to fake being unconscious.

'You've killed her.'

'What if she's only pretending to be dead?'

'It won't do her any good. There's a quarry two miles from here. We're taking her and the others there tomorrow morning.'

Diana was filled with dread. It was apparent the Gestapo were planning to execute her along with the Mariettes' servants.

'I'm hungry.'

'So am I.'

'Which way is the kitchen –?'

The two officers left the room, locking the door behind them, unaware that a radio transmitter and two hand grenades were hidden in a secret cavity beneath the floorboards.

Despite being in terrible pain, Diana removed the two hand grenades from the cavity and concealed them in the folds of her thick skirt. Next, she used the radio transmitter to send an urgent message to a nearby splinter group of the Resistance. Relief surged through her when her comrades radioed back promising to do all they could to help. Diana hoped for everyone's sake they would reach the quarry before morning and avoid capture themselves. After returning the radio transmitter to its hiding place and replacing the floorboards, she lay down on the floor, unable to sleep, her will to live fuelled by hatred.

Now, as Diana stood shivering in the clearing by the side of the quarry, she sensed the Mariettes' servants were exhausted from having spent the night packing up their employers' antiques and heirlooms. Diana had seen the expression on their faces in the back of the truck that had brought them here. They all had a blazing look of fervour in their eyes because they knew that freedom is the only thing worth living for.

The silence in the clearing was deep and profound. The pungent smell of the damp earth and mouldering leaves mingled with the even stronger smell of fear.

'You have been found guilty of treason,' said Captain Dietrich, 'and it is now time for you to die.'

Further along the line, one of the Mariettes' maids fell to the ground in a fit of coughing. Poor Léonie was weakened by pleurisy. It was a miracle she and her unborn child had survived the night. Diana uttered a silent prayer for their souls. She reached behind her back and drew a hand grenade out of a concealed pocket in the folds of her skirt. The other hand grenade in Diana's possession had already passed surreptitiously behind her comrades' backs all the way down the line to the Mariettes' elderly gardener Jacques. The speed of his actions saved her life.

The guards standing by the truck were taken by surprise. The hand grenade Jacques hurled at them landed on the bonnet of the vehicle and exploded with a terrifying, ear-splitting sound that shook the earth. Debris from the explosion shot up into the sky and showered down on them, instantly killing three of the guards. The air was rife with plumes of smoke and the stench of burning rubber.

Simultaneously fourteen members of a splinter group of the French Resistance - alerted by Diana's urgent radio message - burst out of the woods with their tommy guns and opened fire on the Germans in a deafening cacophony of flying shrapnel.

Diana tossed her hand grenade at Captain Dietrich, then turned and ran. It rolled past him along the sloping ground and came to rest under the command car. The force of the explosion ripped open the petrol tank, engulfing the command car in flames and flipping it over onto its side.

Glancing back over her shoulder, Diana saw Captain Dietrich being flung through the air by the blast, his face alive with fury. As she plunged into the woods, her heart was pounding with fear and she prayed for a miracle to deliver her and her comrades from evil.

PART 1

1

Hermione Bradbury was reading a seed catalogue while she waited for the kettle to boil. Above her head she could hear rattling water pipes. These presently fell silent and other sounds ensued – feet thudding on floorboards, the opening of a window and the squeaking of a wardrobe door.

Steam was rising from the spout of the kettle several minutes later when Hermione heard footsteps bounding down the stairs. Her Pre-Raphaelite face softened with a look of pleasurable anticipation and the sunlight streaming through the lead-paned windows brought out the gold tints in her long red hair as Lyle Revel sauntered into the kitchen. Hermione took pride in knowing they were an attractive couple. Lyle was tall and athletic, with a cleft chin, aquiline nose and high cheekbones beneath a sweep of blond hair. His good looks and acting talent had ensured his success in several West End stage plays. It was unusual for him to be late down to breakfast.

'How did you sleep?' she asked in her beguiling cut-glass

English accent.

'Like a dream,' he replied, with a smile that lifted her spirits and made her feel as if she were the only woman in the world.

It was a pleasant summer's day in July 1983. Outside the sunshine warmed the façade of the red-brick, half-timbered Tudor lodge in which they lived by the front gates of Lord Milsham's ancestral property and the perfume of climbing roses drifted in through the open windows. The lodge was called Nettlebed on account of the pine trees that stood nearby – a name Hermione and Lyle not only liked but thought entirely apposite.

The couple had met a year ago at a party to celebrate the West End opening of a revival of Noel Coward's *Private Lives* in which Lyle had played the leading role of Elyot Chase. Hermione had found herself revelling in the intimacy of his twinkling brown eyes and irrepressible smile. Lyle had made all the other men in the room appear like pale ale to his champagne cocktail. The intense attraction they had felt for each other had led to a wonderful night of passion. At the time, Hermione had been residing by herself at Nettlebed. Their decision to live together had received her employer Lord Milsham's blessing and ever since Lyle had helped Hermione run the small estate alongside Mr and Mrs Elliott, the middle-aged caretakers residing in the servants' quarters of Milsham Castle.

During the summer Hermione's and Lyle's privacy went undisturbed for four days of the week; on the other three days tourists came intermittently to see the main house. Milsham Castle was a crenelated Elizabethan manor house which had been in Lord Milsham's family for centuries. It was renowned for its rose and topiary gardens, as well as its rhododendrons which bloomed in a variety of beautiful colours along the driveway leading up to the house.

'Did I remember to tell you I'm going to London this morning?' said Hermione. 'Diana and I are having lunch together.'

'I'm surprised Diana can tear herself away from Arlington,' said Lyle. 'It's truly magnificent.'

Arlington was one of England's most famous stately homes and Hermione's godmother Diana was currently on her second marriage to Gervase Cosgrove, the 10th Duke of Marsden. Hermione shared Lyle's admiration for Arlington and never ceased to be enraptured by its beauty when she went horse riding in its grounds.

Lyle helped himself to a glass of orange juice. 'I've never met anyone like your godmother.'

'I can see you've fallen for Diana's charm,' said Hermione. 'Most people do. Did I tell you Diana's first husband was Sir Hugo Rylander? He saw her picture as a debutante in *Tatler* and fell in love with her soon after they met.'

'His name rings a bell,' said Lyle with a look of surprise. 'Am I right in thinking he manufactured aeroplane parts during the Second World War?'

'Sir Hugo was a wealthy industrialist and philanthropist,' said Hermione. 'Sadly, he died during the Blitz. He was the great love of Diana's life. She was left a very rich widow. Not that she ever cared two hoots about his money.'

'Is it true there was only the one son from the marriage?'

Hermione nodded and said, 'James Rylander took after his father and grew up to become a financial genius in the city. He was still a minor when Sir Hugo died. Diana left their son with relatives in Yorkshire and went to France where she joined the French Resistance. Being Anglo-French, she was determined to help free France from the Nazi's stranglehold. It was only after the war was over that she returned to England and was reunited with her son. James eventually married a banker's daughter. The couple died in a skiing tragedy at Klosters. They left behind two young children in Claudia and Sebastian. Diana raised them almost single-handedly. They couldn't have hoped for a more devoted grandmother.'

'Why did Diana remain a widow for so long?' asked Lyle.

Hermione shrugged. 'Oh, there have been plenty of men who have wanted to marry Diana over the years,' she said. 'She turned them all down until she met Gervase. She's come a long way since she fought as a young woman in the French Resistance. She's now the Duchess of Marsden and chatelaine of Arlington.'

'Diana's life has certainly had its share of ups and downs,' remarked Lyle.

There was a look of empathy in his eyes. He had known Diana for less than six months, but he was completely captivated by her charm and shared Hermione's fascination for her.

'You'd never know Diana once escaped from a Nazi execution squad,' added Hermione. 'She and I are having lunch at the Café Royal. I'm afraid you're going to have a rather dull day compared to me.'

'Not if I can help it,' said Lyle with a determined gleam in his eyes. 'After you went to sleep last night, Oliver Seymour phoned me during the interval at Covent Garden.'

Hermione's interest was piqued. They were friends with the television producer and she was looking forward to seeing the documentary he was making about her godmother's life.

'How is he?'

'Oliver wanted me to know he's got his hands on a murderer's signed confession.'

Hermione was startled. 'You can't be serious.'

Lyle had a penchant for solving crimes and his unexpected disclosure left her feeling a frisson of unease. Soon after she had met him, a member of the Gosford Archery Club had been murdered. The Gosfordshire Constabulary had been baffled until Lyle had identified the culprit in a brilliant display of deductive reasoning.

'How on earth has Oliver got hold of a murderer's signed confession?'

'I haven't the slightest idea,' said Lyle. 'It's an extraordinary piece of luck, isn't it?'

Hermione frowned. 'You must have some idea. I wonder if this has anything to do with the documentary he's making about Diana's life?'

Lyle shrugged. 'Oliver was in a rush when he spoke to me. He plans to tell me the full story later this morning.'

'Perhaps he did you a favour by not satisfying your curiosity,' said Hermione slowly. 'Has he given any thought to his personal safety?'

'Oliver is no fool,' Lyle reassured her. 'He knows how to take care of himself.'

'Surely Oliver must have told you more than that,' insisted Hermione.

'All I know for certain is that Oliver has got hold of a murderer's signed confession,' said Lyle gravely. 'I'm as curious as you to find out what's going on...'

2

Oliver Seymour lived in a small red-brick Queen Anne house at Richmond-upon-Thames. It was a warm Saturday morning, not yet gone half past eleven, when Lyle Revel arrived in his silver convertible, Lady Godiva, and cast an admiring gaze over his friend's beautiful rose and topiary garden.

Alerted by the sound of Lyle's arrival, Oliver came outside and greeted him with a smile. Oliver was as lean as a greyhound, with handsome features, brown hair and twinkling eyes. Despite being in his late fifties, he appeared to have inherited a young gene and kept himself in shape by going jogging every day as well as playing squash on a regular basis.

Oliver's passion in life was movies and his garden. Men liked his air of easy camaraderie while women of all ages enjoyed his charming and gracious personality. There was an air of eternal boyishness about him. The reason he and Lyle were such good friends – despite an age gap of at least thirty years – was due to their inquisitive minds which kept them both young in spirit and contributed to their zest for living.

Lyle was taken to the study where his host poured them both a generous scotch.

'Life seems improbably sweet at the moment,' said Oliver, above the tinkle of ice-cubs. 'Valiant Productions is doing very well for itself. Two rival networks are interested in screening the documentary about Diana's life. What's more, *Faces and Places* is growing in popularity.'

'Hermione and I are delighted you're on to a winner after all these years,' said Lyle. 'We watch *Faces and Places* whenever we can.'

Faces and Places celebrated the eccentricity of the British people taking afternoon tea and was shown each weekday just before the early evening news. Each ten-minute episode featured a guest talking about the minutiae of his or her normal everyday life. The show was about real people and had a policy of shunning celebrities hoping to plug their latest film or book.

Oliver gave a self-satisfied smile. 'My current success makes up for all the years of hard slog,' he said, with heartfelt sincerity. 'I'm lucky to have Diana's granddaughter working for me. I couldn't hope for a more loyal employee. *Faces and Places* is Claudia's brainchild. But I've never known anyone to be so guarded about their private life. Claudia once told me she prefers horses to men. Has some fellow hurt her in the past?'

Lyle nodded. 'Hermione thinks it will take some time before the wounds heal.'

Oliver's expression brightened. 'I must be making progress. Claudia recently drove me down to Arlington to film several scenes for her grandmother's documentary. I was blown away by its amazing beauty. Claudia even offered to collect the keys from the south lodge and introduce me to the occupants.'

Lyle frowned. 'Why was it locked up?'

'The lodge keeper goes away on holiday each June,' said Oliver with a chortle. 'I felt a complete idiot when Claudia told me I was admiring the mausoleum. She couldn't stop laughing at my gaffe.'

'Oliver, you old dog, are you attracted to Claudia?'

'There's no denying she's a beautiful girl,' said Oliver lightly. 'But she's out of my league.'

'You're being too hard on yourself,' insisted Lyle. 'Oliver, you were awfully mysterious when you rang me last night. What's this talk about you having found a murderer's signed confession of all things?'

'It's a tragic business.' Oliver's mood sobered. 'At the time of the episode I'm going to tell you about, Diana was living in German-occupied France. Along with other members of the French Resistance, she was involved in the bombing of the Hotel de Louvre. Several of Hitler's highest-ranking officers were killed or badly injured. Diana was lucky to have loyal friends in Theodore and Odette Mariette who hid her from the Nazis at their chateau on the outskirts of L'Evette.'

'What exactly happened?'

Oliver's voice resonated with anger. 'During a raid on the chateau, the Gestapo tied the Mariettes to chairs in the cellar. They were forced to watch each other being interrogated and tortured before the leader of the Gestapo, a certain Captain Dietrich, killed them –'

'Oh, my God...'

'They endured the horror of having their throats slit and watching each other die. The Gestapo took Diana and the couple's servants to a nearby quarry to execute them the following morning.'

'Oliver, this story gets more nauseating by the minute...'

Oliver drained his scotch. 'A splinter group of the French Resistance ambushed the execution squad,' he said. 'There were heavy casualties on both sides. The remaining Gestapo members fled for their lives. Diana and the Mariettes' valet Marcel Depardieu were lucky to survive the massacre.'

'Thank God for small mercies, Oliver.'

'Diana's courage was nothing short of exemplary.' Oliver spoke with a mixture of pride and affection. 'Earlier this week I received a letter from Theodore and Odette Mariettes' son. Armand was twelve years old when his parents were murdered. He avoided being caught up in the raid because he was away spending the weekend with relatives.'

'I would hate to have lost my parents at that age,' said Lyle with a shudder. 'Was he able to tell you much?'

'A great deal as it turns out. Armand is now curator of L'Evette Museum which is based in a wing of his parents' chateau. The raid took place on 5 February 1944. Later that night, Captain Dietrich wrote a draft report that was addressed to his commandant. It was left behind at the chateau for reasons that aren't clear and for many years has formed part of the museum's collection. Captain Dietrich's draft report describes how he killed the Mariettes and ordered his men to loot the chateau. He also boasts of his plans to execute their servants the following morning. Armand sent me a copy of the draft report a few days ago.'

'I'd like to see it,' said Lyle quickly.

'It's sitting on my desk at Valiant Productions,' said Oliver with a twinge of regret in his voice. 'I forgot to bring it home. The draft report is handwritten in German, but Armand also sent me a transcript of it in English, along with a cover letter providing the background details to the case. I don't mind admitting, Lyle, I was shocked to find myself reading a murderer's signed confession.'

'Do you know if Captain Dietrich is still alive?' asked Lyle.

Oliver paused for a moment while he refilled his glass with scotch. 'Captain Dietrich is a wanted Nazi war fugitive. The authorities have amassed quite a dossier on him. His cruelty and violence are beyond belief.'

'What do you suppose happened to him?'

'Captain Dietrich disappeared after the massacre by the side of the quarry,' replied Oliver. 'No one knows why the Gestapo didn't return to the chateau and finish looting it.'

'Perhaps they were too badly injured,' suggested Lyle. 'Or they could have feared further reprisal from the French Resistance.'

'It's a well-documented fact,' said Oliver, 'that after the Second World War a lot of Nazis used fake passports and fled to Egypt and Argentina. Others were caught and indicted, but there's no record of his capture.'

Lyle was watching his friend closely. 'Oliver, do you have any theories on what happened to Captain Dietrich?'

Oliver shrugged. 'Captain Dietrich disappeared decades ago. The authorities suspect he fled to Argentina. In light of what he did to Diana and her friends it's only right he should be found and punished for his crimes.'

'After you blackmail him for every penny he owns and publicly expose him in your latest television documentary,' said Lyle with a flash of humour. 'I know what you're like, Oliver!'

Oliver grinned suddenly. 'The kudos for bringing him to justice would be enormous! Captain Dietrich has an extremely elegant signature. I'd recognise it again even if he were using a different name.'

A thought suddenly occurred to Lyle. 'Oliver, you don't *know* where Captain Dietrich is, do you?'

He wondered if it was his imagination or did Oliver hesitate before he answered?

'A lot of people would like to know the answer to that question – including myself.'

Lyle recalled the brilliant research that had gone into Oliver's television documentaries and felt a sudden sense of misgiving.

'A man with a past like Captain Dietrich won't want his new identity or current way of life exposed,' he said. 'He might even be prepared to kill to keep his past a secret. Oliver, I don't want you to risk your life in pursuit of a noble ideal. If you know something *tell me now...*'

Oliver was silent for a moment. 'I can't help remembering something Diana said during my visit to Arlington,' he said slowly. '"Peace in our time is taken for granted, but for others who have suffered and still remember *justice is equally important.*"'

Lyle felt a tremor of unease. 'Oliver, if your intention is to find Captain Dietrich, I wish you all the luck in the world. I really do.'

There was another silence, then Oliver raised his glass in a toast and said, 'Here's to the elusive Captain Dietrich.

For the sake of Diana's fallen comrades, I'd like to see him go to prison for the rest of his life so he can never hurt anyone else ever again...'

3

Over lunch in the gold and red opulence of the Grill Room at the Café Royal in London, Hermione Bradbury gazed fondly at her godmother. The splendour of their surroundings seemed entirely appropriate for Diana whose love of haute couture was exceeded only by her glamour.

An aureole of brunette curls surrounded Diana's heart-shaped face with its soft rose-leaf complexion and clear green eyes. She was looking extremely elegant in a black Chanel suit, with pearl stud earrings and a triple-tier of pearls around her neck. People were often astonished when they met Diana. She had been described as lovely in her youth, but loveliness is not something anyone expects to see in a woman of her advanced years.

'You're looking at a proud grandmother,' said Diana in her soft, melodious voice. 'Sebastian's wedding to Gabriella is taking place in three months' time.'

'You must be relieved at how well Sebastian has turned his life around,' said Hermione. 'I never thought the day would come when he would want to settle down and start a family.'

'I still shudder when I think how Sebastian's race car almost became his funeral pyre,' said Diana. 'If given half a chance he would have returned to the Formula One car racing circuit. As his grandmother, I wasn't about to let that happen. I was right to cut off his allowance.'

Hermione said with a faint catch in her voice, 'I don't recall him thanking you at the time, Diana.'

'Falling in love with Gabriella has changed Sebastian's life for the better,' said Diana contentedly. 'He's no longer the bitter, angry grandson he once was. I've made it clear to him – *and* his sister Claudia, for that matter – that I'll only reinstate them both in my will after they're married and have started families of their own.' She added with a hard edge to her voice, 'I warned Claudia against going off to America and chasing after that married fellow. No good will come of it I told her. Luckily, she came to her senses and returned to England earlier this year.'

Hermione decided it would be prudent to change the subject. 'What's this I hear about you taking part in a television documentary about your life?'

Diana smiled indulgently. 'Sebastian introduced me to Oliver Seymour at a charity function – oh, it must have been two months ago now. I wasn't altogether surprised when Oliver phoned me a few days later. As CEO of Valiant Productions, he persuaded me the time is right to talk about my experiences in the French Resistance.'

Hermione was puzzled by Diana's attitude. 'You've turned down offers in the past. What was so different this time?'

Diana replied with a lilt of laughter in her voice, 'I told

myself that *anyone* who could persuade Sebastian and Claudia to work together in adult harmony, as Oliver has done, has got to be a special person.'

'It must be a relief knowing Sebastian and Claudia have outgrown their childhood bickering,' remarked Hermione.

'I'm as baffled as everyone else to know *how* they ended up working together at Valiant Productions,' said Diana. 'Sebastian is lazy and gets by on flashes of inspiration. Claudia, on the other hand, is a lot more like me. She's conscientious and hard-working.'

A few minutes later, a waiter showed an attractive woman to a nearby table. Angelique de Breteuil was around the same age as Diana and wore her fair hair in a chignon. She was the only woman Hermione knew who came close to matching Diana's elegance. Angelique was also something of an enigma and Hermione was intrigued by her a great deal. She had an interior decorating business in Mayfair and her long list of clients read like a *Who's Who* of British upper-class society. Her husband Jean-Luc ran a successful practice in Harley Street.

'Diana, it's lovely to see you,' exclaimed Angelique in a creamy, languid voice.

'Angelique, this is a surprise,' said Diana with a charming smile. 'Are you lunching alone?'

'No, I'm expecting Jean-Luc. It won't be long now before Gabriella marries Sebastian.'

'You're lucky to have such a delightful goddaughter.'

Angelique smiled contentedly. 'Everyone says that about Gabriella. I'd like to get together with you sometime soon and plan the details of the wedding.'

'That won't be possible,' said Diana. 'I'm organizing the wedding myself along with Gabriella's father. Frederick has really been extremely helpful. However, there is something you can do for me, Angelique.'

'What's that –?'

'In light of the rumours concerning your affair with my husband, *I want you to stay away from Gervase.*'

Angelique was quick to reassure her. 'Diana, there's absolutely *no* truth in the rumours. Jean-Luc and I have been happily married for years. We're absolutely devoted to each other.'

Angelique broke off and smiled adoringly at her husband who had just entered the restaurant and was making his way towards them.

Jean-Luc de Breteuil was a short, dapper man of sixty, some ten years or so younger than his wife, and somewhat pompous of manner, with grey hair that was combed back from a noble-looking brow. He greeted his wife with a kiss on both cheeks and then turned to Diana.

'Diana, what a delightful surprise.' Despite his French lineage Jean-Luc spoke impeccable English. 'The last time we saw each other was in the Royal Enclosure at Ascot.'

'It was a fun day, wasn't it?' said Diana. 'I'd love to stay and chat, Jean-Luc, but I've promised to take Hermione shopping –'

Hermione admired Diana's poise as they left the restaurant together. When Diana had married the Duke of Marsden two years ago unkind rumour had suggested he was only interested in her money because he needed it to maintain Arlington. It now saddened Hermione to think there might be some basis of truth in the rumour.

'Diana, how long has Gervase's affair been going on?'

Diana's tone hardened. 'Gervase and Angelique have

been friends for years. Long before he married me, in fact.'

'Have you confronted Gervase?'

'No, not yet...' There was a troubled look in Diana's eyes. 'I'm genuinely looking forward to Sebastian's and Gabriella's wedding. But I do wish Gabriella *wasn't* Angelique's goddaughter. It makes everything so much more complicated...'

4

On Monday 1 August Hermione woke at Nettlebed to find the grounds of Milsham Castle scattered with debris from the previous night's storm. Rhododendron blooms lay discarded like red and white blood corpuscles along the driveway. The sun shone from a blue sky and another warm summer's day was imminent. She sipped an aromatic cup of coffee and gazed out of the kitchen window as the familiar voice of the local newsreader came over the radio:

'The Duke of Marsden's herd of deer have escaped from Arlington. A branch from an oak tree on his property came down during last night's gale and knocked a hole in the boundary wall. Fifty deer are currently roaming the Gosfordshire countryside and police are appealing to motorists to take extra care...'

'I've never seen the garden looking so beautiful,' remarked Hermione on Lyle's return from his early morning jog. 'You'd think the opposite would be true after a storm.'

'You're far more beautiful and ravishing,' said Lyle, standing behind her and nuzzling her neck. 'The *Evening Standard* critic was saying last night that you remind him of Rossetti's *La Ghirlandata* and play the cello like an angel. You must be feeling ecstatic after the brilliant performance you gave.'

Hermione smiled contentedly. 'It's going to take a while to come back down to earth. I feel as if I'm walking on sunshine...'

She was glad her rehearsals had paid off with the Gosfordshire Symphony Orchestra and her performance at the Proms the previous night had been a thundering success. The Elgar Concerto, with its serious beauty and hints of autumn, along with its frequent changes of mood and tempo, had posed formidable interpretative problems, and she had felt distinctly nervous as she stepped out on stage with her fellow musicians. Her technical anxieties had evaporated as soon as she started playing the cello. She had looked a picture of self-possession during the twenty-nine-minute course. There had been no return of the repetitive strain injury that had kept her away from the music profession for the last six months, and her bottled-up emotions had erupted in a histrionic performance that had brought the audience at the Royal Albert Hall to their feet in a ten-minute standing ovation. Hermione's happiness was more complete for knowing that Lyle had witnessed her triumph, along with her godmother Diana and the latter's husband Gervase.

Lyle glanced at his watch. 'I've got a busy day ahead of me,' he said. 'I'm narrating the documentary I told you about for Creative Television. And Oliver is anxious to have lunch with me.'

'What on earth for?' asked Hermione.

Lyle frowned. 'I don't know. He phoned me earlier this morning. He was in a rush to go to a meeting. I got the distinct impression he was excited about something.'

'It's been two weeks since you saw him,' said Hermione. 'A lot can happen in that time. Perhaps he's found Captain Dietrich.'

'On the whole, it doesn't seem likely,' said Lyle with a twinkle in his eyes.

'That sort of knowledge could get him killed,' warned Hermione.

'Oliver is no fool,' Lyle reassured her. 'He can look after himself better than most people I know...'

In the London-based offices of Valiant Productions, Oliver Seymour was speaking on the phone to the curator of L'Evette War Museum in France. There could be no mistaking the emotion in Armand Mariette's deep, guttural voice.

'Oliver, why are you interested in Captain Dietrich? Is it – would this be because you know his current whereabouts?'

Oliver drew a deep breath. 'Yes, I do. Against all the odds, I've found him, Armand.'

'I'm prepared to help you bring him to justice in any way I can,' vowed Armand.

'The only photo I have of Captain Dietrich is slightly out of focus,' said Oliver. 'Do you have a clearer image of him?'

'You're in luck as it happens.' Armand's voice momentarily faltered. The memory of how the Gestapo officer had brutally murdered his parents would be with him for the rest of his life. 'Since I last spoke to you, I've got hold of a head and shoulders shot of Captain Dietrich in full Gestapo uniform. It was published some time ago in a book on wanted Nazi fugitives.'

Oliver nodded in satisfaction. 'That sounds perfect.'

'I'll send it to you straightaway. Captain Dietrich was a barbaric monster. He's escaped justice for too long.'

'I couldn't agree with you more. Trust me, Armand, the draft report Captain Dietrich signed is going to convict him of your parents' murders and ensure he spends the rest of his life in prison...'

Oliver terminated the call and thought excitedly, *It was only a fortnight ago that I boasted to Lyle that I'd like to locate Captain Dietrich. Thanks to the most colossal piece of luck I've found him living incognito as a member of British high society. Now all I've got to do is confront him and then –*

Later that morning, Lyle Revel arrived at Creative Television in London. The studio was situated in Leyton Street in Covent Garden and was owned by Buzz Malone, a big bear of a man, who had hired him to narrate a two-part documentary on the life of Shakespeare.

After an enjoyable exchange of show-biz gossip, work got under way in the recording studio. It was slow going because the script Buzz Malone had commissioned was too long and required cutting in several places. Lyle also spotted a couple of factual errors which resulted in further delays and rewrites. It was three o'clock before he looked at his watch and realized how late it was. He found a phone and rang his friend at Valiant Productions.

'Oliver, I'm really sorry. I forgot I was meeting you for lunch –'

'Don't let it bother you,' said Oliver generously. 'What I was planning to tell you can wait.'

Lyle was puzzled by the excited undertone in his friend's voice. 'What is it?'

'I've discovered the answer to one of life's most enduring mysteries.'

'Oliver, are we talking about your quest to find Captain Dietrich?'

Oliver laughed. 'I'm deliriously happy and I don't give a damn who knows it.'

'Have you fallen in love after all these years?'

'You can mock me now, Lyle, but one day soon I'll announce I've found Captain Dietrich and make the entire world sit up and gasp in admiration.'

'I'm sure you will.'

'I'm about to do something completely reckless and irresponsible,' added Oliver and laughed again. 'Something I should have done before now – if I'd only had the courage.'

'Oliver, I haven't got time to speak to you now. We'll catch up soon, I promise.'

As Lyle returned to the recording studio, he wondered if Oliver had fallen in love with Diana's granddaughter. Claudia Rylander was an attractive brunette and had worked alongside Oliver at Valiant Productions for the past six months. It surely can't have escaped Claudia's notice that Oliver was an exceedingly attractive man. She might do a lot worse than fall for him – even if he was her boss...

A moment later a more disturbing thought dropped into Lyle's mind. *I wonder if Oliver has found Captain Dietrich or was he simply pulling my leg...?*

Lyle Revel dismissed the idea as too fanciful. If Oliver had found the wanted Nazi fugitive, he would have told him. He recalled Oliver's euphoric laughter and the word 'fey' slipped into his mind. It was associated with approaching danger...

At Arlington, Diana's marriage had reached breaking point. She was packing her suitcase when Gervase walked into her bedroom.

'Diana, what are you doing?'

'What does it look like, Gervase? I'm leaving you for Oliver Seymour.'

Gervase struggled to keep a grip on his emotions. He was a melancholic-looking man of seventy, with a long nose, heavy-lidded blue eyes and grey hair. Having married her husband in ignorance of his flaws, Diana was now only too well aware that Gervase's gracious manner masked a ruthless ego. His first love was Arlington. He often claimed he had no wish to be treated differently to other people, but the truth of the matter is that he took his title and position in life very seriously and was quick to vent his anger when others opposed his wishes.

'Now, Diana, listen to me – *please*. I don't want to lose you.'

Diana's voice rose. 'You should have considered that before you hired Angelique to redecorate the breakfast-room.'

'Angelique is not my mistress,' protested Gervase.

Diana glared at him. 'The reason she came here this afternoon is because she thought I was going to Market Chadwell. You both thought the coast would be clear.'

Market Chadwell was a village thirty miles away in the neighbouring county of Aldershire. The tapestries Diana had been planning to buy at an auction for Arlington's Long Gallery were now forgotten in the wake of Oliver Seymour's marriage proposal.

'Diana, I would never have hired Angelique to redecorate the breakfast-room if I'd known it would upset you,' said Gervase with an edge of desperation to his voice. 'Whatever has gone wrong between us can be put right. We owe it to ourselves to give our marriage another chance.'

Diana was in no mood to be placated. 'Gervase, I want a divorce. I intend to marry Oliver.'

Anger lanced Gervase's voice. 'You're prepared to heap disgrace and humiliation on us both by going off with that fellow, are you?'

'Our marriage is over,' said Diana coldly. 'You're the only person who's in denial of the fact.'

Over the last two months, Oliver had made her feel so special. He had worked tirelessly on the television documentary about her life. She had admired his professionalism, adored his sense of humour and had pined for his company when he was absent from her side. Despite the fact he was fourteen years younger than her, she had recognised she was deeply attracted to him because he possessed so many wonderful qualities. In addition to being modest and erudite, witty and amusing, he was a fascinating conversationalist and a sympathetic listener. Diana's awareness of her feelings for Oliver had initially filled her with trepidation. She was a married woman, the wife of the 10th Duke of Marsden, no less. But the sad truth of the matter is that Gervase had not been a proper husband to her for some time, preferring instead to concentrate on his duties in the House of Lords when he wasn't running Arlington or spending time with his mistress Angelique de Breteuil. Despite several pangs of guilt, Diana had entered into an affair with Oliver after he had told her how much she meant to him.

An hour ago, Oliver had phoned her and said, *'Diana, I want to marry you. If you're not waiting for me when I get to Arlington I'm going to turn around and drive right out of your life.'*

Glancing out of the window, Diana saw Oliver's white Jaguar pull up outside in the driveway. She hadn't realized how much time had passed since his phone call. Time spent agonising over her decision whether to end her marriage.

'Gervase, I'm fed up with paying the bills for Arlington. This house means more to you than I do.'

Gervase's voice was choked with emotion. 'I can't believe you're serious about going off with Oliver Seymour. He's a second-rate television producer.'

'No one else thinks so,' said Diana coldly.

Picking up her suitcase, she hurried outside. She was dressed in a white Yves St Laurent outfit and a wide brimmed hat, beneath which she was wearing a headscarf and sunglasses. Gervase followed her, desperate to save his marriage. He glanced up momentarily at Arlington's façade and a look of agony marred his features.

Arlington was a baroque palace built from honeyed stone, with a large dome rising majestically above the central wing. It always looked its best, as it did now, in summer when it gleamed golden in the sunlight. The grounds featured a walled kitchen garden, an arboretum and the Cosgrove maze while the surrounding parkland, together with the lake, had been designed by Capability Brown.

Gervase's face was suffused with blood. 'Diana, I won't allow you to humiliate me like this.'

Diana's voice rang out sharply. *'Let go of my arm, Gervase.'*

Gervase reluctantly complied with her request. 'Oliver isn't taking you away from me,' he vowed. 'If he wants a fight, I'll give him one.'

Diana stood in the shadow of Arlington's portico and watched Gervase stride over to Oliver. The men's confrontation took place by the side of the water terrace, an enormous square pool featuring five ornate tinkling fountains that had been constructed adjacent to Arlington's west wing by one of Gervase's predecessors, the 6th Duke of Marsden, in collusion with one of the most famous French landscape designers of the day.

'I'm ordering you to leave, Seymour.'

'I'm not going anywhere until I get what I've come for,' insisted Oliver.

'Diana is my wife.'

'She wants to be with me, Marsden.'

'I'm damned if I'll divorce her,' snarled Gervase. 'You've wasted your time coming here.'

Oliver refused to back down. 'Your herd of deer has deserted you and your wife is about to follow suit.'

By now Gervase was incandescent with rage. He pushed Oliver aside, reached in through the open window of the Jaguar and removed the set of keys from the ignition.

'What are you doing?' demanded Oliver.

Diana watched in dismay as her husband hurled Oliver's car keys into the water terrace. The keys vanished beneath the surface of the water leaving behind a few tell-tale ripples that quickly disappeared.

Gervase glared at him. 'I'm teaching you a lesson in wife-snatching etiquette you won't forget in a hurry. If you're still here in ten minutes' time, *I'll have you put down like one of my injured hounds.'* He stormed back inside the house.

Furious at her husband's attempt to stop them from leaving, Diana said imperiously, 'Oliver, you'll never find your car keys now. We'll take the Daimler. Gervase can't stop us. The keys are in the ignition.'

Diana's Daimler, a 1959 Majestic model, was parked in front of the portico. Hemmings the chauffeur had brought the car around earlier from the garage before she had changed her mind about going to Market Chadwell.

Oliver put Diana's suitcase, along with his briefcase, on the back seat of the Daimler. As they drove away from Arlington, Diana sensed Oliver's euphoria at having started their new life together and urged him to drive carefully. Less than two minutes later, the road in front of them snaked through a dark, sinister belt of trees that formed the south-east tip of Pelham Wood.

'Diana, there's something you ought to know. I've made an amazing discovery. In my briefcase there are some documents in a blue folder that I want you to see.'

There was something oddly infectious about Oliver's excitement. Diana found herself laughing along with him, too.

'What are you talking about?' she asked.

'I know where Captain Dietrich is. He's alive and

masquerading as a member of British high society –'

'You can't be serious! How on earth –?'

Diana's blood ran cold as a stag with a magnificent set of antlers suddenly appeared like an apparition. It bolted across the road in front of the Daimler. Oliver swerved in a frantic bid to avoid the animal. Diana was relieved when the stag reached the far side of the road unscathed and darted off amongst the trees. But the danger was far from over.

'My God, I don't believe it...'

The Daimler was careering wildly down the road. Oliver was pumping his foot repeatedly against the brake pedal. It hit the floor each time.

'What's the matter?' cried Diana.

'Something's wrong with the brakes...'

They were going too fast. There was no way they were going to make it around the bend in the road.

'Look out – there's a car coming towards us...'

Lyle Revel was approaching them in a blur of flashing silver. He had finished narrating the documentary about Shakespeare's life for Creative Television and was driving home in Lady Godiva.

The two cars were seconds away from a head-on collision.

Diana screamed –

There was a sudden screeching of tyres as the Daimler shot off the road, narrowing avoiding Lyle's convertible. With a terrifying sense of inevitability, a large oak tree loomed up in front of Diana and Oliver. Then the sound of crunching metal was succeeded by the incessant blaring of the Daimler's horn...

5

Hermione Bradbury fought down a sense of rising panic as she arrived at the St. Francis Xavier Hospital in Gosford. She had been watching *Faces and Places* on television at Nettlebed when the complacency of her afternoon had been shattered by Lyle's brief phone call telling her about the car accident.

Over the years Hermione had nurtured an image of herself as someone who was dependable and made rational decisions in a crisis, but her nerves had been stretched almost to breaking point during the ten-mile drive to the cathedral town. She rode the lift impatiently to the second floor of the hospital. The doors opened in front of her with a blinging sound. At the far end of the corridor, she saw Lyle pacing up and down in the waiting area.

Hurrying up to him, she said in a breathless rush, 'Thank goodness you're all right!'

The concern and anxiety they were feeling for each other was communicated in their fierce hug.

'There's no need to worry,' said Lyle. 'I'm perfectly

fine.'

'Are you sure?' she whispered, pressing her face against his neck. 'I don't want you saying you're fine if you're not.'

'I'm okay – really.'

Hermione was reassured by his words. 'How's Diana?' she asked swiftly.

'Dr Sutherland says she's well enough to go home,' replied Lyle. 'Your godmother is lucky to have survived the car crash.'

A shudder passed through Hermione. 'It's nothing short of a miracle.'

Lyle's next words filled Hermione with horror and pity. 'Oliver's condition has deteriorated. He's in a coma. The doctors say he's unlikely to survive the next twenty-four hours.'

'Oh, my God...'

Hermione hated thinking of Oliver lying in a coma. She was going to miss his air of boyish charm, his essential niceness and humanity. Tears pricked her eyes, but she fought against them.

'Hermione, there's no easy way to say this. Diana was leaving her husband for Oliver.'

Hermione was stunned. 'But Diana and Oliver have only known each other for a couple of months,' she protested. 'How can you be sure they're lovers?'

'Diana broke down and told me everything in the back of the ambulance,' said Lyle.

A heavy silence hung between them and Hermione could tell Lyle was having the same doubts as her. Could the Oliver Seymour they knew be a different person to the friend they had grown to admire and respect? English by birth, Oliver had been raised by elderly foster parents who were now dead. By his own account he had left school at the age of fourteen and had taken on a variety of unsatisfactory jobs in order to keep his body and soul together. During the Second World War, he had served briefly in the Royal Navy as a wireless operator before being demobbed. Having concluded that only a fool works for someone else, Oliver admitted to gambling his life savings on a couple of real estate ventures some years ago that had reaped moderate dividends and enabled him to set up his own television production company.

Lyle drew a deep breath before he went on. 'Gervase was furious when Oliver arrived in his Jaguar at Arlington. He threw Oliver's car keys into the water terrace to prevent him from leaving with Diana. The pair drove away from Arlington in Diana's Daimler. The brakes failed soon afterwards...'

'How could the brakes have failed?' demanded Hermione.

Lyle's answer hung heavily in the air. 'No one knows...'

Hermione recalled his flair for solving murders and her voice trembled as she said, 'Gervase will find it difficult to keep Arlington if Diana divorces him. Has anyone told Sebastian and Claudia about the car crash?'

'I rang Sebastian at Valiant Productions a short while ago,' said Lyle. 'Why do you suppose he sounded so angry when I told him about his grandmother's affair with Oliver?'

'Diana is a rich woman,' said Hermione. 'Sebastian and Claudia won't ever be happy unless their grandmother reinstates them in her will and leaves all her money to them.' She frowned and added, 'Unless I'm mistaken,

Gervase has a hold over Sebastian.'

'What sort of hold?'

'According to Claudia,' said Hermione, 'Sebastian has made rather a hash of George Lowestoft's finances. In fact, the word embezzlement springs readily to mind.'

Lyle stared at her in surprise. 'I don't like the sound of that!'

'George Lowestoft is a fool when it comes to money,' added Hermione succinctly, 'not to mention Gervase's best friend.'

A blinging sound intruded on their thoughts. Further down the corridor the doors of the lift had opened. Sebastian Rylander stepped outside and glanced around impatiently as he took in his surroundings.

Gazing over Hermione's shoulder, Lyle said urgently, 'Here's Sebastian. You'll have to be quick if you want to speak to Diana before the rest of her family descends on her.'

'Where is she?'

'Praying for Oliver in the chapel. I'll keep Sebastian talking for as long as I can.'

The way to the chapel was well sign-posted and Hermione hurried away.

As Sebastian strode down the length of the corridor towards Lyle, the latter's thoughts returned to his dying friend. Was it possible Oliver had located Captain Dietrich after all these years? In the back of the ambulance on the journey to the hospital the matter had been uppermost in Lyle's mind.

'Diana, what did Oliver talk about after you left Arlington together? By any chance, did he refer to Captain

Dietrich?'

Diana's startled expression had told Lyle at once that his suspicions were justified. *'Oliver insisted Captain Dietrich is still alive and living under a false name as a member of British high society,'* she said.

'Did he tell you under what name?'

Diana wiped the tears from her cheeks. *'The Daimler plunged off the side of the road before Oliver could tell me. Why are you asking me these questions? Do you think it could have some bearing on the car accident?'*

'Captain Dietrich is a dangerous man,' Lyle reminded her. *'If he's still alive he won't have forgotten you witnessed the raid on the Mariettes' chateau.'*

'That was almost forty years ago,' protested Diana.

'Diana, until the police verify the car crash was an accident and not an act of sabotage, I want you to take extra care of yourself...'

The thought chilled Lyle and he wished he had questioned Oliver more closely when he had phoned him earlier that afternoon. How on earth had Oliver discovered Captain Dietrich's new identity and current whereabouts? The sharp rap of approaching footsteps broke the thread of Lyle's thoughts. He looked up as Sebastian Rylander greeted him with an abrupt nod.

'How's my grandmother?' he demanded in a voice tight with emotion.

'You'll be pleased to know Diana is out of the woods,' said Lyle.

Sebastian looked relieved. Beneath his dark cropped hair, his angular face could look either ugly or attractive, depending on the light or the mood he was in. When he was in a good mood his large black eyes gleamed ebulliently. Or if, like now, he was in a bad mood, his eyes were unfathomable. Following his professional car racing crash two years ago, he had made a full recovery from his physical injuries, except for some burn scars on the right side of his face, which, when he was still, gave the illusion of a partially melted waxwork. He had never spoken about his ordeal, and Lyle knew better than to ask him about it. He had always known there was a line one did not cross with Sebastian if one wanted to retain his friendship.

'Was that Hermione I saw just now?' asked Sebastian.

'She's gone to the chapel to pray.'

Sebastian frowned and said brusquely, 'I hope I can rely on you both to persuade Diana to do the sensible thing. She should never have walked out on her marriage to Gervase.'

Lyle wondered if he had done the right thing by telling Sebastian about his grandmother's affair with Oliver. 'Hermione and I both want what's best for Diana.'

'If I'd known Oliver would try to wreck my grandmother's marriage, I wouldn't have spent the last eighteen months working for him,' said Sebastian bluntly. 'How is he?'

Lyle's throat constricted with anger and grief. 'Oliver has lapsed into a life-threatening coma.'

'It serves him right.'

Sebastian's response left Lyle feeling tight-chested with shock. 'Oliver is your boss. I thought you'd be more concerned about him.'

'Wrong,' said Sebastian coldly. 'Claudia and I have Gervase to thank for letting us live at Arlington so my loyalties rest entirely with him. I'm damned if I'll go on looking after Oliver's business affairs after today –'

Sebastian broke off as a blinging sound caught his attention. Claudia Rylander had emerged from the lift and was hurrying down the corridor towards them.

'I didn't realize you felt so strongly in the matter,' murmured Lyle.

He wondered if there was any truth in Hermione's suggestion that Sebastian had been embezzling Gervase's best friend George Lowestoft.

Sebastian had difficulty returning Lyle's gaze. 'Let's just say I owe Gervase a favour – and leave it at that,' he said awkwardly. 'Now run along, Lyle. I want to speak to my sister alone.'

6

Hermione and Lyle were sitting on a pew in the hospital chapel listening to Diana confide her reasons for ending her marriage to Gervase. Her eyes shone with tears and the couple recognized she was going through a form of catharsis.

Hermione had taken it upon herself to warn Diana that her granddaughter Claudia Rylander was in love with Oliver. Claudia had spoken to Hermione on the subject the last time they had gone horse riding together in the grounds of Arlington. The reason Claudia hadn't told Oliver about her feelings for him is because his life revolved around Valiant Productions and it was apparent he saw her as nothing more than a reliable employee. The news of her granddaughter's infatuation with Oliver came as a total shock to Diana and exacerbated her feelings of survivor's guilt.

It seemed to Hermione to be tempting fate to consider what might happen *if* Oliver were to wake from his coma and eventually regain his health. But miracles, she reminded herself, have been known to happen. Diana, being the older woman with more experience of life, would almost certainly give Oliver up and stand aside so as not to cause Claudia any further unhappiness. But would Claudia be mature enough to appreciate her grandmother's sacrifice? Or would she resort to blame, as the young so often do, and refuse to forgive Diana for involving Oliver in the car crash? Whatever happened, Claudia was bound to suffer the most. She would have to reconcile herself to the fact that Oliver had fallen in love with her grandmother instead of her. Oliver and Diana, in turn, would have to live with the knowledge that they had caused more unhappiness and regret to themselves and the people they loved than they had ever intended.

Claudia entered the chapel and walked up the aisle to her grandmother. She was a lovely brunette with long glossy hair. Her grey eyes radiated pride, sensitivity and courage. She had spent the day directing an episode of *Faces and Places* for Valiant Productions and had no doubt been envisaging having dinner with her family at Arlington. Now, owing to the car crash, the depth of her love for Oliver, along with her suffering, was written on her face for everyone to see.

Claudia's soft, velvety voice was ragged with emotion. 'Is it true you were leaving Gervase for Oliver?'

'Yes, it's true...' Diana's eyes filled with fresh tears and each word was agony for her. 'I wish it was me fighting for my life – instead of Oliver... If I'd known how much he means to you, Claudia, I would never have agreed to go away with him.'

The intensity of Claudia's gaze was extraordinary. 'No, I can see that,' she said after a noticeable silence.

She turned and began walking away.

'Where are you going?' asked Diana anxiously.

Claudia swung back around to face her. 'Gervase has arrived,' she said in a voice that was barely above a whisper. 'He's speaking with Dr Sutherland. One of us needs to be with Oliver.'

She hurried outside, ignoring her brother Sebastian who had just entered the chapel and was approaching their grandmother.

'Oliver should never have taken you away from Arlington,' he said.

Diana's expression was a mixture of pain and torment – and some other emotion Hermione couldn't read.

'Why are you telling me this?'

Sebastian spoke firmly. 'Gervase is your husband and I don't want to see you make a mistake.'

Diana's eyes narrowed suspiciously. 'There was a time when you questioned if I ought to marry Gervase.'

Sebastian flushed. 'I didn't know then what I know now,' he said harshly. 'Gervase is a perfectly decent fellow. You should never have left him.' He added almost as an afterthought, 'Why is Claudia looking so upset?'

'Your sister is worried about Oliver,' said Diana. 'She wants to be with him.'

Sebastian's hard, unfathomable expression was devoid of understanding and sympathy.

'You owe it to Gervase to give your marriage another chance,' he reiterated.

There was a long silence.

It had fallen so quiet in the chapel that everyone was startled by the sound of footsteps close at hand. Diana turned and saw her husband Gervase walking towards her. Hermione and Lyle had never seen him looking so contrite and embarrassed.

'Diana, I've spoken to Dr Sutherland. He told me about your car accident. I was horrified when I heard what had happened. I'm sorry we argued. Pride got in the way of reason. I'll always love you, no matter what.'

Hermione and Lyle exchanged glances - uncertain if Gervase was telling the truth.

Diana's gaze softened and she was seized with guilt and confusion. 'Are you saying you forgive me?'

'Please don't walk out on our marriage,' said Gervase. 'I'm asking you - no, I'm *begging* you - please, give me another chance.'

'There's only room for two people in a marriage,' stipulated Diana.

Gervase winced as if a raw nerve had been struck. 'That's how I want it to be from now on,' he said. 'Diana, if you return to Arlington with me, I promise not to remind you of what happened today. Or refer to the matter ever again.'

There was a pause and then Diana said with a tremor in her voice, 'I want you to take me home...'

On the journey back to Arlington, the Duke of Marsden recognised he was a lucky man - far luckier than he deserved to be.

I should never have lost my temper with Diana this afternoon, thought Gervase. *It made her even more determined to go off with Oliver. From now on I'm going to have to be a more attentive husband. I can't risk losing her again.*

Arlington was looking melancholic in the encroaching dusk. It was the great misfortune of Gervase's life that his eldest brother Mortimer and their father had died in quick succession. The death taxes had almost crippled Gervase. He had always liked to believe there was mutual admiration and respect between him and Diana when they married, that she had simply not been after his title although he had certainly been aware that her money would enable him to save his family seat.

The Rolls Royce drew up in the great forecourt and the driver got out and opened the door. Light spilled from the central wing and Bosworth, the elderly and dignified butler, came outside to assist them.

Gervase and Diana passed through the vestibule, across the long corridor that intersected it and stood for a moment in the Great Hall. He was dismayed at how forlorn she looked. There wasn't the slightest flicker of relief or pleasure in her eyes at being back at Arlington. He looked around and saw nothing amiss.

The Great Hall's design was undoubtedly Arlington's crowning masterpiece. Seen from outside during the day, the dome and its gilded lantern created a unique silhouette while from within the dome dwarfed everyone who gazed up at its grandiloquent beauty. Four massive stone columns, etched with carvings, rose from the corners of the hall. High above the first-floor landing and higher still above the four arches that connected the columns was a circular balcony and gallery, replete with eight large windows, topped by the dome's ceiling, which was decorated with a mural by Pellegrini depicting *The Siege of Troy*. The effect was like a baroque cathedral and Gervase shuddered as he recalled how close he had come to losing his ancestral home earlier that day.

Alerted by the sound of their arrival, Gervase's son Rupert emerged from the High Saloon with a book in his hand and stood for a moment on the first-floor landing looking down at his father and stepmother. A U-shaped staircase bordered the outer walls of the Great Hall. Discarding the book on a table, he hurried downstairs and along the corridor towards them.

'Diana, I've been so dreadfully worried about you...'

Rupert's words struck the right notes – kindly and reassuring. Diana's expression softened and she looked relieved to see him.

Rupert was tall and thin, like a quivering popular, and nearly always gave the impression of being in a breathless flurry of activity. His cadaverous face, with its intelligent dark eyes, looked longer than it was on account of his floppy brown hair.

Gervase felt a wave of gratitude and affection. Good old Rupert – he was an affectionate son who could be relied on in an emergency. He was aware Diana not only liked and trusted Rupert, but also regarded her stepson as an ally. Rupert had recently celebrated his fortieth birthday and it was a cause of concern to Gervase that his son had not yet married and produced an heir and spare.

'I'm taking Diana to her room,' said Gervase. 'It's late and she's tired.'

After settling her for the night, he came back downstairs. He was at once intercepted by Bosworth. The butler had been in service with Gervase's family for many years and he trusted Bosworth implicitly.

'Your Grace, there's a phone call on your private line in the study. Mrs de Breteuil is calling from London.'

'Thank you, Bosworth.

Gervase's mouth tightened into a grim line. He went to the study, shut the door firmly behind him and picked up the phone.

'Angelique, you should know better than to call me at a time like this.'

Angelique's voice was low and restrained. 'I'm worried about you, Gervase.'

'I'm perfectly fine,' said Gervase. 'Diana was upset because you visited Arlington this afternoon.'

'How were we supposed to know she would cancel her plans to go to the auction at Market Chadwell?'

'That's not the point,' said Gervase. 'We ought to have been more discreet. I should never have hired your firm to redecorate the breakfast-room.'

'The original firm hired by Diana didn't carry out her wishes properly –'

'I'm afraid Diana doesn't see it quite like that. Your being here only inflamed her suspicions. It made it easier for Oliver Seymour to come and take her away from me. Now he's in a coma in hospital – fighting for his life.'

'What happened?'

'Diana says there was something wrong with the Daimler's brakes. The police have launched an investigation.'

'What do you mean?' asked Angelique sharply.

'Angelique, it's time we stopped seeing each other.'

'Are the past eight years supposed to count for nothing?'

Gervase's voice hardened. 'Diana needs me right now.'

'Diana won't always control the purse strings at Arlington,' Angelique reminded him.

'Now what do you mean by that?'

'She can't live forever. Rich wives die. You said so yourself.'

'Angelique, stop it!' Gervase's voice was tight with anger. '*Our affair has got to end before anyone else gets hurt. Do you hear me?'*

It was well after midnight by the time Hermione and Lyle returned to Nettlebed. They were feeling tired and overwrought.

They had left Claudia Rylander sitting by Oliver's bedside at the St. Francis Xavier Hospital, her face etched with anguish and grief. The time Hermione and Lyle had spent praying for their comatose friend had seemed unbearably long. They hated thinking of Oliver lying in a hospital room, his hair hacked off, tubes going into him all over the place and a machine breathing for him. The doctors had added to their distress by telling them that he was not expected to survive the night.

'What is it you're not telling me?' asked Hermione.

'Before the car accident, Oliver told Diana that he had located Captain Dietrich's whereabouts,' said Lyle in a strained voice. 'He said Captain Dietrich had rebuilt his life and had created a new identity for himself as a member of British high society. He was unable to tell her anything else before the brakes on the Daimler failed.'

'Why didn't you mention this earlier?' demanded

Hermione.

Lyle's anxious gaze locked with hers. 'Because I didn't want you to worry... Oliver holds the key to Captain Dietrich's new identity and whereabouts – and we've no way of getting him to tell us what he knows...'

'Are you sure Oliver didn't leave any clues behind?' asked Hermione.

Lyle shook his head. 'Before the paramedics arrived at the scene of the crash, I transferred Oliver's briefcase from the back seat of the Daimler to the boot of my car for safekeeping. Inside the briefcase there's a blue folder containing Captain Dietrich's draft report confessing to the murders of Theodore and Odette Mariette. But no further clue to his identity.'

'I don't see how Oliver could have found Captain Dietrich after all this time,' said Hermione bewilderedly.

'Nor do I,' said Lyle heavily.

Hermione felt her blood run cold. 'You don't think Captain Dietrich – whoever he is – could have orchestrated the car crash, do you?'

Lyle's eyes shone with dread. 'Hermione, my inner voice is warning me this might not have been an accident. I don't mind admitting I'm afraid of what might happen next...'

7

Beneath the canopy of her George III bed, with its exotic plumes and diamond-shaped pendants, Diana was having breakfast. Several days had passed since the car crash and she had given a lot of thought to Hermione's and Lyle's suggestion that Captain Dietrich was still alive after all these years and had infiltrated British high society. It seemed incredible – inconceivable – that Captain Dietrich had survived the massacre by the side of the quarry. She had a fleeting memory of throwing her hand grenade at the Gestapo officer at the same moment the splinter group of the French Resistance had burst out of the woods. She was convinced he was dead. Two days after her return to Arlington, she had discussed the episode with Hermione and Lyle at considerable length.

'Can you be absolutely certain, Diana, that Captain Dietrich was killed by the force of the explosion?'

Diana's voice faltered as she answered Hermione's question. *'No – not entirely. I was busy fleeing for my life, but I assumed – quite naturally under the circumstances –*

that he died by the side of quarry...'

'Diana, did Captain Dietrich have any distinctive features? An unusual way of speaking or walking? Is there anything you can remember that would help us to identify him if we were to meet him?'

'It's all so long ago, Lyle. His face is a blur in my memory. All I can tell you for certain is that Captain Dietrich was young and totally ruthless and evil. It seems utterly incredible that he could still be alive. Oliver must have been misled by someone with a passing resemblance to Captain Dietrich.'

Now, as Diana finished her breakfast, she was far more concerned about Oliver than the long dead Gestapo officer. According to the doctors at the St. Francis Xavier Hospital, Oliver was still in a coma. They were amazed he had survived this long. In their professional opinion it was only a matter of time before he died.

God is keeping Oliver alive to punish me for being an unfaithful wife, thought Diana. *I don't want him to suffer any more than he has. I wish he was alive and well. I – I can't bear to think of him suffering like this...*

Diana thought of her granddaughter and blamed herself for not realizing sooner that Claudia was in love with Oliver. Claudia and Oliver had worked in close proximity with each other at Valiant Productions for the last six months. It was obvious Claudia was looking for a father figure to replace the one she had lost as a child.

Diana went in search of Claudia. Her room was empty and her bed did not appear to have been slept in. As far as Diana was aware, Claudia had been spending all her time at the hospital by Oliver's side praying for his recovery.

Diana sighed and wished there was *something* she could

do to take away Claudia's heartbreak and suffering...

Poor child – what must she be going through...?

At the St. Francis Xavier Hospital, Hermione and Lyle were standing in the corridor outside Oliver's room, gazing at their critically ill friend through a glass partition in the wall. It was heartbreaking to see him trapped in a coma, suspended in limbo somewhere between life and death. The couple had never known such a feeling of anger and grief, such a feeling of total helplessness. They were worried, too, about Claudia Rylander. She was refusing to leave Oliver's side. She had lost weight and wasn't eating properly. If Claudia was not careful, she was going to become ill. Hermione was aware there had been an unspoken tension emanating from Lyle ever since Claudia had told them the outcome of the police investigation into the car crash.

'Is something the matter?'

'What do you mean?' replied Lyle in a stifled voice.

'You've got that preoccupied look in your eyes,' said Hermione. 'The one you get when your inner voice is telling you something.'

'Diana's and Oliver's car crash was too coincidental for my liking.'

'The police have confirmed the car crash was an accident,' said Hermione. 'The holes in the brake lines were caused by corrosion and rust.'

'Hermione, the police could be *wrong* to assume the brake fluid leaked out of the holes in the brake lines.'

'What are you saying?'

'Someone might have *emptied* the brake fluid reservoir beneath the Daimler's bonnet before the car crash – unaware the brake lines were already leaking brake fluid. We've got to face the fact that *Captain Dietrich might have tried to kill Diana and Oliver.*'

Hermione drew a deep breath. 'I was beginning to relax – to imagine this business with Captain Dietrich was a figment of our imaginations.'

'My mind keeps going back to the day of the car crash,' said Lyle shakily. 'I wish to God I'd persuaded Oliver to tell me everything he knew about Captain Dietrich. You've no idea how *angry* I am with myself for letting that chance slip through my fingers.'

'You mustn't blame yourself.'

'Hermione, if Captain Dietrich has infiltrated British high society, he isn't going to want his new identity and current way of life threatened. Here at the hospital Oliver is surrounded by twenty-four-hour care from the staff. The CCTV cameras record everyone who comes and goes. But Diana doesn't have this sort of protection at Arlington. She might still be in danger…'

Hermione's confident response was not enough to quell the nagging unease in her mind.

'Diana's experience in the French Resistance taught her to never underestimate her enemies,' she said firmly. 'If Captain Dietrich is still alive, he won't find it easy to harm her…'

Later that morning, Diana visited Arlington's private chapel and stood lost in anguished contemplation before the

Burne-Jones stained glass windows. After lighting a candle and praying for Oliver, she decided to send some freshly cut flowers to the St. Francis Xavier Hospital for him along with a food hamper for Claudia.

Diana was crossing the Great Hall when the phone rang. 'Hello, this is Diana speaking,' she said, taking up the receiver.

There was a moment's hesitation, then a breathless voice, almost schoolgirlish in tone, came across the line. 'Oh, hello, Your Grace. I hope I'm not disturbing you – it's Poppy Carter calling.'

It immediately crossed Diana's mind that Poppy had been hoping Gervase's son Rupert would answer the phone. An image came to her of a pixie-faced girl in her late twenties, with large blue eyes and a slightly vacant expression, who was always changing her hair colour. On one occasion Poppy's hair had been a startling fuchsia pink. The time before that it had been an even more unbecoming shade of ginger. More recently she had taken to wearing her hair in a blonde bob. Poppy lived in Brimhurst, the nearest village to Arlington. She gave the impression of being simple, but as Diana knew she could be disconcertingly shrewd at times.

'Poppy, how are you, my dear?' asked Diana fondly.

'Oh, I can't complain,' said Poppy. 'Everyone in the village was so sorry to hear about your car accident. Did you get your bottle of Tagamet capsules okay?'

'Yes, thank you.'

Diana was aware Poppy had two part-time jobs in the village. She worked for her father at the Brimhurst Pharmacy and served behind the bar of the Drunken Admiral which was run by her uncle. Both establishments were situated in Brimhurst's High Street.

'Dad and I were watching television on the evening of the car accident,' said Poppy. 'One of the servants from Arlington knocked us up at home. I made your prescription up straightaway.'

'It was very kind of you, my dear,' said Diana gratefully. 'Dr Sutherland says the capsules should counteract any aches and pains.'

'We all want to see you make a full recovery,' insisted Poppy. 'I'm ringing on behalf of my cousin Bridget to confirm your weekly hairdressing appointment. This coming Monday – two o'clock.'

'Thank you for reminding me.' Diana suspected this was not Poppy's real reason for calling. 'I know I can always rely on Bridget to look after me.'

'I can't remember if she said it was a wash and set or –'

'It's a wash and cut this time,' confirmed Diana. 'I have one every six weeks since my hair is so thick.'

'I'll be sure to let Bridget know,' said Poppy quickly. 'Well, I must go –'

Aware of the forlorn note in the other's voice, Diana said quickly, 'Poppy, I'm aware of how much Rupert likes you. Do you want me to ask him to return your call?'

Gervase hated Poppy and would be furious if he found out his son Rupert was seeing her behind his back. Diana wished there was something she could do to help the couple. After all, it wasn't as if the police had ever charged Poppy with the death of Gervase's older brother Mortimer four years ago.

Poppy replied in a startled voice, 'Oh, I'm sure that won't be necessary, Your Grace,' and quickly rang off.

Diana thought with a sigh, *Gervase is determined Rupert should marry Venetia Campbell-Scott. What sort of man expects his son to marry a rich society heiress?* Despite her love for Gervase, Diana couldn't help feeling worried and depressed. *Did Gervase only marry me for my money?* She recalled the love and tenderness in Gervase's eyes that night at the hospital. *I – I mustn't think like this. Of course, Gervase loves me...*

'It seems strange to be going to Arlington,' said Hermione.

'We could certainly do with cheering up,' said Lyle, adjusting his wing collar and bow tie. 'I was surprised when you told me Diana and Gervase are celebrating their wedding anniversary with a lavish party tonight. The timing seems odd considering all that's happened.'

The couple was in their bedroom at Nettlebed getting dressed for dinner. The last month had taken its toll on their nerves. The strain of juggling their duties around Milsham Castle with their visits to the St. Francis Xavier Hospital had been made easier by Mr and Mrs Elliott, who as joint caretakers of the estate had gone out of their way to help them. Oliver Seymour was still in a coma and unable to breathe without the aid of a ventilator. Although Lyle was not normally superstitious, he couldn't help wondering if his friend's spirit was refusing to die while Captain Dietrich still posed a threat to the living.

'The invitations went out months ago,' said Hermione, clipping on a pair of earrings. 'Diana and Gervase are obviously determined to make a success of their marriage or they wouldn't be going ahead with tonight's celebrations. It won't be long before Diana's grandson Sebastian ties the knot with Gabriella Steen. Their wedding is taking place in a months' time.'

Lyle's eyebrows shot up. 'Is it really that soon?'

Hermione nodded and said, 'It's bound to be the society wedding of the year. The only time Sebastian seems genuinely happy is when he's with Gabriella. She's one of the nicest people I know. He's lucky to have found her. Gabriella absolutely adores her father. Did I tell you Frederick Steen is a Polish Jew? He was interned in a concentration camp during the Second World War. I can't begin to imagine how awful it must have been for him.'

'It sounds horrendous,' said Lyle, running a brush through his blond hair. 'Frederick Steen must count himself lucky to have survived.'

'I'm looking forward to meeting him tonight,' said Hermione. 'According to Gabriella, he's a wonderful raconteur. As a young man, he went to work for the Astex Pharmaceutical Corporation. He ended up marrying the boss's only daughter. Old man Astex left everything to Gabriella's mother. Frederick Steen was widowed some years ago. He's an immensely wealthy man as a result. Gabriella is an only child. He absolutely dotes on her. By the way, did I tell you George and Irene Lowestoft are spending the weekend at Arlington?'

'I feel quite envious of their good fortune.'

Hermione stared at Lyle in surprise. 'It's not like you to be envious of anyone,' she said. 'You're going to enjoy tonight. Everything at Arlington is done on a lavish scale.'

'I don't mind admitting Arlington has cast its spell on me,' conceded Lyle with a smile. 'The Lowestofts won't be happy if they find out Sebastian is embezzling them. What can you tell me about them?'

Hermione sprayed some perfume on her wrists. 'Diana and Irene are distant cousins and dislike each other intensely. It's my belief that as a young naval officer George secretly fancied Diana. When he found out she wasn't available he consoled himself by marrying Irene instead.'

Lyle suppressed the urge to smile. 'I presume Irene wouldn't be too happy if she found out?' he murmured.

'George is a perfectly charming old fuddy duddy,' said Hermione with an indulgent smile. 'He lets Irene walk all over him which isn't a quality Diana admires in a man. She and George would never have been well suited to each other. When you meet Irene tonight don't be fooled by her pretence of feminine helplessness. She's more resilient than a lot of people think. During the Second World War she was a FANY and drove an ambulance in the Blitz. Give Irene a spanner and she can fix any problem beneath the bonnet of a vehicle.'

'It sounds as if she's more than capable of emptying the brake fluid reservoir of Diana's Daimler,' remarked Lyle.

Hermione caught the ironic gleam in his eyes and conceded with a faint smile, 'Personally, I wouldn't trust Irene as far as I could throw her.'

'Are there any children from the Lowestofts' marriage?'

'Irene doesn't need a child – she has George,' said Hermione. 'Ever since Diana married Gervase there's nothing Irene would like more than to be married to a Duke herself.'

Lyle brushed a piece of lint from the sleeve of his tuxedo. 'You've told me why Irene is jealous of Diana,' he said shrewdly. 'Now tell me why Diana is jealous of Irene.'

'Diana isn't jealous of anyone –'

'There must be something that niggles Diana about

Irene. Cousins don't dislike each other for no reason at all.'

'It's odd you're saying that,' said Hermione slowly. 'As Sebastian's grandmother, Diana feels she ought to have first call on his affections. It annoys her that Sebastian gets on so well with George and Irene.'

'Is that why you dislike Sebastian?' asked Lyle.

'Call me old-fashioned if you will,' said Hermione, 'but I have an aversion to embezzlers –'

'So do most people.'

'Irene and George go to church every Sunday. I doubt if Sebastian has ever been to church in his entire life. He wouldn't know the meaning of repentance.'

'We only have Claudia's word for it that her brother is embezzling George,' pointed out Lyle. 'She might be wrong.'

Hermione fell silent. 'Dislike is a strong word,' she said at last. 'Indifference best sums up my attitude towards Sebastian. At least it did until he met Gabriella. I really value her friendship. When I'm in her company I truly find myself believing her love will redeem Sebastian and make him a less selfish person. There's only one person Gabriella loves more than Sebastian and that's her father. It's a foregone conclusion she won't be entirely successful in making Sebastian turn over a new leaf, but I hope he changes sufficiently so the life they share together is devoid of conflict. I've got a theory Sebastian loves Gabriella on account of all the goodness he finds in her which he knows is absent in himself. Gabriella is special. I know I'll never forgive him if he ever hurts her –'

The sound of the ringing phone reached them from the kitchen. Lyle hurried downstairs and took the call while Hermione stayed in their bedroom putting the finishing touches to her make-up. A minute or so later she came downstairs and entered the kitchen as Lyle was hanging up.

'Who was that on the phone?'

'Sebastian – of all people,' replied Lyle with a puzzled expression on his face. 'Diana must have told him I've got Oliver's briefcase. He asked me to bring it to Arlington tonight.'

'Why is Sebastian suddenly interested in Oliver's briefcase?' asked Hermione suspiciously. 'He told you he wasn't prepared to go on working for Oliver in light of his affair with Diana.'

Lyle shrugged. 'I'm as surprised as you, but I couldn't see any reason for refusing Sebastian's request.'

Outside in the driveway, the evening sunlight was bathing Lady Godiva in a warm glow. As they drove away from Nettlebed, Hermione was unable to shake off a sense of misgiving.

'I'm worried about tonight,' she said. 'I don't want anything to go wrong for Diana's sake.'

'Let's hope George Lowestoft doesn't get murdered during the party,' said Lyle lightly. 'We both know *who* the number one suspect would be if *that* happened.'

'Don't say that,' Hermione scolded him. 'The last time we joked about a murder happening it wasn't long afterwards that we found a body.'

8

Hermione and Lyle arrived at Arlington shortly before six-thirty. They were greeted in the Great Hall by Diana's grandson Sebastian Rylander.

'What beautiful lilies!' exclaimed Hermione, gazing at the large bouquet gracing the octagonal table beneath the dome. 'The scent is unusually strong – almost overpowering.'

A mild flicker of disregard appeared in Sebastian's eyes. 'Is that Oliver's briefcase?' he asked, deliberately ignoring her.

Lyle nodded in response to the question and put the briefcase on the table. 'One of the locks is stiff and the lid slides shut unless you hold it open. There's not much inside. Oliver's address book, a copy of *The Times,* several contracts and a blue folder.'

Hermione said suspiciously, 'You told Lyle after the car crash that you were no longer prepared to work for Oliver.'

'I can't just wash my hands of Valiant Productions – as much as I'd like to,' said Sebastian. 'My signature is on a number of contracts. Several clients are expecting me to deliver the goods. I promised my grandmother I'd stick it out for a bit longer – until I'm married at any rate.'

He glanced idly through the pages of the address book, put it back inside the briefcase, picked up the blue folder and examined the documents inside it.

'Who is Armand Mariette and why was he writing to Oliver?' asked Sebastian.

'Armand Mariette is curator of L'Evette War Museum in France,' explained Lyle. 'Oliver was curious about a raid that took place there during the Second World War. You might like to read the correspondence for yourself since it involves Diana. It should only take you a few minutes.'

After complying with Lyle's suggestion, Sebastian remarked in a matter-of-fact voice, 'Captain Dietrich sounds a perfectly despicable fellow. Most of the people involved in the raid are probably dead. I've never heard my grandmother talk about the episode.'

'You're looking at the written confession of a murderer,' said Hermione. 'The draft report is signed with an unmistakable flourish – Captain Helmut Dietrich.'

While the trio were talking, the lid of the briefcase slid shut. Sebastian put the documents back inside the blue folder and dropped it on top of the briefcase.

'What became of Captain Dietrich, do you know?'

'A lot of war criminals are still unaccounted for,' replied Lyle. 'Captain Dietrich is one of them.'

'My hunch is that he's dead along with everyone else involved in the affair,' said Sebastian. 'That's apart from my grandmother, of course. Let's join the others for a drink, shall we?'

Hermione glanced upwards and saw the figure of a bitter-looking old maid, with a dark blotched complexion, standing on the first-floor landing near one of the pillars supporting the dome. Something in the women's stare made Hermione feel uncomfortable, then it occurred to her that she was probably admiring the lilies.

Uncertain if the maid had overheard their conversation, Hermione followed the men from the Great Hall.

The Duke of Marsden was having a drink before dinner in his study with his friend. George Lowestoft was a bluff, hearty fellow, with an underlying sense of his own inferiority, who cherished the mistaken belief that he had married above him when, in fact, the exact opposite was true. At that moment the retired naval commander was listening to the lamentations of his host.

'Diana has so many splendid characteristics,' Gervase was saying. 'She's beautiful, charismatic, warm and loving – and generous to a fault... Yet she's also easily bored and becomes difficult when she doesn't get her own way. I wish I knew where I stood with her. Take Oliver Seymour, for example. How does she feel about him *now?* Is she in love with him or did she use him in a bid to make me jealous? We got on so well together in the early days of our marriage.'

George tended to speak in an overly loud voice. 'You've got to find a way to build on that, Gervase. I'm surprised Diana's head was turned so easily. The fellow's hardly out of the top drawer. The car crash was a nasty business. In my experience brakes don't fail unless they haven't been properly serviced. Accidents are best avoided, eh?'

Although Gervase was surprised at the number of questions George had asked about the car crash, his manner showed no signs of exasperation as he steered his friend away from the subject. 'I wish I knew what to do to make Diana happy again.'

'What does Rupert have to say in the matter?' asked George suddenly.

'My son tells me I'm too much of a fusspot,' replied Gervase. 'Am I being one now?'

'Rupert's a sensible fellow,' said George with conviction. 'You should listen to him more. It's your second wedding anniversary, Gervase. You've got to make tonight special for Diana in every way you can. I know what I'm talking about, old boy, because I've been married to Irene for close on forty years. As you know, we met at a debutante dance before the outbreak of the Second World War –'

Gervase leaned back in his chair and resolved himself to listen patiently to the other's flood of happy reminiscences. George Lowestoft was a faithful old friend – one of the very best. But owing to his garrulous and well-meaning nature he was a poor listener.

'It took me five years to persuade Irene to marry me,' continued George. 'I had a lot of competition on account of her being such a lovely girl.'

'It was undoubtedly your dancing that won Irene over in the end,' declared Gervase loyally.

A smile of gratitude lit up George's face. 'That was also the opinion of Irene's father. He was an agreeable fellow. Only ever met him the once and that was at a ball in London. I'm told he had expensive tastes – jewelled boxes, Chippendale furniture and Spode china – but in the end horses and gambling did for him. He lost the lot, poor devil.

Thurlestone Hall in Yorkshire had been in his family for generations. I never stayed there myself. It was reduced to a shell during the war. Irene's family was lucky to be in Scotland at the time. The Luftwaffe caused a lot of damage with their bombs.'

'Hitler did his best to destroy London, but he didn't succeed,' said Gervase grimly. 'I doubt if my generation will ever forget seeing the dome of St. Paul's Cathedral standing firm as fire and destruction raged all around.'

George stared broodingly into space for a few moments. 'After all these years, I wouldn't be surprised if there were still a number of Nazi war criminals knocking about. The thought is enough to make a man's blood boil. I wouldn't mind bagging one of the beggars myself.' He added gruffly, 'You're lucky to have kept hold of Arlington.'

'As you know, it was requisitioned as a hospital during the war,' said Gervase. 'A bomb flattened one of the outlying farmhouses without loss of life, thank goodness.'

'I wasn't referring to the war, Gervase. I was thinking of more recent times. It was only four years ago that your brother died.'

Gervase frowned and a pained look came into his eyes. 'I try not to remind myself of Mortimer's death and the bungled investigation into it. The police should have arrested Poppy Carter. If I find out Rupert is seeing her against my express wishes –'

George cut him off. 'Rupert wouldn't be that foolish. He's a lot more like you than you realize.'

Gervase pulled himself together with difficulty. 'You know us both so well,' he said, a colourless smile flitting across his face. 'Mortimer's death was followed six months later by my father's. He died of a broken heart. There's no point denying it. Mortimer always was his favourite son. Arlington is a sadder place without them. I rely on my old friends like you, George, to help keep my spirits up.'

George released a sigh. 'You're not the only one with problems, Gervase. I could do with some luck now, couldn't I, old boy?'

'You're teetering on bankruptcy, I'm afraid,' said Gervase gently.

George made a gruff sound like an old dog momentarily roused out of its apathy. 'I made the right decision to sell the town house last year,' he said. 'Irene was tired of London, the traffic, the foreigners, the exorbitant prices. The idea of living in the country appealed to us both. The small manor house we found in Market Chadwell was a bargain –'

'It was still above your means,' said Gervase. 'Unfortunately, you didn't ask Sebastian for his advice at the time. You ought to have settled for a smaller property.'

'Irene had her heart set on it,' said George, with a hangdog air as if this explained everything. 'What do you propose I do? Sell the manor house – find somewhere cheaper?'

'Your debts currently exceed your assets,' said Gervase. 'The best advice I can give you is to ask Diana for help.'

'You seriously think she would come to my rescue?' asked George eagerly.

'Provided you make it clear you've done everything possible to economise.'

'I don't see how I could have done more.' George shook his head in bewilderment. 'Sebastian has done his best to look after my finances. He blames my difficulties on the government. They've nothing better to do than overtax law abiding citizens like myself –'

'By the way, George, it might be better if Diana thought the idea of approaching her was *yours* rather than mine. Now drink up...'

Dinner was served at half past seven in the opulence of the Grand Saloon. The interior was sixty feet long and seventy feet high, with hand-frescoed walls and white marble door cases designed by Grinling Gibbons. Everyone sat in high-backed gilt red-damask chairs around a long dining-table which was adorned with a Venetian tablecloth, Georgian silver and gold candelabra.

Some of Diana's and Gervase's guests were known to Hermione, others were not. Her host and hostess looked the picture of a loving couple. Anyone who did not know of Diana's and Gervase's recent marital problems would have found it impossible to believe they were not happily married. Diana was sipping her favourite drink Cuervo tequila and looking lovely in a gold lamé evening dress.

Diana's stepson Rupert was sitting next to Venetia Campbell-Scott who had a tinny voice and was sniggering at one of her own jokes. Hermione suspected the socialite's invitation had probably been issued by Gervase who was no doubt hoping for a marriage alliance between Rupert and the rich heiress. Rupert was being perfectly charming to her. Venetia Campbell-Scott, for her part, seemed to be enjoying Rupert's company. Perhaps she was envisaging marrying him and becoming the Marchioness of Willoughby.

Diana's grandson Sebastian and his fiancée Gabriella drew the most attention at dinner. The couple seemed totally wrapped up in each other. Although lacking Diana's elegance and charisma, no one could deny that Gabriella was lovely. She had the body of a woman and the face of a girl. She was as slim as a willow reed, with long silky blonde hair, and her mouth, even when it was in repose, formed a sensual pout. There was an air of purity and innocence about Gabriella that made others feel sullied by life and better for having spent time in her company.

Sitting next to Hermione was Gabriella's father Frederick Steen. He was an elderly, distinguished-looking man, with intelligent green eyes and dark grey hair that was going white at the sides. While Hermione was undecided as to whether it was his own hair or a toupée, she had heard it said that his charming personality and impeccable manners meant he was a favoured guest at A-list functions and country house parties.

'The opening of Gabriella's new art gallery in London has been a great success,' Frederick was saying. 'I'm enormously proud of her.'

'Has she always been interested in art?' asked Hermione.

'Ever since I can remember. After Gabriella's mother died, I made a conscious decision not to send her away to boarding school. She lives with me in London. On her school holidays I used to take her abroad two or three times a year. There's hardly an art gallery in America we haven't visited together.'

Hermione's gaze moved on to Lyle. He was conversing with Diana's cousin Irene Lowestoft. Hermione had warned him that Irene was the sort of woman who would create a scene if she didn't feel she was getting enough attention and Lyle was doing his utmost to keep her happy by flirting outrageously with her.

'You and Diana look so alike,' he flattered her. 'I could easily mistake you both for sisters.'

Irene smiled delightedly at him. She was wearing a plum-coloured velvet evening gown that had seen better days, but no amount of make-up or carefully coiffured brown hair could disguise the fact that she was a coarse-looking woman in her late seventies, with the dry skin and the pursed lips of a habitual smoker. She couldn't have provided a harsher contrast to her younger and more elegant cousin.

'Diana is extraordinarily vain about her appearance,' remarked Irene. 'I'm sure her hairdresser puts highlights in her hair although she would never admit it. It's amazing how Diana survived the car crash, isn't it? More recently, she suffered the most awful bout of food poisoning – *or so she says.'*

'You're not suggesting she was play-acting, are you?' asked Lyle.

'Diana does it on *purpose* to get Gervase's attention,' said Irene. 'Now if *I* had a husband as important as Gervase, I'd treat him differently. Gervase married beneath him. Now he's suffering the consequences. He'd be a lot happier if Diana treated him as well as I treat my George.'

Turning to Sebastian, Irene tackled a cause that was close to her heart in a self-consciously loud voice that reached several other guests.

'Sebastian, I *must* have a word with you about George. A few months ago, he agreed it was a good idea for us to go to South Africa this winter. Now he's gone and changed his mind. There isn't anything wrong with our finances, is there?'

'Not at all,' said Sebastian quickly.

Hermione's enjoyment of the meal, along with everyone else's, was soon undermined by Irene Lowestoft who engaged in subversive tactics to get her husband George to change his mind about taking her to South Africa. Her method of attack involved recalling the pleasures of her privileged upbringing at Thurlestone Hall in Yorkshire and taking digs at George's finances.

'We had the most wonderful house parties at Thurlestone Hall before the war. There were thirty indoor servants although the number could triple by the time the guests arrived with their own servants. We had so many footmen they were all called Henry. It seems curiously self-indulgent now, but at the time we had a total of forty-one gardeners. The head gardener and several under-gardeners would decorate the ballroom in swathes of flowers. There's many a wealthy young man who proposed to me in my day, but I've never regretted turning them all down in favour of my poor George. He says there isn't *anything* he wouldn't do for me.'

By the end of dinner, George was looking thoroughly miserable. 'Marrying you was the wisest decision I've ever made, old girl,' he mumbled. 'Since it means so much to you of course we'll go to South Africa for Christmas.'

Irene was clearly delighted. 'The warm weather will do *wonders* for my bronchitis! It's nice to know I won't be relying on my furs this winter.'

Gervase intervened diplomatically. 'The rest of tonight's celebrations will be taking place in the Long Gallery. It won't be long now before the other guests arrive.'

'That's if I remembered to issue the invitations, Father.'

Rupert's frown of comical alarm drew a ripple of

amusement from around the table. As much as Hermione liked Rupert, she wasn't deceived by his apparent vagueness or scattershot remarks which were usually a ploy on his behalf to melt his father's reserve. She was aware Rupert's facetious behaviour sometimes tested Gervase's patience sorely, but the two men had a genuine affection for each other and Rupert was every bit as intelligent as his father.

Gervase's smile turned to affectionate forbearance. 'Thank you for your concern, Rupert, but I made sure the invitations were sent out myself. Tonight is a very special occasion for Diana and me since we're celebrating our second wedding anniversary. I can assure you I've left nothing to chance...'

By nine o'clock two hundred additional guests had arrived and were celebrating in the Long Gallery.

Having detached himself from the others, Sebastian stood alone on the circular balcony far above the Great Hall. Above him, adorning the ceiling of the dome, was *The Siege of Troy.* Despite his excellent vantage point from which to view Pellegrini's ravishing masterpiece, Sebastian's thoughts were racing and his eyes remained downcast.

Only that afternoon George Lowestoft had mentioned he would like to go over his accounts with Sebastion before his departure the following day...

Sebastian was filled with dread. Was it possible George suspected he was being embezzled?

It had never occurred to Sebastian that he might be found out by George. The feelings of alienation, the frustration of being unable to resume his car racing career because his grandmother had cut off his allowance and disinherited him following his near fatal car crash, the black moods that had darkened his days and left him feeling dissociated – all these had vanished after Sebastian had met Gabriella on a skiing holiday in Switzerland a year and a half ago.

Yet, despite falling in love with her, he had still gone on embezzling George Lowestoft. He had no plausible excuse to offer for his actions. The old boy had never done him any harm. The reason he had embezzled George is because he was bored – *that was the simple truth of it!*

Sebastian swallowed a mouthful of bourbon. He was still filled with wonder that a woman as wonderful as Gabriella could love him. If Diana found out what he had done to George, Sebastian would forfeit any chance of being reinstated in his grandmother's will.

Sebastian gripped the balcony rail and far below him saw the marble floor of the Great Hall. It was a hell of a long way to fall.

I love Gabriella too much to risk losing her over this, thought Sebastian desperately. *I've got to find a way out of this mess – preferably before tonight is out...*

9

In his bedroom at Arlington, Rupert was lying on some cushions and staring up at the mural on the ceiling. It depicted cherubs floating on clouds against an idyllically blue sky. Poppy Carter was resting her head on his shoulder.

'George Lowestoft was in my uncle's pub earlier this week,' she said, breaking the companionable silence. 'He wouldn't stop talking about Diana's car crash.'

'He's an even bigger fusspot than my father,' said Rupert. 'Did you tell him the police confirmed it was an accident?'

'I'm not sure it did the least bit of good,' said Poppy. 'When George has had a pint or two he doesn't half go on. Some of his conspiracy theories are too lurid for words. You should hear him on the subject of the moon landings.'

'My father would be furious if he knew we were lying here in each other's arms.'

Poppy's large blue eyes gazed anxiously at Rupert through her wispy blonde fringe. 'Is Gervase still on at you to marry Venetia Campbell-what's-her-face?'

'I'm afraid so,' said Rupert. 'It's a bloody awful thought, but if my stepmother Diana had died in the car crash her money would have gone to my father. If that had happened, he wouldn't be kicking up such a fuss about marrying me off to Venetia. He's desperately worried about the future of Arlington.'

Poppy sat up abruptly, staring down into his face. 'Rupert, I'm not sure I can go on waiting for you. There are times when I feel as if I'm wasting my life away. Dad's become so set in his ways since Mum died. I'm fed up working in the chemist. I'd marry you tomorrow if I could but we both know Gervase would be dead set against it.'

'You're wrong to imagine my father hates you –'

Poppy said with a shudder, 'Oh, let's not go into that again. I would never have joined the *League Against Cruelty to Animals* if I'd known they were sabotaging the local hunt. I thought they were a peaceful organisation.'

'Uncle Mortimer was a careless rider.' Rupert spoke in a stifled voice. 'He was too fond of getting tanked up before he went out with the hunt.'

'Rupert, the whole village of Brimhurst knows it was my green van that blared its horn and frightened Mortimer's horse into bolting. Gervase blames *me* for your uncle's death. That's not easy for me to live with.'

The colour ebbed from Rupert's face. 'It was a terrible business all round – what with my grandfather dying of grief six months later,' he said, swallowing hard. 'Uncle Mortimer was his favourite son.'

'Gervase holds me responsible for both their deaths,' said Poppy fretfully. 'I can't see him ever agreeing to us marrying.'

'No – you mustn't say that. It's not true. He's worried about the future of Arlington, that's all.'

Poppy sighed wistfully. 'Where does that leave us?'

'My father is bound to inherit a bundle when Diana dies,' said Rupert with a curious intonation in his voice. 'We simply need to be patient a little while longer and everything will turn out all right in the end – I promise...'

Lyle and Diana were dancing in the Long Gallery to the strains of an excellent string quartet. As Diana glanced over Lyle's shoulder, he saw her eyes narrow in displeasure.

'Is anything the matter?' he asked.

'Jean-Luc de Breteuil and his wife Angelique are dancing together,' said Diana in a low voice. 'It must be quite a novelty for her since she normally prefers to dance with my husband.'

'Does Jean-Luc know about Angelique's affair with Gervase?'

Diana shook her head. 'Jean-Luc worships the ground his wife walks on. If he were to find out the truth, it would go down as well as a cyanide capsule.'

'Perhaps you'll get lucky and the de Breteuils will murder each other,' said Lyle light-heartedly.

'That would certainly put an end to my problems,' said Diana. 'Gervase recently went behind my back and hired Angelique to redecorate the breakfast-room. I intend to wipe the smile off her face before tonight is out.' She saw Lyle wince and added, 'Are you all right?'

Lyle smiled ruefully. 'I'm overdue a visit to the dentist. Here's hoping I don't need to go under the drill.'

'Make sure you avoid an amalgam filling if you do,' said Diana. 'It would be a shame to spoil the whiteness of your smile. Porcelain fillings are best.'

Lyle remembered something Irene Lowestoft had told him during dinner. 'Diana, is it true you recently suffered a bout of food poisoning?'

'Oh, that – it was *nothing...*'

Diana spoke so dismissively of the incident that Lyle was immediately reassured. Jean-Luc and Angelique de Breteuil passed them on the dance floor.

'Diana, it's lovely to see you,' gushed Angelique.

Jean-Luc gave the impression of having drunk too much. 'We're delighted you're looking so well after your recent ordeal.'

'I received a lot of lovely gifts after my car accident,' said Diana graciously. 'The Belgian chocolates you both sent me were delicious.' She paused to make sure she had the couple's full attention before she added, 'Gervase has given me the most wonderful Sèvres breakfast service as a wedding anniversary present. Sadly, it clashes with the current wallpaper in the breakfast-room, so I've decided to have the breakfast-room refurbished all over again. I've already consulted the most *wonderful* decorator.'

Angelique held on to her smile with difficulty. 'I'm sure it will look terrific. You've always been a woman of exquisite taste, Diana.'

As Diana and Lyle moved off, they couldn't help overhearing Jean-Luc's exchange with his wife.

'Weren't you saying Gervase hired *you* to refurbish the breakfast-room?'

'Darling, you must have misunderstood,' said Angelique

quickly. 'My work schedule has me tied up for months...'

Towards the end of the night, Lyle found himself dancing with Hermione in the Great Hall beneath the dome. There was an amorous gleam in his eyes and they were both looking forward to making love when they got home.

George Lowestoft came downstairs. He ignored Hermione when she spoke to him. He walked down the vaulted corridor and went into the gun room.

'I wonder what's the matter with George?' murmured Hermione.

'Perhaps he didn't hear you,' said Lyle. 'That's odd...'

'What is it?'

Lyle was staring at the briefcase on the octagonal table. 'The blue folder containing Captain Dietrich's draft report is gone. Sebastian left it on top of Oliver's briefcase.'

Lyle opened the briefcase and glanced inside. There was no sign of the draft report.

'It can't have just disappeared,' said Hermione frowning.

A couple of minutes later, Gabriella emerged from the Garden Room. Hermione couldn't help thinking that Frederick Steen was lucky to have such a beautiful daughter. Gabriella was holding a bottle of champagne and two crystal flutes in her hands.

'I've been admiring the murals in the Garden Room while I wait for Sebastian,' she said, her face radiating the happiness of a woman who is engaged to the man she loves.

'Where is he?' asked Lyle.

'Sebastian has gone upstairs to change his shirt. He spilt some red wine on it.'

Hermione smiled. 'You must be looking forward to

your wedding.'

Gabriella's eyes shone enthusiastically. 'As soon as we're married, we're going to start a family and give my father the grandchildren he deserves. Sebastian thinks I'm mad to hope for twins since the odds are against me, but I'm determined to have them and that's all there is to it. One pregnancy will be so much easier on my figure. It's important to me to replace the family my father lost.'

'Your father was interned in a concentration camp during the Second World War, wasn't he?' said Hermione sympathetically.

Gabriella nodded and said sadly, 'How he retained his sanity after his entire family was wiped out by the Nazis, I'll never know. Their treatment of the Poles was barbaric.'

Sebastian denied all knowledge of the blue folder's whereabouts when he came downstairs a minute or so later.

'Gabriella and I are about to go outside and have some champagne by the water terrace,' he added. 'Why don't you both join us?'

Glancing uneasily at Hermione, Lyle murmured, 'It might be an idea to check on George first.'

'Is something the matter with him?' asked Sebastian.

'He seemed rather distracted when he went into the gun room a few minutes ago,' replied Lyle.

'He shouldn't be around guns when he's had too much to drink,' said Sebastian. 'Come on, Lyle.'

His concern surprised Hermione who watched the two men hurry down the vaulted corridor towards the gun room. Coming towards them in the opposite direction was George's wife Irene Lowestoft.

'The band is playing my favourite tune in the Long

Gallery,' she said. 'George and I always enjoy dancing to it. Have you seen –?'

A loud shot shattered the silence from behind the closed door of the gun room.

There was a moment's horrified silence – and then Lyle and Sebastian dashed into the gun room ahead of the others.

George Lowestoft was lying in the middle of the room. A pistol was on the floor a few inches away from his left hand.

'Oh, my God,' gasped Gabriella. *'Is he badly injured?'*

Hermione and Lyle exchanged startled glances. There was no doubt in their minds that the ex-naval commander was dead.

Irene murmured in a stricken voice, 'George – George, speak to me...' She began to howl like a grief-stricken banshee.

There was a sound of running footsteps outside in the corridor. Gervase and Rupert burst into the gun room.

Gervase turned to his son. *'Rupert, call an ambulance – quickly!'*

Rupert rushed out of the gun room almost colliding in the doorway with his stepmother. 'Diana, don't go in there. George has shot himself.'

'The pistol must have gone off accidentally while George was cleaning it,' said Sebastian quickly.

Diana was looking horrified. *'Oh, God, please tell me this isn't happening,'* she whispered.

'Lyle, don't just stand there,' snapped Gervase. 'Take the women outside. This is no place for them to be.'

Outside in the corridor the small group of women stood

uncertainly around Lyle. He had closed the door of the gun room behind him, but they could still hear Gervase and Sebastian trying to comfort Irene who was sobbing uncontrollably.

Hermione saw Irene Lowestoft's maid at the end of the corridor and hurried up to her. Marjorie Pym was standing next to a life-sized marble statue called the Goddess of Fortune. Earlier in the night, she had stood on the first-floor landing admiring the lilies in the Great Hall and had later entered the Grand Saloon and placed her mistress's cigarette lighter on the table next to her.

'Pym, you were in the corridor when Mr Revel and I went past several minutes ago. Did anyone go into the gun room ahead of Mr Lowestoft?'

'No, ma'am,' replied Pym in a flat voice. 'I would have seen if anyone had gone in or come out. The only person who went into the gun room was Mr Lowestoft himself.'

PART 2

10

'Did you find out what Irene Lowestoft's maid was doing in the corridor?' asked Lyle.

'Pym says she was listening to the music coming from the Long Gallery,' said Hermione. 'Apparently, she was there half an hour or more. The door of the gun room was in her sight the entire time. She claims the only person to enter the gun room before we heard the shot was George Lowestoft. I'm convinced she knows more than she's letting on, but I couldn't make her tell me.'

The couple was talking in hushed voices in the Great Hall. Before the arrival of the police, the last of the guests had left through a side door of the Long Gallery without getting wind of the tragedy.

'The pistol that fired the fatal bullet was a Walther PPK,' said Lyle. 'Gervase had no difficulty identifying it because his initials are engraved on the handle.'

'George Lowestoft chose an unusual time to go to the gun room,' said Hermione frowning.

Lyle nodded in agreement. 'What we don't know yet is

whether it was an accident, suicide or murder.'

'It can't have been suicide,' objected Hermione. 'George was a devout Roman Catholic. They regard suicide as a mortal sin.'

'That makes suicide seem less probable,' said Lyle thoughtfully. 'The bullet entered behind George's left ear. There was no scorching of the skin consistent with him having pressed the muzzle of the pistol against the side of his head.'

'The absence of a suicide note along with the lack of scorching points to murder,' said Hermione. 'I'm convinced Sebastian was embezzling George.'

'Sebastian and I were standing in the vaulted corridor when we heard the shot,' Lyle reminded her. 'No one came out of the gun room before we entered and found the body. The windows were locked on the inside.'

'A pistol shot is easily faked,' insisted Hermione. 'George could have pushed Sebastian too far by threatening to go to the police.'

'Let's assume George *was* murdered,' conceded Lyle. 'Pym could be telling the truth when she says she saw no one enter or leave the gun room. It appears we have a locked-room murder on our hands.'

Hermione came to a decision. 'It's late and we ought to be going home,' she said. 'But before we leave, I want to make sure Diana is all right.'

'George was a good man,' said Diana, in a soft, tremulous voice. 'He genuinely cared about people and was always quick to help someone in need. I'm going to miss him more than I can say.'

Hermione was listening to her godmother's confidences in the privacy of her sitting-room. Diana was looking devastated by George's death. She had known him since he was a young officer in the Navy before the outbreak of the Second World War.

'George's death has come as such a shock,' continued Diana. 'I'd like someone to tell me this isn't happening. It might have been better if I hadn't gone to the High Saloon with him before he shot himself.' It was obvious from her expression that she had acceded reluctantly to the dead man's wishes. 'I was angry with him.'

'Because of George's impromptu speech during the party?' queried Hermione gently.

Diana nodded. 'After all that's happened lately, I only agreed to go ahead with tonight's celebrations provided there were *no* speeches. I really didn't want George or anyone else congratulating Gervase and me on our perfect marriage. George was quite crestfallen when I refused to accept his apology. His talk descended into foolishness, no doubt exacerbated by all the alcohol he'd drunk. He said he still had feelings for me, that the only reason he'd married Irene is because I was already accounted for.'

'What did you say to *that?'* exclaimed Hermione.

'I told George I regarded him as a good family friend. Nothing more. The scene went from bad to worse. He said it still wasn't too late for us to divorce our partners and marry each other.'

Hermione's eyes widened incredulously. *'I can't believe George asked you to marry him.* The two of you have known each other for years. Did he really expect you to take him seriously?'

The colour rose in Diana's cheeks. 'I immediately poured cold water on the idea,' she said. 'I'm afraid I lost my temper and said too much. George proposed for old times' sake, as he put it, that I help him out of his current financial difficulties. Irene would have been furious if she had heard him talking to me like that. She's been jealous of me ever since we were girls.'

'There's something almost pathological about your cousin's jealousy,' murmured Hermione with a shiver.

'George was such a muddle-head,' said Diana in a tired voice. 'I knew he couldn't possibly be in financial trouble. Sebastian has been taking care of his investments for him. I couldn't ask for a more astute grandson.'

Hermione was tempted to tell Diana there was a possibility Sebastian had embezzled George, but she couldn't bring herself to add to her godmother's distress.

'George was always having panic attacks,' added Diana, 'and crying pauper when there was *nothing* actually wrong. I pointed out his finances couldn't be as bad as he imagined or he wouldn't be planning to take Irene to South Africa this winter. I was relieved when George left me. A quarter of an hour later, Bosworth saw George go to Irene's room and leave a bouquet of flowers on her pillow.'

Hermione stared at her. 'A bouquet of flowers?'

'Yes.'

'How odd...'

'That's what I thought,' said Diana.

Hermione frowned. 'George must have gone to the gun room immediately afterwards,' she said. 'It would have been a few minutes after midnight when we heard the shot.'

Diana shuddered. 'I can't believe there was anything

seriously *wrong* with George's finances.'

'Men say the most foolish things when they've had too much to drink,' said Hermione quickly. 'George's death was an *accident*. He loved life too much to kill himself.' There was a soothing note in her voice and doubt in her heart as she added, 'Once you've had a good night's sleep, I'm sure you'll come around to my way of thinking.'

Downstairs in the Great Hall, Lyle was pacing up and down, unable to forget the moment he and Sebastian had burst into the gun room and found George Lowestoft's body. The scene kept looping around in his mind like a spool of cinema film and he wished he hadn't drunk so much champagne.

Lyle had already supplied the police with a witness statement regarding George Lowestoft's final movements. He had also questioned a couple of the servants, but they were unable to shed any light on the disappearance of the blue folder. Was it possible George Lowestoft had seen who had taken the blue folder and had made the fatal mistake of confronting the person with the fact –?

Hermione came downstairs.

'How did you get on with Diana?' asked Lyle.

'George's death has come as a huge shock to her.'

'Did you tell Diana about the missing folder?'

Hermione shook her head. 'I didn't want to upset her unnecessarily.'

Lyle frowned. 'Sebastian left the folder on top of Oliver's briefcase. Someone must have taken it during the party.'

'I expect it's been mislaid,' said Hermione.

Lyle was not so easily convinced. 'I'm glad I photocopied the documents inside the folder. I've hidden them in Lord Milsham's library. Did you find out anything useful from Diana?'

'George told Diana that he was in desperate need of money,' said Hermione. 'But when the police arrived earlier tonight, I overheard Gervase saying there was nothing wrong with George's finances. Who are we supposed to believe?'

'Judging by the look of hatred Gervase gave Sebastian when the body was found,' said Lyle, 'I'd say he thinks George committed suicide rather than face bankruptcy –'

He broke off as Diana's stepson Rupert came along the corridor towards them.

'Lyle – Hermione, I didn't know you were still here.' Rupert looked faintly displeased.

'How's Irene?' asked Lyle.

'Dr Cheadle has come over from Brimhurst. George's death has come as a terrible blow to her. They were married for a long time.'

'Was that Venetia Campbell-Scott we saw leaving earlier?' said Hermione.

Rupert nodded. 'My father is hoping I'll marry Venetia,' he said bitterly. 'It was his idea to invite her here tonight. I'm simply a passing fancy of hers. She's gone back to London. She told me she doesn't care to be caught up in any unpleasant business. My God, a man is dead and all she cares about is her social position!'

'The two of you seemed smitten with each other at dinner,' remarked Hermione.

'If you must know I've got my eyes set on a girl in the village who's hardly got a penny to her name,' confided Rupert.

'Poppy Carter?'

Rupert was startled. 'Yes, how did you –?'

'Your secret is safe with me,' said Hermione. 'I'm a friend of Poppy's. It wasn't hard to guess the truth.'

'I'd give anything to marry Poppy,' said Rupert with a sigh. 'Not that I dare admit as much to my father. He hates her with every fibre of his being. Presumably you know my uncle died four years ago after falling from his horse?'

'Lyle doesn't,' said Hermione.

Turning to Lyle, Rupert said unhappily, 'My father is convinced Poppy was driving the green van that startled Uncle Mortimer's horse into bolting. He refuses to believe she's innocent. My uncle died from a broken neck.'

'There was a loudhailer on the roof which was connected to the van's horn,' added Hermione for Lyle's benefit. 'It was the sound of the amplified horn that startled Mortimer's horse into throwing him to the ground. The van drove off at high speed. Witnesses were unable to see who was driving it.'

Lyle's eyes narrowed. 'Are you saying your uncle's death was the result of a deliberate act of sabotage?'

'That had nothing to do with Poppy,' insisted Rupert.

'Rupert, can you seriously blame your father for feeling the way he does?' said Hermione. 'Poppy joined the *League Against Cruelty to Animals* of her own free will.'

'That was before she realized they were sabotaging the local hunts,' said Rupert, flushing.

'It's a well-known fact the green van belonged to Poppy,'

pointed out Hermione.

'Hermione, you know as well as I do that the police found Poppy's van abandoned in Pelham Wood. It had been wiped clean of fingerprints.'

'You've got a difficult task ahead of you if you're going to persuade Gervase of Poppy's innocence,' said Hermione.

Rupert looked distinctly annoyed. 'George said exactly the same thing to me. In fact, he took quite an interest in Uncle Mortimer's death. He promised to have a word with my father and see if he could bring him around.'

'What would you have done if George had gone to your father and told him that he'd uncovered proof of Poppy's guilt?' asked Hermione boldly.

Rupert gave her an agitated look. 'I would have stopped him – I mean, I would have reasoned with George. Convinced him he was mistaken. Really, Hermione, you ask the most impertinent questions.'

'I can't imagine George having an enemy in the world,' said Hermione. 'Can you?'

'Of course not!' Rupert frowned irritably. 'The shooting could have been avoided if I'd kept the gun room locked...' He swallowed hard in the grip of a deep emotion.

'Rupert, is there any truth in the suggestion that George had money difficulties?' said Lyle.

'Nothing could be further from the truth,' said Rupert sharply. 'Along with everyone else, Irene accepts George died accidentally. The best advice I can give you both is to go home and forget this dreadful business...'

11

On their way home, Hermione and Lyle made a detour and stopped off at the St. Francis Xavier Hospital to speak to Claudia Rylander. Oliver was still in a coma, and she was sitting next to his bed looking miserable and haggard with grief. Her reaction to George Lowestoft's death was surprisingly matter of fact.

'Poor George... I was fond of him in my own way. I know this makes me sound awful but it's simply his stuck up wife Irene who I can't stand... She must be devastated by his death...'

'You suggested some time ago that your brother Sebastian had made a hash of managing George's finances,' said Hermione. 'Is it possible the situation worsened? Might George have been on the brink of bankruptcy?'

Claudia shook her head slowly. 'I have no idea. Do you think it might be important?'

'If Sebastian was embezzling George, it could have a bearing on why he shot himself,' said Hermione.

Claudia came to a decision. 'Leave this to me. I know

someone who can give me an answer to your question. I'll get back to you both as soon as I can.'

As they drove away from the hospital, Hermione said, 'We should know more about George's finances once Claudia gets back to us.'

'My inner voice is telling me that we'll get a phone call from Claudia in a day or two's time,' said Lyle. 'She'll probably insist there was nothing wrong with George's finances. The family will close ranks to ensure the coroner returns a verdict of accidental death.'

'Claudia and I have been friends for years,' protested Hermione. 'I can't imagine her lying for Sebastian's sake.'

'Sebastian isn't the only person with a motive for shooting George,' said Lyle bluntly. 'We only have Claudia's word that she found out about her grandmother's affair with Oliver *after* the car crash. Claudia could have siphoned the brake fluid from Diana's Daimler before that in order to rid herself of a rival for Oliver's affections. What Claudia had no way of knowing is that Oliver would be in the Daimler with Diana when it plunged off the side of the road.'

Hermione was startled. 'I can't believe I'm hearing this. Claudia loves Diana –'

'After the car crash Claudia didn't once express concern for her grandmother's well-being,' continued Lyle relentlessly. 'Her only thoughts were for Oliver. I think deep down Claudia resents – possibly even *hates* – Diana for surviving the car crash instead of Oliver.'

Hermione's anger flared. 'Are you saying Claudia shot George because he found out she had tampered with the Daimler's brakes –?'

'It would have been easy for Claudia to slip away from

the hospital tonight,' said Lyle, 'and shoot George to prevent him from exposing her.'

Hermione was too upset to argue the point. Her loyalty to Claudia was shaken and she wondered if Lyle was right to suspect Claudia of being the killer. It was well after two a.m. by the time they reached Nettlebed. Lyle surprised Hermione by driving up to the main house.

'There's a book I want to consult in Lord Milsham's library,' he said, switching off Lady Godiva's engine. 'It might shed light on tonight's tragic events. I can't believe I didn't think of it sooner.'

Hermione knew better than to argue with Lyle since he was looking like a thundercloud. Fortunately, Lord Milsham was not in a position to object to them using his library because he was currently living in tax exile in Switzerland.

'I'll go to the kitchen and make some coffee,' said Hermione in a strained voice.

Ten minutes later there was a rattle of crockery as she entered the oak panelled library carrying a tray with cups and a pot of coffee. Several wall sconces had been switched on and were emitting a soft radiance over Lord Milsham's ancestral portraits and leather bound volumes. Lyle's former moodiness had lifted and he had the pleased air of a conjuror who has successfully mastered a new trick.

Pouring out the coffee, Hermione asked, 'What are you reading?'

'A book called *Arlington: The Life and Times of a Stately Home.* I now know how George Lowestoft's murder could have been made to look like suicide. According to the author, Arlington was built with servants' passages between the walls of the main reception rooms. This enables the servants to go about their duties without being seen by the family and their guests.'

'That explains why Bosworth is always materialising out of nowhere,' exclaimed Hermione. 'Does one of the servants' passages lead to the gun room?'

'A former maid from the thirties is quoted as saying one of the house guests tried to chat her up,' replied Lyle. 'He was about to pounce on her when one of the footmen entered the gun room through the servants' passage and put a stop to it.'

Hermione passed him a cup of coffee. 'I don't suppose the book mentioned where the entrance to the servants' passage is?'

'No, but I'll bet Sebastian knows where to find it,' said Lyle confidently. 'He's bound to have seen the servants using it. Let's re-examine his actions tonight in light of our new knowledge. Shortly before the shooting, Sebastian went to his room and changed his shirt because he had spilt some red wine on it. He says he spoke to George after the latter left Diana in the High Saloon. But we've only got *Sebastian's* word that George said he was looking forward to target practice tomorrow morning.'

Hermione's pulse quickened. 'I wouldn't be surprised if Sebastian was preparing the way for George's murder –'

Lyle nodded and went on, 'Suppose Sebastian asked George to go downstairs to the gun room and wait for him so they could have a private chat? It would have been easy for Sebastian to enter the gun room via the servants' passage in the central wing. The servants were all in the west wing attending to the party. George was possibly admiring Gervase's gun collection and never realized anyone was with him until it was too late.'

'How is it that no one heard the shot?' asked Hermione.

'It's easy enough to attach a silencer to a Walther PPK,' said Lyle. 'All Sebastian had to do after he shot George was to remove the silencer and leave the pistol by the body with a nice set of the dead man's fingerprints on it. I can't imagine it would have taken Sebastian long to light a firecracker in the servants' passage before hurrying back upstairs. My guess is that there was a long fuse attached to the firecracker and he knew there would be a delay of a couple of minutes before it went off with a loud bang. By then Sebastian had joined us in the Great Hall.'

'Is this your way of saying you no longer think Claudia is the killer?' asked Hermione with a hint of reproof in her voice.

'What if we're right about the *method* and altogether *wrong about the killer's identity?'* countered Lyle calmly. 'Before George died, he took a considerable interest in your godmother's car accident. Suppose he found out that the person who emptied the Daimler's brake fluid reservoir was Gervase?'

'George is the sort of person who would have stewed the matter over in his mind,' said Hermione slowly. 'He wouldn't have wanted to believe that his best friend Gervase was capable of trying to murder Diana for her money! Being a rather transparent person, George would probably have dropped a lot of hints to Gervase. It would have been his way of seeking psychological reassurance from Gervase that his suspicions were untrue.'

'George's need for psychological reassurance could have cost him his life,' said Lyle. 'On the other hand, *Diana might have shot George.'*

Hermione stared at him in astonishment. 'What

possible motive could my godmother have for killing him?'

'Diana claims George begged her to divorce Gervase so they could go off together,' Lyle reminded her. 'But what if she made the mistake of spurning George *before* he told her that Sebastian was embezzling him? How do you suppose an old codger like George would have felt?'

'I don't know.' Hermione paused for a moment to consider. 'Possibly angry, humiliated – vengeful...' She broke off uneasily.

'George could have turned on Diana completely,' said Lyle, 'and made it clear he was going to send Sebastian to prison. Diana could have shot him rather than let him wreck Sebastian's future.'

Hermione said indignantly, 'You won't convince me Diana killed George, no matter what you say. I've known Diana longer than you. She's a warm and loving human being. Sebastian is far more likely to have murdered George than Diana.'

'Perhaps.'

Lyle's soft utterance infuriated Hermione. She was filled with a terrible sense of foreboding. Diana had killed in the past. Her survival in the French Resistance had depended on her doing so.

'In a case of murder everyone is a suspect *until proven innocent*,' insisted Lyle. 'Gabriella is planning to marry Sebastian. She might very well have shot George to protect the man she loves. We only have Gabriella's word that she was in the Garden Room admiring the murals. Remember – she only joined us a couple of minutes *after* we saw George go into the gun room.'

'I'd forgotten about that,' murmured Hermione, wondering if he was right to suspect Gabriella. 'If we're to find out who killed George, I suppose we have to be honest with each other,' she added reluctantly. 'Who do you think really did it?'

Lyle hesitated and then said, 'If I were to tell you who I think the killer is I couldn't trust you not to go around staring at that person and giving the game away. Your manner was embarrassingly direct when you questioned Rupert tonight. I don't want you putting yourself in danger. *We can't trust anyone – not even your godmother.*'

Hermione's voice hardened. 'You're accusing me of letting my heart rule my head, is that it?'

'Hermione, we mustn't overlook the possibility that Captain Dietrich removed the blue folder from the table in the Great Hall tonight. If George saw him the fact might have been enough to sign his death warrant.'

Hermione's eyes widened in shock. 'Are you suggesting Captain Dietrich was one of the guests at the party?'

'Precisely.'

'There were over two hundred guests in the Long Gallery.'

'The fact had not escaped me,' said Lyle grimly.

There was a long pause.

'What are you thinking?' he asked.

'For some reason I can't get Irene Lowestoft's maid out of my mind,' said Hermione in frustration. 'I'm convinced Pym knows more about George's murder than she's letting on...'

12

On Wednesday morning Lyle Revel took the train up to London. The disappearance of the blue folder was uppermost in his mind. Had Captain Dietrich stolen it and murdered George Lowestoft to conceal the truth about his past?

Lyle arrived at 98 Harley Street with ten minutes to spare before his dental appointment with Dr Galbraith. There was a new nameplate next to the others on the front of the building: *Jean-Luc de Breteuil, F.D.S, R.C.P.S., B.D.S., L.D.S, R.C.S.* His eyebrows rose – it seemed quite a coincidence.

'I see you have a new tenant on the floor below,' remarked Lyle a few minutes later as he settled himself into his dentist's chair.

Dr Galbraith, a big, hearty man with gold-rimmed spectacles, launched into an explanation. 'Jean-Luc de Breteuil was forced to move out of his old business premises at 20 Harley Street. Some of his elderly patients were refusing to visit him.'

'Oh – why?'

'A clinic for sexual diseases had recently opened on the third floor. They were horrified at the idea of people thinking they might be visiting the *clinic* instead of his surgery. Jean-Luc de Breteuil moved into 98 Harley Street just over a year ago. His predecessor Solomon Atkinson was anxious to retire. He sold the lease to the surgery and his list of clients to Jean-Luc de Breteuil.'

Lyle expressed mild surprise, then explained the reasons for his visit. A sore tooth on the right side of his lower jaw.

After a preliminary examination of Lyle's teeth, Dr Galbraith was able to reassure him, 'There's no need for you to go under the drill like your friend and have a porcelain filling. Diana was awarded the *Croix de Guerre* with Palm and Bar by the French for her work during the Second World War.'

'She's a brave woman,' said Lyle. 'Why is my gum sore?'

'It's mildly inflamed by a build up of plaque around the bottom of the tooth. A clean and polish will set you right –'

Half an hour later, Lyle emerged from the surgery after a friendly reminder from Dr Galbraith to visit him again in six months' time. Lyle paused for a moment on the second-floor landing to look at a framed print of Monet's *Bridge Over a Pool of Water Lilies.*

A door opened on the far side of the landing and Lyle heard a man saying in an agitated voice, *'Your demands have got to stop. This is all the money I'm going to give you.'*

Lyle swung around and saw Jean-Luc de Breteuil standing in the doorway of his surgery speaking to a woman who was wearing a maroon coat, black cloche hat and black gloves. She was standing with her back to Lyle and he was unable to see her face.

Even so, he had a clear view of Jean-Luc's face. His expression was one of malign hatred as he thrust a wad of notes into her hand. The woman put the money in her handbag and walked off down the stairs.

Jean-Luc became aware of Lyle's presence. He wrestled briefly with his social conscience and then decided he would condescend to speak to Lyle.

'My wife and I were at Arlington on Sunday night to celebrate the Duke and Duchess of Marsdens' wedding anniversary. I seem to recall you were one of the guests.'

'Yes, my name is Lyle Revel.' Lyle stifled his dislike of Jean-Luc's obsequious manner and shook hands with him. 'I've been visiting my dentist.'

'I understand you're an actor, Mr Revel.' Jean-Luc's tone implied Lyle's profession was further down the social ladder than his own.

Lyle wisely changed the subject. 'Is that one of your more troublesome patients?' he asked, nodding in the direction of the woman disappearing down the stairs.

Jean-Luc's expression momentarily froze, then he tapped his forehead and murmured, 'Yes, she constantly asks me for donations for her church. Religious mania, I fear.'

'You ought to raise your consultation fee to cover the cost of your donations,' suggested Lyle with a twinkle in his eyes. 'Did you speak to George Lowestoft at Arlington on Sunday night?'

Jean-Luc leaned forward, his eyes alight with pleasurable anticipation. 'He's a most agreeable fellow. Ex-naval commander. A highly distinguished career, I believe. Is there something I should know?'

'Shortly after midnight George shot himself.'

A look of horror spread across Jean-Luc's face. 'I – I can't believe it. He's not –?'

'Dead, I'm afraid,' said Lyle gently. 'What time did you leave Arlington?'

'Eleven o'clock or thereabouts. My wife had a headache so we didn't stay as late as some of the guests.'

'It seems George asked a lot of questions about Diana's car accident. Did he discuss the matter with you?'

'The misfortune of a fellow guest, who was barely known to me, is hardly a subject for gossip,' said Jean-Luc abruptly. 'Good morning, Mr Revel.' He retreated into his surgery and closed the door.

Lyle's eyebrows rose and he slowly shook his head. Outside in the street, he hailed a taxi to take him to the station. He recalled the thick wad of notes Jean-Luc de Breteuil had thrust into the woman's hand. He wondered who she was and, more importantly, what possible reason she could have for blackmailing him.

Lyle's train arrived at Compton Sutton railway station shortly before midday. Hermione was waiting for him outside in the yard in her 1948 red MG TC roadster.

On the journey back to Nettlebed, Lyle asked, 'How was this morning's inquest?'

'It was rather dull,' Hermione complained above the hum of Casanova's engine. 'I was hoping to speak to Diana, but she wasn't there. After Gervase and Sebastian testified that George Lowestoft's finances were in order the verdict of accidental death was a foregone conclusion. I didn't know he suffered from arthritis in both his hands –'

'Nor did I –'

'Until I heard his doctor's testimony. I could see him dropping the pistol and accidentally firing a bullet into his brain. I owe you an apology for being so irate with you after George was shot. It's obvious the family closed ranks just as you said they would. His death appears to have been hushed up very nicely.'

'M'mm...I think you're right,' said Lyle. 'What can you tell me about Jean-Luc de Breteuil?'

'The way Jean-Luc looks at me sometimes makes me feel quite uncomfortable,' said Hermione. 'He's got the hots for me, but he's too frightened to do anything about it because his wife's money funds their comfortable lifestyle. For someone who claims to be related to the Huguenots, he's remarkably servile to Angelique's wishes. I wouldn't be surprised if he made that up so she would marry him.'

'Social climbers?' suggested Lyle.

'Oh, they both are,' declared Hermione. 'It's a pity Angelique is Gabriella's godmother. Angelique's and Jean-Luc's invitation to dinner last night was withdrawn at Diana's insistence. Gervase could hardly refuse her request since he's trying to make their marriage work. The excuse he gave Angelique and Jean-Luc is that too many people had already been asked to dinner. Their invitation was restricted to the party afterwards in the Long Gallery.'

'Do you know what time they left Arlington?'

Hermione cast her mind back. 'George died soon after midnight. It would have been several minutes before that when we left the Long Gallery. Angelique and Jean-Luc were still there.'

'Now that is interesting,' murmured Lyle. 'Jean-Luc told me they left around eleven o'clock.'

'There's nothing wrong with my eyesight,' said Hermione. 'I wonder if he was mistaken – or if he has something to hide?'

Once they were clear of the village, she applied pressure to Casanova's accelerator, negotiating the turns in the road with consummate ease. Hedgerows and green fields flashed past and a warm breeze swept over them.

'Does Jean-Luc know his wife is having an affair with Gervase?' asked Lyle.

'If Jean-Luc knows about Angelique's affair with Gervase I would expect him to mind a great deal,' said Hermione. 'He's an extremely fastidious man, full of his own self-importance. But as long as they're discreet he's not in a position to complain, is he? I suspect having titled friends is more important to Jean-Luc than his wife's adultery.'

'Can you think of anyone who has a reason for blackmailing him?'

Hermione heard the curious undertone in Lyle's voice and said, 'Why do you ask?'

Lyle told her about the conversation he had overheard in London that morning.

Hermione's eyebrows rose. *'"Your demands have got to stop. This is all the money I'm going to give you,"'* she repeated. 'How odd. No, I can't – not off the top of my head. I would have thought it would be far more likely for someone to blackmail Angelique and Gervase over their affair.'

On the couple's return to Nettlebed they found a letter had been hand-delivered through the front door letter flap in their absence. It bore Arlington's crest and was written in Diana's neat, slanting handwriting.

Dear Lyle,

Here at your request is a list of all the guests who attended my wedding anniversary party. You were awfully mysterious when you phoned me. Were you frightened someone might be listening into our conversation?

Once the inquest is over this morning, Gervase and I will be going away for a couple of days. We've been invited by Mrs Thatcher to a house party at Chequers. All very political and not as glamorous as it sounds. I shall expect you to tell me everything on my return.

Much love,

Diana

P.S. I've just remembered the Mariettes' valet Marcel Depardieu once said Captain Dietrich had the coldest ice-blue eyes of any man he had ever seen.

'You seem decidedly pleased with yourself,' remarked Hermione.

Lyle was smiling to himself. 'According to Diana, Captain Dietrich has blue eyes,' he explained, '*and so does Jean-Luc de Breteuil.* I'm now more curious than ever to find out *why* someone is blackmailing him. I wonder if we're closer to the truth than we realize?'

13

Hermione drove Lyle to Brimhurst that afternoon in Casanova so he could collect Lady Godiva from the local garage. She had been teasing Lyle for some time that Lady Godiva needed a facelift and he had put her in for a silver spray paint job the previous day to restore her lustre.

Built on a Saxon site, Brimhurst abutted the south-east boundary wall of Arlington and was a regular winner of the most beautiful village in Gosfordshire. The elegant Georgian houses with their brightly polished door knockers and ivy clad facades were interspersed with village shops that discreetly sold their wares, a town hall and a church.

On the way home, the couple stopped off at the Drunken Admiral. After buying their drinks from the bar they settled themselves in a sunny alcove by a window overlooking the High Street.

'I'd give anything to know for certain if Jean-Luc de Breteuil is Captain Dietrich,' said Hermione impatiently.

'We need to devise a plan to flush him out,' said Lyle.

'If we can get hold of Jean-Luc's signature, we'll be able

to compare it with Captain Dietrich's signature,' said Hermione. 'In the event their handwriting is identical, we'll know for certain Jean-Luc stole the blue folder and shot George Lowestoft.'

She lapsed into silence while her fertile mind went to work.

'I think I'll write to Jean-Luc and invite him to a cello recital at Milsham Castle. He's a snob so he ought to write back if I pretend Lord Milsham and a few titled friends will be attending.'

Lyle nodded in approval of the idea. 'What will you do if Jean-Luc accepts your invitation?'

Hermione sounded distinctly unrepentant. 'I'll cancel the recital by pretending I have something highly infectious and unpleasant –'

She broke off as a door marked 'Staff Only' opened and her pixie-faced friend Poppy Carter entered the bar, saw them and approached their table. Beneath her wispy blonde fringe Poppy's eyes were a limpid blue. She exuded an air of wholesome amiability and reminded Hermione of a puppy that was anxious to please. She liked Poppy a lot although she was forced to admit she didn't know a great deal about her. Within the last two years Poppy's mother had died after a short illness and she now kept house for her father who was the local chemist. Poppy was known for wearing knitted cardigans and going for walks with her two bulldogs Cornelius and Daisy. In addition to fussing over their health, Poppy knitted colourful hats and vests for them to wear. It was rather amusing to see the two canines in all their finery, with bells attached to their collars, trotting down Brimhurst High Street.

'Hermione, it's lovely to see you. What brings you to

this neck of the woods?'

'We're here to collect Lyle's car. Lady Godiva needed a spray paint to freshen her up. I forgot – you haven't met Lyle, have you? Lyle, meet Poppy Carter – *Rupert's secret mistress.*'

'I wish I wasn't such a secret,' said Poppy good-humouredly. 'I never get to see enough of Rupert as it is.'

'I expect you've heard about George Lowestoft's death,' said Hermione.

'Rupert has taken charge of the funeral arrangements,' said Poppy. 'I knew George quite well. He used to come in here for a drink and a chat.'

'Did George speak to you about Diana's car accident?'

'Poor love, he was beside himself with worry when he first heard about it,' said Poppy. 'It was a miracle Diana survived, he said. I couldn't help wondering if he was a bit soft on her. The way he went on about the accident you could have been excused for thinking it was sabotage. Rupert was saying Irene is ever so upset by George's death. She's really not up to organising the funeral by herself.'

'They were married for a long time,' said Lyle.

Poppy sighed. 'Being the partner who's left behind is always difficult. Dad still hasn't got over the loss of Mum.'

'I'm told Rupert is smitten by you,' said Hermione, hoping to lift her friend's spirits. 'If you play your cards right, you might one day end up becoming lady of the manor.'

Poppy rolled her eyes and said despondently, 'That would certainly be a turn up for the books. Along with my cousin Bridget, I used to work at Arlington.'

'I didn't know that,' said Hermione with an air of lively

curiosity.

'It was only for a short period after we both left school when they needed extra staff for the larger functions they put on. Bosworth the butler is a terrible stickler for detail. He used to scare the life out of us. Bridget's done all right for herself since then. She now owns the only hairdressing salon in the village.'

'Are the servants' passages as cold as one imagines?' said Lyle with an ingratiating smile.

'Only in winter.' Poppy essayed a mock shiver. 'I was glad when my uncle offered me a part-time job here in his pub. The hours are regular and he lets me do my job without looking over my shoulder. It wasn't long afterwards that my father's part-time chemist assistant left to have a baby and I took her place. I'm the only person in the village who has two jobs.' She grinned impishly at the thought.

'I bet that's led to envy and charges of nepotism,' said Hermione sympathetically. 'Has there been any improvement in your relationship with Rupert's father?'

Poppy grimaced. 'Gervase still blames me for his brother's death. I don't know who was driving my van that day, but it certainly wasn't me who startled Mortimer's horse into bolting.' She bit her lower lip and shook her head in despair.

'Who do you think it was?' asked Lyle.

Poppy blinked back tears. 'I shouldn't wonder if it was one of the local hunt protesters. They go by the name of the *League Against Cruelty to Animals*. I had no idea they were into dangerous sabotage activities until after Mortimer's death. Since then I've had nothing to do with them. There are about forty members. They're known to one another on a first name basis only. It's their way of enforcing security and avoiding discovery by the police when their mischief gets out of hand.'

'Poppy, I'm really sorry to see you in so much distress,' said Hermione gently. 'Is there anything Lyle and I can do to help?'

Poppy's voice trembled. 'Believe me, if there was anything I would have asked for your help a long time ago. Gervase's father died of a broken heart after Mortimer's death. I'm tired of living under the shadow of suspicion –'

She broke off as a group of American tourists came into the pub. After taking a moment to pull herself together, she went behind the bar to help her uncle serve them.

'That was quite an outburst,' observed Lyle.

Puzzled by the tone in his voice, Hermione asked, 'What are you implying?'

Lyle took a pull on his dark rum and Coke. 'If George Lowestoft uncovered irrefutable proof of Poppy's guilt, she might have shot him to stop him from going to the police with the truth.'

Hermione stared at him and said sharply, 'Rupert swears blue in the face that he was making love to Poppy when his uncle was killed. I could be wrong, but I refuse to believe she was responsible for Mortimer's riding accident. Poppy is a real sweetie. I can't believe it's in her nature to be vindictive and violent.'

'I happen to know for a fact Poppy was at Arlington on the night of George Lowestoft's death,' said Lyle calmly.

'How can you possibly know that?' demanded Hermione.

'Because I saw Rupert taking a bottle of champagne and a couple of glasses to his room,' replied Lyle. 'He smuggled

Poppy into the house so he could engage in some private pleasures. He later came up to me in the Long Gallery and asked me not to tell anyone. It wasn't long afterwards that George went to the gun room.'

'Which begs the question where was Poppy when he was shot shortly after midnight?' said Hermione with a slither of apprehension.

'By her own admission she's worked at Arlington in the past,' said Lyle gravely, 'and *she knows the layout of the servants' passages.*'

He broke off abruptly as Claudia Rylander entered the pub from the High Street and approached them.

14

Claudia Rylander greeted them with an air of easy familiarity. 'I just popped into the Brimhurst Pharmacy to get some hay fever tablets,' she said, as she sat down opposite them in the alcove. 'This warm weather has me suffering like mad without them.'

'Several of my friends suffer from hay fever, too,' said Lyle. 'It's a curse, isn't it?' He extracted his wallet from his pocket and asked, 'What would you like to drink?'

'A gin and tonic, please.'

Claudia smiled gratefully at Lyle as he went off to the bar, then she turned to Hermione and said, 'I'm glad I saw the two of you sitting by the window as I came out of the chemist. I've been meaning to contact you, but with one thing and another I completely forgot. I spoke to Gervase – discreetly, of course – and he assures me George's finances are in excellent order.'

'A few months ago you were convinced Sebastian was up to no good,' said Hermione, stifling her frustration.

'My suspicions of my wayward brother were unfounded,

I'm afraid.' Claudia spoke in an apologetic voice. 'I've rather an unfortunate habit of suspecting the worst of Sebastian. A throwback to our bickering childhood, I daresay.'

'At the time you seemed so *sure*.'

'George had reservations about investing in some shares,' said Claudia. 'In fact, he got quite worked up over it. Sebastian talked him around in the end. The shares have since doubled in price. I suppose it's good news for George's wife Irene. At least she'll be well provided for as a widow.'

She looked up appreciatively as Lyle returned from the bar with her drink. He sat down and put a question to her.

'Claudia, on the night of the party Sebastian asked us to bring Oliver's briefcase to Arlington. Is it true he's running Valiant Productions in Oliver's absence?'

Claudia nodded complacently. 'Sebastian was planning to quit straightaway. But he's decided to stay on – partly to impress Gabriella and partly because I told him our grandmother would be sure to approve of his selflessness. Why are you both looking so concerned?'

'I've never known Sebastian to be considerate of others,' said Hermione. 'He only is if there's something in it for him. You don't think he'd try and target Oliver's bank account, do you?'

Claudia sipped her gin and tonic. 'Sebastian would be wasting his time trying to embezzle Oliver. A week before the car accident, Oliver signed a legal document giving me power of attorney over his business affairs.'

'Why did he do that?' asked Lyle with a quickening of interest.

Claudia shrugged. 'Oliver wanted to safeguard against

the possibility he might become ill or incapacitated one day. He told me that if anything happened to him I was to take charge of Valiant Productions until he was well enough to assume control again.'

Hermione felt the blood draining from her cheeks as she said, 'I wonder if Oliver had a premonition about the car accident?'

'If he did, he certainly didn't tell me about it,' said Claudia. 'You're wrong to be suspicious of Sebastian. Valiant Productions is quite safe in his hands. Every document has to be approved and countersigned by me. Playing the dutiful grandson is top of Sebastian's list of priorities. Diana's car crash reminded him she can't live forever.'

'Who would have inherited Diana's money if she had been killed?' asked Hermione.

Claudia's voice tightened. 'Gervase would have got the lot as her husband. Diana is adamant that she'll only reinstate Sebastian and me in her will once we're both married and raising families of our own. I used to think my brother was beyond redemption, but now Sebastian has fallen in love with Gabriella I'm not so sure.'

Lyle spoke. 'What do you think of Gabriella?'

'I've got a lot of respect for her,' replied Claudia. 'She's got a kind heart and a capable business head on her shoulders. Her new art gallery in London has established a first-rate reputation in a remarkably short space of time.'

'Claudia, does the name Captain Dietrich mean anything to you?' said Hermione gravely.

Claudia shook her head. 'It doesn't ring any bells. Why?'

'Oliver was on the track of a Nazi war criminal called

Captain Dietrich. He told Lyle as much on the day of the car crash.'

Claudia's look of surprise quickly gave way to bewilderment. 'Oliver certainly never mentioned the matter to me. He usually confided in me about most things –'

She chatted to them for another twenty minutes, finished her drink, and then left. They knew, without having to ask, that she was returning to the hospital to continue her vigil by Oliver's bedside. Nowadays she was only seen at Arlington when she needed a change of clothes or a few personal necessities.

Lyle said thoughtfully, 'My inner voice is beginning to discern a sequence of events involving Oliver's search for Captain Dietrich.'

'I still don't see how Oliver could have found him,' objected Hermione, 'unless he had second sight. The whole thing's too fantastic – too absurd.'

Lyle took another swig of his dark rum and Coke. 'Oliver told me, *"Captain Dietrich has an extremely elegant signature. I'd recognise it again even if he were using a different nam*e." Hermione, suppose that's exactly what happened? Oliver must have known confronting Captain Dietrich over the past would involve a certain degree of risk. As a contingency plan he assigned power of attorney over his business affairs to Claudia – just in case anything happened to him.'

'And a week later it did,' said Hermione with a catch in her voice. 'Are you forgetting it was Diana's Daimler – rather than Oliver's Jaguar – that crashed off the side of the road?'

'No, I haven't forgotten,' said Lyle. 'Oliver might have spoken to Captain Dietrich. He might have let slip that

Diana was still alive and that he was going to see her because she had witnessed what happened at the chateau the night Theodore and Odette Mariette were murdered. Captain Dietrich might have feared Diana would recognise him if they came face to face again, so his immediate goal was to dispose of her. What he had no way of predicting is that *Oliver would be in the Daimler with Diana when the brakes failed.*'

'Captain Dietrich must be an old man by now, his face and body victim to the ravages of time,' said Hermione thoughtfully. 'He's bound to look completely different to the young Gestapo officer Diana briefly knew.'

'A man as ruthless as Captain Dietrich wouldn't be prepared to take the risk that Diana might recognize him,' said Lyle. 'It was a miracle she and Oliver weren't killed outright when the Daimler plunged off the side of the road. We know the brakes failed, but we've no way of knowing for sure if the brake fluid leaked away through the rusted holes in the brake lines. *Or if Captain Dietrich deliberately emptied the brake fluid reservoir shortly before the car crash.* My inner voice is telling me that George Lowestoft saw Captain Dietrich take the blue folder from the table in the Great Hall.'

'If we're right and Jean-Luc de Breteuil is Captain Dietrich, it shouldn't take us long to find out,' said Hermione confidently. 'If I write to him tonight, we should get a reply by the end of the week. By the way, we've been invited to George's funeral on Saturday. The least we can do is go and offer our moral support to his grieving widow. Diana and Gervase will have returned from Chequers by then. Afterwards everyone is going back to Arlington for the wake.'

'You wouldn't be planning to find the servants' passage, by any chance, would you?' said Lyle with a twinkle in his eyes.

'What do you think?' said Hermione. 'Of course, I might find the servants' passage is blocked up. If the only access to the gun room is from the vaulted corridor at least we'll have the satisfaction of knowing George *wasn't* murdered by Captain Dietrich or anyone else.'

15

'George was a wonderful man,' said Irene Lowestoft with a tearful note of pride in her voice. 'No one knows that more than I do. But even I'm surprised at how *many* people attended his funeral.'

'George was a lucky man to have you as his wife,' said Lyle gallantly.

George Lowestoft's funeral was over and the drawing-room at Arlington was thronging with family and invited guests who were attending the ex-naval commander's wake. Out of the corner of his eye, Lyle saw Hermione slip out of the drawing-room.

'The two of you danced so beautifully together,' he added.

Irene smiled in gratitude. 'Yes, we did. George was a very distinguished man in everything he did –'

It was Hermione's intention to go straight to the gun room

and look for the entrance to the servants' passage. But she altered her plans the moment she saw Irene Lowestoft's maid. Hermione hurried upstairs after the old woman. By the time she reached the first-floor landing Pym was gone. She saw Bosworth coming along the central corridor towards her.

'Bosworth, have you seen Mrs Lowestoft's maid? I'd like to speak to her.'

'No, I haven't, miss.'

Since Hermione was on friendly terms with the butler she had no difficulty engaging him in conversation. He agreed that Mr Lowestoft's death had been very sad for his wife.

'My godmother tells me you saw him leave some flowers on his wife's pillow on the night he died,' remarked Hermione.

'Quite lovely flowers they were, too. Taken from some of the vases in the corridor.'

'What sort of flowers were they?'

Bosworth cast his mind back. 'If memory serves me correctly, the bouquet was made up of purple hyacinths, red roses, sweet scabious, dog roses, butterfly weeds, globe amaranths, meadow saffron, francisca latifolia, gum cistus and a single pansy with a broken flower. Quite a fragrant bouquet, you might say.'

Frowning, Hermione asked, 'Why should Mr Lowestoft leave a bouquet on his wife's pillow? I'm told there was already a vase of lilies in the room.'

Bosworth coughed delicately. 'It's a romantic tradition for a gentleman to leave flowers on his wife's pillow to indicate his amorous intentions towards her. If the flowers are still there when he calls to say goodnight, he knows he's welcome to spend the night with her.'

Hermione stared at him in surprise. *George's actions don't make sense,* she thought. *Shortly before he put the flowers on Irene's pillow, he asked Diana to go away with him. George must have had another reason for leaving the flowers in Irene's room. I wonder what it was...?* Out loud, she said, 'Bosworth, did Mr Lowestoft do anything on the night he died that struck you as unusual?'

Bosworth hesitated for a moment. 'Before Mr Lowestoft went downstairs to the gun room, he removed a photo of Mr Sebastian from the table in the corridor. He put it on the round table before the window in Mrs Lowestoft's room. Next to the photo he left a sprig of ivy and dogsbane. He also opened the curtains.'

'Opened the curtains,' repeated Hermione. 'What an odd thing for him to do, especially since it was dark outside. It would have been impossible to see anything.'

'Quite so, miss. During the day, you can see a black mulberry tree in the middle of the lawn, of course.'

'I don't suppose we'll ever know exactly what was going through Mr Lowestoft's mind. I'm interested in the history of Arlington. Would you mind showing me the entrance to the servants' passage?'

Bosworth's indulgent smile suggested he was used to accommodating the unconventional whims of young people. 'There are entrances all over the house,' he said, 'provided you know where to look for them.'

He crossed to the panelled wall behind Hermione and pushed a hidden spring. A section of the wall swung inward, revealing a dark recess. Reaching inside he flicked on a switch. An explosion of light filled the recess and Hermione saw a flight of wooden steps.

Concealing her nervous exhilaration, she asked, 'Where do the steps lead to?'

'Mainly the downstairs rooms in the central wing,' replied Bosworth, 'including the library and the gun room.'

'My godmother has given me permission to go exploring on my own.'

Bosworth accepted Hermione's lie in good faith and offered to accompany her. It took some ingenuity on her behalf to dissuade him. She reasoned that in the event she found any clues in the passage it might be hard to explain her interest in them without arousing the butler's suspicions.

The stairs were old and creaked under Hermione's weight as she descended to the ground floor of the central wing. She paused and looked around her. The stone passage was lit by overhead strip lighting. A mild coating of dust on the flagstone floor suggested it hadn't been swept for a week or two.

All I need to do now is find the entrance to the gun room, thought Hermione. *This must be the way Sebastian came on the night of the murder. He's far more likely to have shot George than anyone else. Lyle is wrong to suspect Diana murdered George in order to protect Sebastian. I've known her all my life and she simply isn't capable of murdering anyone in cold blood – least of all a family friend like George Lowestoft...*

At strategic intervals along the passage she saw numbers written in chalk on the wall panels. She came at last to panel number four which according to Bosworth marked the entrance to the gun room. Her attention was drawn to a discarded burnt match lying on the floor.

A few feet away, on the opposite side of the passage,

there was a cupboard. She opened the door and saw it was full of boxes containing fireworks, presumably put there in preparation for Guy Fawkes' night. One box was evidently left over from the previous years' celebrations because it was half-empty. It dawned on her as she closed the door that George Lowestoft's killer had been distinctly clever in helping himself to one of the firecrackers from it. After such a lapse of time, no one would know for certain how many firecrackers ought to have remained in the box.

The atmosphere in the passage had become oppressive. Hermione took a moment to steady her nerves, then she activated the spring mechanism on the wall. She found herself holding her breath as she watched the secret panel swing silently inwards on its hinges. Without waiting for the panel to open fully, she slipped through the gap.

A voice inside the gun room demanded, *'What the hell are you doing here?'*

Hermione turned sharply. 'I've loved secret passages ever since I was a child.'

Her glib response sounded false to her own ears and drew a look of derision from Sebastian. She had the curious impression he had been lying in wait for her. He swung the panel shut, thereby preventing her from escaping into the servants' passage.

'There was nothing mysterious about George's death,' said Sebastian. 'The gun room is officially out of bounds. Do you hear?'

'Diana thinks I might have left my bag in here after we found the body.'

Glancing around the gun room, Sebastian said, 'Well, it's not here now. I don't think it ever was.' His unspoken anger was almost palpable. 'Ah, Gervase, there you are,' he added, as the Duke of Marsden entered the gun room from the vaulted corridor.

Looking annoyed at finding the gun room occupied, Gervase said, 'Is everything all right?'

'Hermione was indulging her curiosity,' said Sebastian softly. 'From now on I think you ought to keep the gun room locked. We can do without any more – accidents.'

Outside in the vaulted corridor, Gervase locked the door and put the key in his pocket.

In response to her enquiry as to whether any ghosts inhabited Arlington, Gervase said, 'I'm sorry to disappoint you, Hermione. All the Cosgroves have died peacefully in their sleep.' His voice resonated with irony. 'There's a book about Arlington in the library. There's still time for you to look at it before everyone goes into lunch.'

Annoyed with herself for having been caught snooping, Hermione thanked Gervase for his suggestion and walked off self-consciously down the corridor in the direction of the library. After her terse encounter with Sebastian, she was more convinced than ever that he was the killer. In all probability, he had stolen the blue folder and destroyed it in order to divert suspicion from himself.

As Hermione entered the library, she came face to face with Irene Lowestoft's maid. They stared at each other and then Pym broke the silence by speaking in a low, unhurried, monotonal voice.

'Mrs Lowestoft asked me to find her cigarette lighter. It's not here.'

Hermione found it hard to imagine how the old hag had looked as a young woman. Her face bore the ravages and dark blotches of a hard-lived life. Her eyes were red and watery and her tongue was coated white as if she'd been drinking milk. Or rather – Hermione's glance took in the nearby drinks cabinet – Bailey's Irish cream liquor.

Pym is even more sour-faced than I remembered, thought Hermione. *Trying to befriend the cantankerous old slattern will be a waste of time. My only hope is to startle her into admitting some small fact that might put me on the right track.*

'Pym, I want you to tell me what you overheard on the night of the shooting,' said Hermione firmly.

Pym gave a disapproving sniff. 'I'm sure I don't know what you mean, ma'am.'

Hermione pressed on desperately, 'The only thing we owe the dead is the truth. You heard someone in the gun room talking to Mr Lowestoft. Tell me who it was.'

'I only heard the gunshot – like everyone else.'

'Then you *saw* something everyone else missed,' persisted Hermione. 'We both know George Lowestoft was murdered. Tell me what you saw or heard.'

Pym's reply took Hermione by surprise.

'Sometimes our misconceptions get in the way of our seeing what we should.'

The old maid's gait was unsteady as she left the library and Hermione suspected she was a secret drinker.

Now what do you mean by that, I wonder?

16

Diana was dreaming...

She was a young woman once again living in Nazi occupied France. The Gestapo had raided Theodore and Odette Mariettes' chateau and killed them for colluding with the French Resistance...

In the nearby woods she was standing with the couple's terrified servants by the side of the quarry. She was unable to see Captain Dietrich's face because he was standing beyond the edges of her peripheral vision...

It was a cold February morning in 1944 – and they were waiting for him to give the order for them to die...

Hermione and Lyle were having breakfast at Nettlebed when they heard the metallic clatter of the letter flap in the front door followed by a plopping sound as the day's mail hit the mat. There was only one letter of any interest and it was addressed to Hermione. She saw the London postmark and ripped the envelope open.

'Jean-Luc de Breteuil's letter has arrived,' she said breathlessly. 'He says he's grateful for the invitation to my cello recital at Milsham Castle. But he regrets he and Angelique won't be able to attend because they have a prior engagement.' She turned the letter over and stared at the signature. '*My God, you're not going to believe it...*'

Lyle felt a rush of excitement. 'What is it –?'

'Jean-Luc's signature doesn't resemble Captain Dietrich's signature in the slightest,' she exclaimed. 'His handwriting is totally different.'

Lyle cursed out loud. 'We've made complete fools of ourselves!'

Hermione was bitterly disappointed. 'We were wrong to imagine Jean-Luc is Captain Dietrich.'

Lyle summed up the bewilderment and frustration they were both feeling by saying, 'The trail has gone completely cold. Where do we go from here...?'

Later that day, after discussing various household matters with Bosworth, Diana returned to her bedroom at Arlington and found her cousin sitting in front of the dressing-table. Irene Lowestoft was trying on the pearl necklace Gervase had given Diana for her birthday. There was a look of happy contemplation on her face.

'Irene, what are you doing here in my room?'

Irene was momentarily startled, then she saw Diana's reflection in the mirror and turned to face her. 'I've been waiting for you,' she said in a friendly voice. 'I thought we might talk.'

'Gervase tells me he's invited you to stay with us

indefinitely,' said Diana coldly.

'I'm destitute so I had no choice other than to accept his kind invitation.' Irene played out a tragic pause, then added, 'Gervase is worried about my bronchitis. He's given the adjoining guest bedroom to Pym.'

'Aren't the servants' quarters good enough for her?' asked Diana sarcastically. Her nerves were on edge and she felt angry with herself for betraying the fact. 'Why do you keep her on? She can't be of much use to you. She's incredibly ancient.'

'So am I for that matter,' said Irene gently. 'Youth comes and goes so quickly.' There was an awkward pause, then she added in a tone of quiet desperation, 'I don't imagine you're happy about my being here. I've lost everything. George overextended his finances without telling Sebastian or Gervase. The manor house in Market Chadwell will be going under the auctioneer's hammer in October. I still won't have enough money after it's sold to pay off George's debts.'

'How can you bring yourself to stay at Arlington – after what happened to George?' asked Diana with a shiver.

'What else am I supposed to do? The idea of being alone terrifies me. George and I were together for so long. I – I'm not sure I know how to go on without him.'

'You have your maid.'

'Pym? She ought to have retired years ago. It's not the same as having a wonderful husband and home like you do, Diana. I had everything I wanted – until my husband shot himself. There's nothing worse than losing the man you love.'

Irene's eyes filled with tears as she unfastened Diana's pearls from around her throat. She returned them to the jewellery box on the dressing-table next to Diana's bottle of Tagamet capsules.

'I – I'd like us to put our past rivalries behind us, Diana. We're not silly young girls any more. We both know better. I wouldn't impose on your kindness if Pym and I had anywhere else to live.'

Nothing has changed between Irene and me, thought Diana despondently. *I'd only be fooling myself if I thought it had. George's death has led to a temporary truce between us. It would be nice if it lasted, but I know it won't. Irene has always been jealous of me and coveted everything I have – including my pearls and my husband.*

'Gervase ought to have consulted me before he spoke to you, Irene. I don't want you living at Arlington with us. I'm aware of your fondness for my grandson. You're welcome to stay here until Sebastian marries Gabriella. On the morning after the wedding, I expect you to leave Arlington for good. Your manor house in Market Chadwell isn't being auctioned off until two weeks later. That ought to give you plenty of time to decide what to do with your future.'

'I had hoped from what Gervase said –'

Diana's voice hardened. 'My decision is final, Irene. I'm not prepared to offer you a permanent home here at Arlington. There's nothing else left for us to say to each other. Now would you please leave my room? I wish to be alone.'

'I'm grateful to you for your kindness, Diana.'

Irene's eyes burned with humiliation and her mask of cordiality slipped momentarily to reveal a glimpse of the hatred she was feeling for Diana. Summoning a watery smile, she left the room.

Diana swallowed a Tagamet capsule and thought to

herself, *Irene can't be trusted. She would never forgive me if she thought George killed himself because I refused to help him out of his financial difficulties. I won't be happy until she leaves Arlington...*

That afternoon Diana visited Milsham Castle and said a prayer for George Lowestoft in the small private Roman Catholic chapel near the main house. He was a distant relative of Lord Milsham's and had been laid to rest in the family crypt.

Milsham Castle was closed for the day to the public and Diana was given a private tour around the estate by Hermione and Lyle. Decades before, Diana had attended a dance there as a young debutante. One of the young men with whom she had danced was George Lowestoft. Sadly, his widow Irene had fallen out with Lord Milsham some years ago and the peer had refused to offer her a home at Milsham Castle. Irene was going to have to find somewhere else to live after the manor house in Market Chadwell was sold. Diana felt sorry for her cousin, but this in no way weakened her resolve to ensure Irene left Arlington after Sebastian's and Gabriella's wedding.

Over tea in the drawing-room, as the fragrance of roses drifted in through the window, Diana said, 'I'm sorry Gervase and I had to go to Chequers. Now that Hermione has told me about your flair for solving murders, Lyle, I'm inclined to take your suspicions more seriously. No one was more surprised than I was when George apparently took his own life.'

'I'm convinced the missing blue folder holds the key to the mystery,' said Lyle gravely. 'Have you spoken to

Sebastian?'

'Yes – and he says he has no idea who took it from the Great Hall.'

'What about the servants?' prompted Hermione.

'The servants also deny taking it.'

Lyle exchanged frustrated glances with Hermione. 'Sebastian left the blue folder on top of Oliver's briefcase shortly before dinner,' he recapitulated. 'By the end of the night, it was missing – along with Captain Dietrich's draft report confessing to the murders of Theodore and Odette Mariette.'

Diana looked at him with her remarkably clear green eyes. 'Nothing would give me greater pleasure than to see Captain Dietrich convicted of their murders along with the rest of his war crimes. You were wise to make a copy of the draft report before it disappeared.'

'We think George saw who took the blue folder,' said Hermione.

Diana's eyes widened a little, but she gave no other sign of emotion. 'It's odd you're saying that,' she said slowly. 'Earlier in the night, George told Gervase there was nothing he would like to do more than capture a Nazi war criminal – presumably because a large number have yet to be found and punished for their war crimes. Now I can't help wondering if George knew more about Captain Dietrich's present whereabouts than he was willing to admit at the time.'

'It seems George asked a lot of questions about your car accident,' said Hermione. 'It's possible he discovered Captain Dietrich siphoned the brake fluid from your Daimler.'

'That would certainly explain why the brakes failed,' said

Diana with a shiver. 'I don't believe for one moment Captain Dietrich is one of the servants. Just before the crash, Oliver told me that Captain Dietrich was masquerading as a member of British high society.'

'Pym claims no one other than George went into the gun room,' said Hermione. 'Provided she's telling the truth, that means the killer used the servants' passage to enter and leave the gun room without being seen.'

'I had no idea the gun room was connected to the servants' passage,' said Diana. 'Arlington has over two hundred rooms. I know the main ones, of course.' She fell silent, her expression clouded with anxiety.

'Do you think you could speak to the servants again?' said Hermione. 'And ask them whether they saw anyone in the servants' passage near the gun room shortly before the shooting?'

'I don't imagine there should be any difficulty in my doing that,' said Diana on a more practical note. 'There were just over a hundred couples at my wedding anniversary party. A surprising number of husbands wrote accepting the invitation Gervase and I extended to them and their wives. None of their signatures resembled Captain Dietrich's. I've drawn up a list of those guests who obviously can't be Captain Dietrich for reasons of their age or social standing.'

'How many men are still unaccounted for?' said Lyle.

'Thirty-two,' replied Diana. 'Since their identity is open to doubt, I think it would be a good idea if Hermione and I invented a pretext for writing to them. Once each of them writes back to us, we'll do a comparison with Captain Dietrich's signature and see if we get a match.'

Hermione nodded approvingly. 'That sounds like a good idea. If Captain Dietrich was at Arlington, we shouldn't have any difficulty flushing him out.'

'In the meantime' – Diana turned to Lyle – 'I thought you both might like to have this photo album I put together. On the night George died, nearly all the guests were photographed as they arrived in the Long Gallery. Captain Dietrich won't look at all like the young Gestapo officer who tried to kill me. But it's possible the photos might prove helpful in some way.'

'We're truly grateful for all your help,' said Lyle fervently. 'I know we've asked you this question before, Diana, but can you think of any of the guests who might fit Captain Dietrich's overall description?'

Diana shook her head. 'I've given the matter a great deal of thought,' she said, 'but I really can't think of any one. If Captain Dietrich discovers you've hidden a copy of the draft report in Lord Milsham's library, he could come looking for it. From now on, you need to take extra care...'

A week later, Diana went up to London and visited Frederick Steen at his elegant Georgian terrace house overlooking Regent's Park. No expense had been spared in furnishing the grade I listed property with exquisite antiques and tapestries.

Over afternoon tea in the drawing-room, Diana discussed the details of Gabriella's and Sebastian's forthcoming nuptials with her host. It was apparent Frederick Steen adored his only daughter.

'My only regret,' he said, 'is that Gabriella's mother is not alive. She would have been so proud to see Gabriella get married.'

'I imagine you loved your wife very much,' said Diana

gently.

'Eleanor was the most wonderful woman I've ever known,' said Frederick simply.

Glancing at the painting above the mantelpiece, Diana remarked, 'Gabriella bears a striking resemblance to the portrait of your wife.' Her gaze flitted around the drawing-room and came to rest on an antique easel. The painting on it seemed somehow familiar. 'What an exquisite painting!'

Frederick smiled proudly. 'I'm glad you like it. I thought you saw it the last time you were here?'

'No, there was another painting on the easel.'

Diana stopped. She had been about to say she had never seen the painting before. But she had a curious feeling that wasn't true. It depicted a woman reclining naked against a piece of velvet.

'It's called *Nu Dans Sa Chambre*,' said Frederick. 'It's by a little-known French artist called –'

'Michel Dupree,' blurted Diana. 'I knew him well.'

Frederick accepted the coincidence with perfect *savoir faire*. 'The painting was given to me by a married couple. I've had it for many years now.'

'Perhaps I might know them,' said Diana curiously.

'Their name escapes me,' said Frederick. 'You know the translation of the title?'

'Nude in her Bedroom,' replied Diana. Her surprise at seeing the painting was so profound she had difficulty focusing her thoughts. *I feel as if I've encountered a long-forgotten ghost from my past,* she thought. Out loud, she said, 'I'm actually Anglo-French. My father came from Yorkshire. As a teenager, I was raised in Paris by my mother

which is why I speak such impeccable French. She was a celebrated Parisian dressmaker. During the Second World War, I became a member of the French Resistance. For a time, I was the most wanted female enemy agent in France. My codename was the Vixen.' She stopped, unable to account for the reason why she had mentioned the war.

'What an extraordinary life you've led.'

'The painting was originally owned by friends of mine – Theodore and Odette Mariette,' continued Diana. 'They lived in a chateau just outside L'Evette. Michel Dupree died of emphysema in the early stages of the war. He left all his artwork to them. They were a charming middle-aged couple.'

'Diana, you're looking pale. Are you feeling all right?'

'I was remembering the Mariettes. They died at the hands of the Gestapo.'

'I'm sorry your memories are painful ones.'

Diana spoke with a shudder. 'The officer who killed them was a brutal man called Captain Helmut Dietrich.'

The coffee spoon slipped from Frederick's fingers and fell against the side of the saucer. Dragged back in time against her will, Diana was hardly conscious of the rattling sound.

'Memory is such a strange thing,' she went on. 'I can recall Captain Dietrich's name easily enough, but after all these years his face is a blur in my mind.'

Frederick said, 'My family were Polish Jews. We suffered a terrible fate when Germany invaded Poland. My entire family was wiped out. I spent the duration of the war in a concentration camp. It was a terrible experience.'

Diana swallowed a lump in her throat. 'I'm sorry to have

touched on such distressing memories, Frederick. The war claimed so many innocent lives.'

'The couple from whom I bought the painting after the war ended were very young,' said Frederick. 'They told me they needed the money in order to marry each other. I hope they have a long and happy life. I want the same for Gabriella and Sebastian. They love each other so much.'

Diana was reassured by his words. 'With our help, I'm sure they will, Frederick – I'm sure they will...'

17

At last the day of the wedding had come. A banner, emblazoned with the words *Congratulations Sebastian and Gabriella,* hung from the first-floor balcony rail in Arlington's Great Hall. Hundreds of helium-filled balloons of every conceivable colour were tied with long ribbons to everything in sight to prevent them from rising to the ceiling of the dome.

By four o'clock that evening the private chapel was packed to capacity. Everyone's attention was on Gabriella, looking exquisitely lovely in her ivory tower of lace, as she glided up the aisle on the arm of her father. Frederick Steen was beaming with paternal pride. Sebastian, dapper in dove grey tails, was standing before the altar. A smile ravished Gabriella's lips when she saw him and he was transported with happiness. There was complete love and trust in their eyes for each other. It was a joyful occasion with no portent of the tragedy that was about to unfold.

Diana was sitting on a front-row pew gazing at her grandson's bride. *Gabriella looks so beautiful,* she thought.

My friend Michel Dupree would have enjoyed painting her in the nude.

As the ceremony began, Diana found herself thinking about Michel Dupree's painting *Nu Dans Sa Chambre.* The last time she had seen it was at the Mariettes' chateau on the night they were murdered. The fact had eluded her memory until now. She shuddered as she recalled how Captain Dietrich had slit their throats and helped himself to their possessions.

Diana's nightmare had returned last night. Only this time, as she stood with the Mariettes' servants by the side of the quarry, she had seen Captain Dietrich's cruel young face and cold blue eyes. Rather than wake up terrified, she had gone on dreaming. He had been standing so close to her that she could see every line and pore on his face.

I should never have agreed to make the television documentary about my life, thought Diana sadly. *It's brought back so many ghosts, so many memories... I lost so many courageous, wonderful friends during the war... If Michel Dupree hadn't died of emphysema, he would have gone on to be recognised as a truly great artist.* Her gaze fell on Gabriella's father and her next thought filled her with hope. *I wonder if Frederick might be persuaded to sell* Nu Dans Sa Chambre *to me?*

Suddenly, with a terrible sense of conviction, Diana realized *she was looking at Captain Helmut Dietrich.* It was as if a mist in front of her eyes had cleared. She had seen Frederick Steen's face many times before, but never from this angle or in such a translucent light. The bones of the jaw and cheek looked more pronounced than usual. She had been wrong to assume he had died by the side of the quarry...

The priest was intoning, *'Should any one present know of any reason that this couple should not be joined in holy matrimony, speak now or forever hold your peace...'*

Diana rose to her feet. Her horror and unwavering certainty were compounded by an urgent desire.

Sebastian's marriage to Gabriella mustn't go ahead, she thought. *I won't allow my grandson to marry the daughter of a Nazi murderer.*

Frederick Steen, hearing an inarticulate cry of pain, turned and looked directly at Diana.

'Stop – stop the wedding!' she cried.

Diana looked into the eyes of the brutal Gestapo officer who had murdered her friends... Frederick Steen's eyes – instead of being blue like Captain Dietrich's – were a vivid green. She realized at once that he must be wearing coloured eye contact lenses. The signature on the letters he had sent to her, discussing the details of the wedding, bore no resemblance to Captain Dietrich's signature; it was obvious the letters must have been written and signed for him by someone else – *like his daughter Gabriella...*

Suddenly, Diana clutched her midriff as a shaft of pain seared through her stomach. 'I – I don't feel well,' she gasped.

She belatedly remembered the advice of Dr Cheadle who had attended her throughout her recent attacks of gastroenteritis.

'At your time of life, Diana, you need to be more careful about your diet. Avoid rich foods such as shellfish, fried food and chocolates – and, above all else, avoid stress.'

The congregation gave a collective sigh of dismay as she slid to the floor in a dead faint.

By eight o'clock that night, the wedding celebrations were in full swing in the Long Gallery. Rupert had reassured everyone that his stepmother Diana had recovered from her fainting spell and was chatting to her guests in various rooms around the house. His explanation went unchallenged.

Lyle Revel was looking forward to taking Hermione to the Norfolk Broads the following day for a fortnight's holiday. They planned to leave behind the demands of their everyday lives by hiring a cabin cruiser to explore the waterways. He envisaged days of hazy sunshine - spent sunbathing, birdwatching, and fishing - as well as the occasional skinny-dipping expedition in the moonlight. He was about to help himself to some food from the cold buffet when his attention was caught by Irene Lowestoft's maid. Pym was standing in the doorway of the Long Gallery.

'Excuse me, sir. Would you mind telling Mr Steen there's an urgent phone call for him in the library? His solicitor is calling from London.'

Frederick Steen was talking to a group of friends. His face registered mild surprise when Lyle spoke to him. He thanked Lyle for the message and left the Long Gallery.

A couple of minutes later, Frederick Steen entered the library. The call from his solicitor must be important although he was at a loss to understand what the problem might be. He adored his daughter Gabriella almost to the point of obsession and was anxious to get back to the party.

The receiver was lying on the desk next to the phone.

He picked it up and frowned when he heard the dial tone.

'You can hang up. The line is dead.'

Startled, Frederick turned to face the person who had issued the command. 'I was told I was wanted on the phone,' he said.

'That was a ruse on my part to get you alone,' said Pym. 'It must be an exciting day for you – seeing your daughter get married.'

'I'm very proud of Gabriella.'

'Just how proud is she of you?' asked Pym.

Frederick had not survived the Second World War without having a fine instinct for danger and every fibre in his being urged him to be on his guard, especially at the mention of his daughter. There was something malevolent in the old woman's gaze.

'Who are you?' he asked.

'I'm Mrs Lowestoft's maid – Marjorie Pym. I want to speak to you about the past.'

Frederick grew tense. Good God, surely she couldn't – *no,* it was impossible! He had covered his tracks so well after the defeat of Germany. Fleeing from the smouldering embers of his country with a fake passport and a new identity, he had gone to South America and rebuilt his life from scratch as a hard-working chemist whose good luck it had been to marry an English pharmaceutical heiress. Eleanor's death four years into their marriage had left him a very rich, albeit lonely, man with a young daughter to raise by himself. He was widely respected as a pharmaceutical giant and his position in British high society was unassailable. This old crone couldn't possibly know the truth.

Frederick smiled politely. 'The past must hold happy memories for you,' he said, stalling for time.

'Orphaned at birth, I was,' said Pym scornfully, 'and I've not had much luck since then. During the war I only got married because my Albert got me in the family way. He was one of the under-gardeners at Thurlestone Hall where I worked as a land girl. Albert and I were both as young and silly as each other. He made the mistake of joining the RAF. In no time at all the Germans shot his plane down over the North Sea. The shock of becoming a widow was too much and I lost our baby.'

'How tragic.'

'The Nazis were an evil lot. They caused a lot of hardship and suffering for everyone.'

Frederick felt nothing but contempt and disgust for her. 'Your past is of no concern to me,' he said coldly. 'Don't waste my time like this again.'

He walked towards the door.

'We haven't spoken yet about your past, Captain Dietrich...'

Frederick slowly turned and looked at Pym. He felt as if an electrical charge had gone through him. Every nerve ending in his body was tingling.

'You've mistaken me for someone else,' he said. 'I was born a poor Polish Jew. My father was a humble tailor. When Germany invaded Poland at the beginning of the war, my entire family was slaughtered. I was the only member of my family to survive. Food was scarce in the concentration camp. On more than one occasion I came close to starving to death. I was forced to capture and eat rats.'

Pym's response was inexorable. 'On 5 February 1944,

as Captain Helmut Dietrich, you raided a French chateau outside L'Evette owned by Theodore and Odette Mariette. I've seen the draft report you wrote to your commanding officer. It's there in the blue folder on the table. You murdered the Mariettes for colluding with the French Resistance. You're very silent, Captain Dietrich. The Mariettes' servants didn't fare any better, did they? Are you remembering how you took them to the quarry the next day to execute them?'

Frederick's heart was racing. This pathetic old woman gave every appearance of being crazy! Yet, somehow, *she knew he was Captain Helmut Dietrich!* How could she have discovered the truth after all these years...?

'Look inside the blue folder if you don't believe me,' instructed Pym. 'The draft report was left on the table in the Great Hall next to the bouquet of lilies you sent to the Duke and Duchess of Marsden on their wedding anniversary. The signature on the draft report is the same as the one on the card attached to the bouquet. If I hadn't admired the lilies so much, I would never have found out your secret.'

Frederick walked over to the desk and examined the contents of the blue folder. He felt a flicker of curiosity as he saw the handwritten card. He caught his breath at the sight of the draft report he had signed decades earlier as Captain Helmut Dietrich. He had always prided himself on his beautiful signature and now it had come back to haunt him. A team of handwriting experts would be able to testify in a court of law that *the signatures of Frederick Steen and Captain Helmut Dietrich were one and the same.*

Instead of feeling fear at having his Nazi past exposed, Frederick Steen felt a curious swelling of pride. The blue folder contained one more document – an excellent translation of his letter from German into English. He nodded his head in approval.

'These are photocopies,' he said sharply. 'Where are the originals?'

'Somewhere safe.'

'You still haven't said what you want from me,' he said.

'Money,' said Pym simply. 'I want you to make a regular cash payment of fifty thousand pounds to me on the first Wednesday of each month until I tell you to stop.'

It wasn't as bad as he had feared. She could have asked him for a lot more. He was an immensely wealthy man. It was obvious she was planning to go on blackmailing him for the rest of her life. *Or was she?*

Frederick's thoughts were racing. *Her husband's plane was shot down over the North Sea by the Luftwaffe. As inconceivable as it seems, she might actually have loved this Albert fellow. She could be planning a widow's revenge – blackmail followed by the exposure of my Nazi past! It would be a mistake to underestimate this malevolent old hag. I must handle her with the utmost care – or it could cost me everything...*

Frederick removed his wallet from his pocket and extracted some notes. 'Here's five hundred pounds as a goodwill gesture,' he said. 'This is all I have on me. You'll get the first instalment of fifty thousand pounds after I visit my bank.'

Pym nodded. 'I want it on Wednesday next week.'

Frederick said, 'I suggest we meet by Nelson's Column in Trafalgar Square at midday. I'll bring the money in a briefcase.'

'I'll be waiting for you,' said Pym.

It was strange how she seemed to have no fear of him. Anyone else in her position would have had the good sense to be terrified. His brow cleared suddenly – he understood the reason for her absence of fear.

She hates being a servant, he thought. *Her hatred of her downtrodden life is stronger than her fear of death.* Out loud, he said, 'I'm grateful to you for coming to me in this matter. All I ask in return is that you don't tell anyone about our private arrangement.'

Pym said primly, 'You have my word' and left the library.

Frederick Steen's face was transformed by fury. *Pym needn't think she can blackmail me forever. Sooner or later all my enemies die...*

Angelique de Breteuil was woken by the sound of the phone on her bedside table. The beautifully decorated house she shared with her husband Jean-Luc in Bruton Street in central London was quiet and still at its centre. A soft, early morning light filtered through the curtains.

Gervase's voice came over the phone line. 'Angelique, is it safe to talk?'

'I've told you before – Jean-Luc and I have separate bedrooms,' she said. 'He's unlikely to be awake.'

Gervase's voice sounded worried. 'I hardly got any sleep last night.'

'It's seven o'clock,' she said. 'Is everything all right?'

'Diana is dead...'

A surge of adrenaline woke Angelique up completely and she was overwhelmed by a feeling of euphoria.

'What happened?' she gasped, struggling to keep a grip on her emotions.

'After Diana fainted in the chapel yesterday, Rupert and I took her upstairs to her room. I phoned for Dr Cheadle, but by the time he reached her side she was dead.'

'It was such a hot day,' murmured Angelique. 'I expect the heat was too much for her.'

Gervase spoke in a stifled voice. 'Rupert and I didn't dare tell another soul what had happened. Sebastian's and Gabriella's wedding celebrations would have been ruined if news of Diana's death had leaked out. You know what this means, don't you?'

There were so many things Angelique wanted to say to Gervase, but her instincts urged caution in case Jean-Luc or one of the servants was using a phone extension to eavesdrop on the conversation.

Diana's death had released Gervase from the shackles of his unhappy marriage. There had been a time, long before Angelique had grown to hate Diana, when she had been grateful to her for marrying Gervase because he had needed her money to save Arlington.

Now that Diana was dead all her money went to Gervase. Her death meant freedom for them both...

'I'm grateful for your call,' said Angelique in a remote voice, her mouth curving upwards in a catlike smile. 'We'll talk again soon, *I promise...*'

18

'Diana died soon after she collapsed in the chapel,' said Hermione, her voice swollen with emotion. 'Part of me feels numb with grief and another part feels really angry. Why couldn't Gervase or Rupert have told us at the time?'

'If word of Diana's death had got out, it would have ruined Sebastian's and Gabriella's wedding celebrations,' said Lyle gently.

Hermione wiped a tear from her cheek. 'I can't believe Gervase and Rupert let us go off to the Norfolk Broads for a fortnight's holiday without telling us what had happened.'

Following their return to Nettlebed earlier that day, they had been shocked to receive a phone call from Rupert telling them the sad news about Diana's death.

Lyle stared moodily out of the living-room window. 'It must have been a hundred times worse for Sebastian and Gabriella,' he said. 'They had to postpone their honeymoon so they could attend Diana's funeral.'

'I'm not sure I'll ever forgive Gervase and Rupert for

denying us the opportunity of paying our final respects to Diana.'

'Hermione, there's something you ought to know,' said Lyle slowly. 'On the night of the wedding, Irene Lowestoft's maid asked me to tell Frederick Steen there was an important phone call for him in the library.'

'Why didn't you tell me sooner?'

'I forgot,' said Lyle with an uncharacteristic hangdog expression.

'It's a breach of protocol for a visiting lady's maid to pass on messages to other guests,' said Hermione with the certainty of someone well-versed on the subject of servants.

Lyle gazed at her uneasily. 'A short while later, I saw Pym coming out of the library. She was looking distinctly pleased with herself.'

Hermione frowned. 'It sounds as if Pym lured Frederick Steen to the library so she could speak to him.'

'I can't help wondering if Pym is blackmailing Frederick Steen because he's Captain Dietrich,' said Lyle quietly.

A look of ridicule sprang up in Hermione's eyes. 'Frederick Steen is a Polish Jew,' she protested. 'He spent the war in a concentration camp.'

'Hermione, I want you to cast your mind back to the night of Diana's and Gervase's wedding anniversary. Pym saw us leave the blue folder containing Captain Dietrich's draft report on the table in the Great Hall.'

'What if she did?''

'Do you remember the bouquet of lilies we saw on the table?'

'How could I forget?' said Hermione. 'The scent was marvellous. They were delivered to Arlington by messenger that afternoon. While we were dining in the Grand Saloon, Diana mentioned they were a gift from Frederick Steen.'

'My inner voice is telling me that after we left the Great Hall,' said Lyle, 'Pym looked through the contents of the blue folder. She must have got a huge surprise when she saw the signature on the card attached to the bouquet was identical to the one on Captain Dietrich's draft report.'

'It's an ingenious theory,' conceded Hermione, taking several moments to assimilate the idea. 'Diana and Gervase received lots of gifts. I doubt if they personally opened them all or read the card attached to the bouquet. Rupert or someone else will have done that and arranged afterwards for thank you letters to be sent out.'

'I'm convinced Frederick Steen is our man,' said Lyle with a look of quiet exaltation in his eyes.

Hermione was not so easily persuaded. 'Are you forgetting Diana and I sent letters to all the men who were possible candidates for Captain Dietrich? She and I came to the inescapable conclusion none of them was Captain Dietrich after receiving handwritten replies from every single one of them.'

'It's obvious the one person you both overlooked is the father of the bride,' said Lyle.

'You could be right,' said Hermione, frowning in an effort of recollection. 'If it makes you feel any better, I can write to Frederick Steen and invite him to a dinner party at Milsham Castle. You'll be able to see his signature for yourself when he writes back to us.'

'Hermione, we may have to face the possibility Diana was murdered...'

Hermione was startled. 'What you're suggesting is ridiculous,' she said. 'Diana died of natural causes. Dr

Cheadle signed her death certificate –'

'What if he was wrong to believe she died of gastroenteritis? What if she was poisoned? Suppose Frederick Steen murdered George Lowestoft and Diana to prevent them from exposing his true identity?'

A look of anger flared in Hermione's eyes. 'Dr Cheadle isn't the fool you're making him out to be,' she said coldly. 'There was nothing suspicious about Diana's death. I would know if there had been.'

'Suppose you're wrong,' persisted Lyle, '*and Diana was murdered...?*'

Hermione fought back tears. 'A fortnight before her death, Diana told me she wasn't making any plans after the New Year. At the time I was surprised and then I later remembered her once telling me, "It's not in my nature to sit around and do nothing. I must keep busy. That will be the case until shortly before the end when I'll suddenly cancel all my appointments and wait to die." You're *wrong* to suspect Diana was poisoned.'

Lyle refused to back down. 'I think we should ask for Diana's body to be exhumed in order to confirm whether she died of natural causes.'

'On the off chance Frederick Steen is Captain Dietrich?' demanded Hermione scornfully. 'Unless their signatures are identical, we'd only be making complete fools of ourselves. You seem to have forgotten *Frederick Steen has green eyes.*'

Lyle stood his ground. 'The Mariettes' valet Marcel Depardieu might have been mistaken when he said Captain Dietrich had the coldest ice-blue eyes of any man he'd ever seen.'

'You can take my word for it that Frederick Steen's past

is entirely blameless,' said Hermione firmly. 'Once I've written to him and you've seen his signature, you'll know you were wrong to suspect him of being Captain Dietrich. We would only be wasting our time asking the authorities to exhume Diana's body. Trust me – *she died a perfectly natural death...*'

At his home in London, Frederick Steen knew he ought to be satisfied with his life now that his daughter Gabriella was married to Sebastian Rylander, but something was bothering him.

On the desk in his study lay a letter from Hermione Bradbury that had arrived in the afternoon post. The letter invited him to attend a dinner party being given by Lord Milsham. He frowned – uncertain whether to accept. The memory of his encounter with Pym was still fresh in his mind. Lyle Revel had seen him go to the library to speak to Pym. He had also been loitering in the corridor chatting to other guests when Pym had left the library a short while later. Was it possible Lyle Revel also suspected the truth about his past?

Frederick found Gabriella and Sebastian playing table tennis in the games room. He was pleased they had decided to share his town house and make it their main residence. Their youth and vivacity brought warmth and spontaneity into his life. Sebastian was putting on a brave face for Gabriella's sake, but he had been furious to discover his grandmother Diana had left her entire fortune to her husband Gervase.

'Gabriella, would you mind coming to my study when you have a moment?'

'Of course. What is it?'

'I need to speak to you about a business matter.'

Gabriella entered the study a short while later.

'Is anything the matter?'

'Gabriella, my arthritis is playing up again. I need you to write a letter for me.'

After Frederick finished dictating the missive to Gabriella, he read it carefully and nodded his head in satisfaction. Her handwriting and signature looked entirely different to his own.

Dear Hermione,

I would be obliged if you could thank Lord Milsham for his kind invitation to dinner. It is with regret that I am unable to accept owing to a prior engagement. I hope the occasion is a great success.

Yours sincerely,

Frederick Steen

'Gabriella, this is to remain our secret,' he said quietly. 'Is that understood?'

She looked at him with total trust and adoration in her eyes. 'Of course, Daddy, I understand...'

The following day, Frederick Steen's letter arrived in the post at Nettlebed. It was immediately apparent to Hermione and Lyle that the handwriting and signature bore no resemblance to Captain Dietrich's.

Lyle cursed out loud. 'I was so sure I was right!'

Hermione's response was totally lacking in sympathy. 'Every guest is now accounted for,' she said. 'You're just going to have to accept Captain Dietrich wasn't at Arlington on the night George Lowestoft was killed.'

Lyle groaned and said, 'We've led ourselves on a wild goose chase.'

'It's just as well I didn't listen to you,' said Hermione. 'The authorities would have wasted their time exhuming Diana's body. No one poisoned her. *She died of natural causes.*'

'Aren't you at all curious to know why the blue folder went missing from the Great Hall?' demanded Lyle.

'It was probably mislaid by one of the servants. We were wrong to imagine George Lowestoft was murdered. I should never have listened to you in the first place.'

Lyle felt a wave of despair. 'I've never known my inner voice to be wrong –'

'We haven't come up with a single shred of proof that Captain Dietrich is still alive,' said Hermione firmly. 'Diana was convinced he died by the side of the quarry. Trust me, it's time we let go of the past – *and get on with our lives...*'

A month after Diana's death, Hermione and Lyle received a phone call that left them euphoric and prompted them to cancel their plans to go punting with friends that afternoon. They arrived at the St. Francis Xavier Hospital in Gosford in a state of breathless excitement. Their eyes widened in delight at the miracle they saw before them.

Oliver, looking frail and pallid, was resting against his pillows, holding Claudia's hand. He was smiling at Claudia and her face was transformed with joy. She had sat with him every day since the car crash until she was ragged with exhaustion, willing him to come out of his coma, even though his doctors had insisted he was going to die. Oliver's eyes gave a flicker of recognition the moment he saw his friends.

'Did the nurse tell you?' asked Claudia excitedly. 'Oliver came out of his coma two hours ago. I couldn't have asked for a more wonderful birthday present. I'm so thrilled to have him back – I – I could burst with happiness...'

'Hello...'

Oliver's voice sounded raspy from lack of use and he gave them a lopsided smile. He was clearly delighted to see them and was looking as happy as a child for whom Christmas has come early.

Lyle's voice was choked with emotion. 'Oliver, it's wonderful to see you again.'

Tears pricked Hermione's eyes. 'We've missed you so much...'

Claudia gave Oliver a bright smile. 'I've been praying for a miracle for the last three months,' she said shakily, 'and now it's finally come true... Everyone is going to be so thrilled when they hear Oliver has finally woken up...'

Hermione and Lyle stood in the hospital corridor watching Oliver through the glass partition in the wall. A week had passed since Oliver had come out of his coma and he was sitting up in bed being spoon-fed by Claudia whose devotion to him knew no bounds.

The couple had entered into a pact with Claudia not to

tell Oliver that Diana had died. He wasn't strong enough yet to cope with bad news of any kind and the last thing they wanted to do was impede his recovery in any way.

Claudia had been pouring all her energy and love into helping Oliver get well again. She was determined to ensure he made a full recovery. Each day was a series of challenges for Oliver and there were some days when the obstacles confronting him seemed insurmountable. His muscles had dwindled alarmingly through lack of use. It was going to take weeks of regular daily sessions with the physio-therapists to help him regain full use of his limbs and walk properly again.

A cloud came over Lyle's eyes. 'Thankfully Oliver hasn't suffered any brain damage,' he said. 'But the doctors say he's unlikely to remember what happened during the week leading up to the car crash...'

Hermione said, 'Trauma usually has that effect. Did you ask him how he traced Captain Dietrich?'

Lyle released a heavy sigh. 'The search for Captain Dietrich has gone cold once again. Oliver doesn't remember a thing...'

The weeks merged into one another and leaves fell from the trees. The Gosfordshire countryside was transformed into a riot of beautiful autumnal colour that gave way to the grip of a cold winter.

A few days before Christmas Oliver was deemed well enough by his doctors to leave the St. Francis Xavier Hospital. His coordination and movement had improved a lot, but he needed a walking stick to help him get about. He wasn't ready to fend for himself or return to his empty house at Richmond-upon-Thames. Hermione and Lyle invited Oliver and Claudia to stay with them at Nettlebed for the duration of his convalescence and they were relieved when the pair gratefully accepted their offer.

After resting for three weeks, Oliver grew bored with being pampered and began to take a more active interest in his surroundings. Although he wasn't able to venture far from Nettlebed without a minder, one of his greatest pleasures each day was to feed the ducks by Lord Milsham's pond. By February he had fallen into the habit each afternoon of accompanying Lyle around Milsham Castle for half an hour and helping him with some of the lighter duties. Another milestone was reached a few weeks later when Oliver was able to dispense with the use of his walking stick.

'I'm determined to return to work later this year,' he told them one afternoon. 'That's if Claudia doesn't object. She like a mother hen and bosses me around more than the doctors.'

'That's because she really cares about you, Oliver,' said Lyle, with a twinkle in his eyes.

Oliver grinned. 'Claudia says Sebastian did an excellent job running Valiant Productions while I was in hospital. It's a pity he's gone to work for Frederick Steen's pharmaceutical corporation.'

'Claudia is pleased with the new fellow she's hired to take Sebastian's place,' said Hermione. 'The doctors are really impressed with your progress, Oliver.'

Oliver was silent absorbing what they had told him, then he added with a puzzled look in his eyes, 'I only wish I could help you both locate Captain Dietrich. But for the life of me I can't remember how I found him in the first place.

How soon will Diana and Gervase be returning to England?'

'Not for another two or three months,' replied Hermione quickly. 'She and Gervase are coming home via Europe.'

Oliver accepted her lie in good faith and went outside to collect the eggs from the henhouse. His strength and coordination had improved a great deal. He was now able to lock up the main house and chapel by himself after the cleaners and various other individuals who took care of the estate had gone home at the end of each day.

'Oliver has a right to know Diana is dead,' said Hermione in a stricken voice.

'We've promised Claudia not to say anything until he's made a complete recovery,' Lyle reminded her.

'I hate lying to him about Diana.'

Lyle shared her concern. 'The news might come as too much of a shock,' he said. 'It could banish any chance Oliver has of remembering what happened in the week leading up to the car crash. Unless he finds a way to unlock his memories, we may never locate Captain Dietrich...'

At the end of March, Oliver announced he was returning to work in a fortnight's time. Against all the odds, he had made a complete recovery from all his injuries. It had been an incredibly long, hard haul with many setbacks along the way. His recovery seemed nothing short of a miracle.

The news of Diana's death subsequently upset Oliver a great deal. They sat down with Claudia and told him at the start of April. At first, Oliver admitted he wasn't sure if he could forgive them for lying to him, but within a couple of hours he relented because their friendship meant so much to him. Shortly after being released from hospital, Oliver had taken to referring to them as his fellow musketeers – 'one for all and all for one' – and as far as he was concerned nothing was going to undermine their special friendship – not even Diana's tragic passing...

Life resumed its normal pattern for Hermione and Lyle. A warm spring gave way to the pleasures of summer, then, on the afternoon of Friday 22 June, their interest in Captain Dietrich was reawakened after Hermione received an unexpected phone call. She hung up as Lyle entered Nettlebed's kitchen with a bag of groceries he had bought in the nearby village of Compton Sutton.

'That was Claudia phoning from Valiant Productions,' she said excitedly. 'Armand Mariette, the curator of L'Evette War Museum, has been in touch with Oliver. One of Armand's contacts has located his parents' former valet – Marcel Depardieu.'

'It's imperative we speak to Marcel Depardieu as soon as possible,' said Lyle urgently. 'He's the only living person who knows what Captain Dietrich once looked like. It's a miracle he and Diana survived the massacre by the side of the quarry.'

'Claudia is too busy to leave London,' continued Hermione.

'What about Oliver?'

'He's on his way to Yorkshire to shoot the latest series of *Faces and Places* –'

'That only leave us,' said Lyle quickly.

'Claudia asked us if we'd be prepared to speak to Marcel Depardieu,' said Hermione. 'I knew you'd want to so I agreed.'

'Where does he live?'

'At a place called Cedar Lodge in Canterbury. We'll have to stay overnight in a hotel and contact Oliver and Claudia on our return tomorrow. I think we should take Diana's photo album with us on the off chance Captain Dietrich *was* at Arlington on the night George Lowestoft was shot. There's a small chance Marcel Depardieu might recognize him in one of the photos.'

Lyle nodded in approval of Hermione's logic. If they were to bring Captain Dietrich to justice after all these years they had to exhaust every possibility - however slim or remote...

The journey to Canterbury was long and uneventful. The couple arrived at Cedar Lodge Nursing Home around five o'clock that evening. It was a well-preserved Victorian mansion set in attractive gardens. The matron received them with an air of kindly indulgence. She took them outside to a sunny terrace where a white-haired old man was sitting.

Hermione's and Lyle's adrenaline was pumping with excitement as they introduced themselves to Marcel Depardieu and explained the purpose of their visit. He listened attentively and then spoke in a soft, mellifluous voice that was wracked with anguish.

'I remember being taken to the quarry with the Mariettes' servants as if it were yesterday. There was a look of gloating pleasure in Captain Dietrich's eyes. They were the coldest looking blue eyes of any man I've ever seen. It was obvious he was looking forward to killing us. Thinking of him now - all these decades later - still makes the hairs on my neck stand up...'

Hermione could barely contain her eagerness as she

produced Diana's photo album. 'Lyle and I would be grateful if you could look at these photos. Does any one in them remind you of Captain Dietrich?'

A pained expression came over Marcel Depardieu's face. 'I'm terribly sorry to have wasted your time,' he said. 'Clearly no one told you.'

'Told us what?' asked Hermione.

'I lost my eyesight ten years ago.'

'What are you saying –?'

'*I'm completely blind...*'

Hermione and Lyle were shocked and apologized profusely for their misunderstanding. The couple had difficulty swallowing their disappointment. It was clear the charming old man sitting opposite them did not know anything that would enable them to locate Captain Dietrich. After listening to Marcel Depardieu talk about his war experiences for almost three hours, they thanked him for his help and left.

Rather than go to the expense of booking into a hotel for the night, Hermione and Lyle dined at a restaurant in Canterbury and then set off home. Lady Godiva disgraced herself by getting a flat tyre along the way and they got lost twice in the dark. It was almost midnight by the time they reached Nettlebed. The lateness of the hour capped off a truly frustrating day and they felt irritable and exhausted as they clambered into their Tudor four-poster bed.

Two hours later, the alarm shattered the silence up at Milsham Castle. The alarm was old and apt to go off for no apparent reason. The cost of installing a new alarm system was so exorbitant that Lord Milsham had vetoed the suggestion despite repeated appeals from Hermione and Lyle. The incessant noise of the alarm penetrated the fog of

Hermione's sleep. She fumbled for the switch of the bedside lamp and blinked as the light came on.

Lyle stirred next to her. 'Whose turn is it to reset the alarm?' he groaned.

'Yours,' insisted Hermione. 'I can guarantee you there won't be any intruders as usual.'

'If Lord Milsham had to put up with this infernal racket on a regular basis you can bet he'd have the decency to get the problem fixed,' muttered Lyle.

He felt a spurt of resentment towards their employer who was doubtlessly sound asleep in his tax haven in Switzerland. Normally, Hermione and Lyle took turns with their fellow caretakers, Mr and Mrs Elliott, in dealing with the security arrangements, but the Elliotts were currently enjoying a fortnight's holiday in Eastbourne.

Cursing under his breath, Lyle got out of bed and pulled on a pair of brown corduroy trousers and a white cable knit jumper. Downstairs in the kitchen, he slid his bare feet into a pair of Wellington boots and removed a torch from the drawer of the dresser. The keys to the main house and chapel were hanging as usual on a hook by Nettlebed's back door. He grabbed them and hurried outside.

Switching on the torch, Lyle trudged up the drive. A cold wind buffeted him and he recognized it had been a mistake not to pull on a jacket before leaving Nettlebed. The clamour of the alarm grated like a buzz saw on his tired, jangled nerves and grew louder as he approached the house.

Milsham Castle was shrouded in darkness except for a light that filtered out of the library windows. A sharp metallic sound drew Lyle's attention. The noise came from somewhere close at hand. Unless he was mistaken, it was the sound of a closing car door.

Lyle walked around the side of the house. The beam of his torch failed to locate a vehicle of any sort. The sound must have come from further away – carried to him on the wind.

He remembered Diana saying, *'If Captain Dietrich discovers you've hidden a copy of the draft report in Lord Milsham's library, he could come looking for it. From now on, you need to take extra care...'*

Lyle shivered in the cold. 'Is anyone there?' he called out.

By way of an answer, Lyle's assailant struck him from behind. A series of stars exploded inside his head, then he pitched forward into darkness and oblivion...

PART 3

19

'Uncle Roly, have another slice of fruit cake,' urged Hermione. 'I made it especially for you.'

She gazed fondly at Sir Roland Anstruther who was sitting by the side of the inglenook fireplace in Nettlebed's living-room enjoying the warmth of the crackling log fire. The middle-aged barrister was possessed of a face like a mournful basset hound, a fruity voice and an engaging dash of theatricality about him which appealed to juries forced to sit through hours of tedious testimony. He duly helped himself to more cake and agreed to Hermione topping up his cup of tea.

'It will soon be December,' said Hermione, gazing dispiritedly out of the window. 'All I want for Christmas this year is Lyle. I'm not sure I could cope if anything else happened to him.'

The cold mist of a winter's afternoon pressed against the leaded panes as she recalled that dreadful summer's night five months ago when the alarm had gone off at Milsham Castle and she had found Lyle lying unconscious outside the library.

'Lyle, what's this I hear about you being attacked during Royal Ascot week?' asked Sir Roland in concern.

Lyle was lolling in an armchair near the fire. Although the blow to his head had left him concussed for a couple of days, the psychological scars had since healed and he was in remarkably good physical health.

'Following a wasted trip to Canterbury on Friday 22 June, Hermione and I got home shortly before midnight,' he said matter-of-factly. 'About two hours later, we were woken by the sound of the alarm going off up at the main house. The alarm was so dodgy we'd got used to being woken up by it for no good reason at all.'

'We didn't realize we had genuine intruders this time,' said Hermione.

'I left Hermione in bed and went up to the house. There was a light coming from inside the library. Before I could investigate further someone hit me over the back of the head. I must have been out cold for half an hour.'

Sir Roland tutted sympathetically. 'What a dreadful business. Was anyone in the house?'

'Mr and Mrs Elliott were away on holiday,' said Lyle. 'The only occupants were Rupert and Poppy –'

Sir Roland frowned. 'What were they doing there?'

'Gervase disapproves of his son's relationship with Poppy,' replied Hermione. 'Despite Poppy's protests of innocence, Gervase refuses to believe she wasn't responsible for his brother Mortimer's death. Before Diana died, she paid Lord Milsham a handsome sum to enable Rupert and Poppy to meet up at Milsham Castle from time to time. They were also woken by the noise of the alarm going off.'

'The police are reasonably confident the alarm went off accidentally,' said Lyle. 'The burglars weren't to know we keep the keys to the main house and the chapel on a hook by Nettlebed's kitchen door.'

'The alarm frightened the burglars off before they had a chance to break into Milsham Castle or the family chapel,' said Hermione. 'Not that there's much in the donation box at the best of times. The police told us afterwards there had been a string of burglaries in the neighbourhood in recent months.'

Lyle poured himself another cup of tea and said, 'After the Elliotts got back from their holidays, they admitted they hadn't set the alarm at nights when it was their turn to supervise the security arrangements. I can't say I blame them. They were just as fed up as we were at being disturbed by the alarm going off for no apparent reason. Lord Milsham has since installed a new alarm system. It's wonderful not being woken up by the old one.'

'Diana died over a year ago,' remarked Hermione. 'As you can imagine, the results of her exhumation came as a terrible shock. Somehow we weren't altogether surprised when Gervase was arrested for poisoning her.'

'He needed Diana's money to keep Arlington,' said Lyle, 'and his affair with Angelique de Breteuil has been going on for years.'

'We were one of the first people to discover Diana was poisoned,' continued Hermione sadly. 'It just so happens we were shopping in Gosford and stopped off at the Golden Eagle for a drink. By pure chance, we bumped into Gavin Bond –'

'You would never guess he's an eminent toxicologist,' said Lyle. 'He has the most appalling sense of humour.'

'We were at Eton together,' remarked Sir Roland. 'Even then, Gavin's idea of what is funny was regarded as perverse by most people. It doesn't bother him in the slightest when others are offended by his jokes.'

'We'd heard rumours that Diana's body was about to be exhumed,' said Hermione, 'but everyone kept denying them. Anyway, I exerted my fatal charm on Gavin Bond and asked him if the rumours were true.'

'What Hermione and I didn't know is the result of the autopsy was already known. Off the record Gavin Bond told us there was a great deal more than split ends in Diana's hair. We were shocked when he told us her hair also contained arsenic.'

'Age certainly hasn't cured Gavin Bond's fondness for gallows humour,' said Sir Roland disapprovingly. 'Toxicologists and pathologists often adopt it as a defence mechanism, of course. Did it never occur to you that Diana might have been poisoned?'

Hermione's eyes filled with tears. 'If we'd known how closely the symptoms of arsenic poisoning mimic gastroenteritis, we would have insisted on an autopsy being carried out immediately after she died. We had no idea she had been suffering from regular bouts of food poisoning. She was rather vain about her health and disliked admitting to any kind of illness.'

'Defending Diana's husband is going to be one of the most challenging briefs of my career,' said Sir Roland. 'The evidence against Gervase is overwhelming – and not just because he inherited all her money.'

'Assuming Gervase is innocent, how do you propose to get him off?' asked Lyle.

'I was hoping *you* could help me, Lyle,' said Sir Roland

with a touch of asperity in his voice. 'Your reputation for solving murders has preceded you. If you were to resurrect Captain Dietrich from the dead, I could argue he poisoned Diana to prevent her from exposing his Nazi past.'

'If I knew his whereabouts, I'd be only too happy to tell you,' said Lyle with a tinge of regret in his voice.

'Uncle Roly, did you know Diana was planning to reinstate Sebastian and Claudia in her will? A week before she died, she told them both that she was going up to London after the wedding in order to see her solicitor and sign her new will.'

Lyle said, 'It looks as if Gervase deliberately administered a fatal dose of arsenic to Diana on the day of the wedding to prevent her from carrying out her plan.'

Sir Roland released a heartfelt sigh. 'It's a pity Diana died before she got around to signing her new will. If she had, who would have been the most obvious suspect – Sebastian or Claudia?'

'I'm convinced Sebastian was embezzling George Lowestoft,' said Hermione firmly. 'But no one else seems to believe me.'

'Gervase has already admitted he destroyed George Lowestoft's financial papers after his death,' said Sir Roland. 'It's possible he was covering up for Sebastian in order to avoid a scandal for Diana's sake. If called to the witness box, Sebastian would naturally deny any such indiscretion. Worse still, he might insist Gervase embezzled George Lowestoft and then poisoned Diana for her money. What I need is incontrovertible proof of the real killer's guilt – provided that person is not my client. As Diana's sole beneficiary, Gervase is the person with the strongest motive for poisoning her. No one else has a financial motive –'

'Unless you take into account Gervase's son,' pointed out Hermione. 'Rupert stands to inherit an enormous fortune after his father dies.'

Sir Roland nodded thoughtfully. 'One could make out a reasonably strong case against Rupert,' he said grimly. 'After all, he was up at the house with Poppy on the night Lyle was attacked...'

20

In court number one of the Old Bailey, Nigel Baldwin's opening speech for the prosecution was drawing to a close.

'...The Duchess of Marsden died on Friday 30 September last year. The defendant Gervase Decimus St. Vincent Cosgrove, 10th Duke of Marsden, claims he is innocent. But the Crown will show that when his first attempt to kill both his wife and her lover Oliver Seymour failed earlier that year on Monday 1 August, he set about systematically poisoning her to death. At the beginning of July this year, some nine months after the Duchess of Marsden was laid to rest, Oliver Seymour's suspicions were aroused and he wrote to the Home Secretary requesting an exhumation. The Duchess of Marsden's body was exhumed and found to contain huge amounts of arsenic....'

A tall, pencil-thin man in his late fifties, with the smooth, unlined face of a bachelor, Nigel Baldwin was an extremely fastidious man who conducted himself with immense dignity. His professional rivals prayed he would not be prosecuting a case they were defending because his bland demeanour masked the ruthlessly efficient mind of a human rottweiler.

'The Crown will demonstrate the Duke of Marsden wanted his wife out of the way so he could get his hands on her vast fortune and marry his mistress Angelique de Breteuil. In the days and weeks ahead, I will present to you, members of the jury, a line up of witnesses, many of them distinguished experts in their fields, whose testimony will enable you to give a true verdict according to the evidence....'

After lunch, Nigel Baldwin rose and said, 'May it please Your Lordship, the first witness I would like to call for the Crown is Oliver Seymour.'

Oliver Seymour's manner was calm and resolute as he picked up the bible and read aloud the customary oath.

'I swear by Almighty God that the evidence I shall give shall be the truth, the whole truth and nothing but the truth.'

'Mr Seymour, how did you first meet the Duchess of Marsden?'

'My television company Valiant Productions made a documentary about her life last year,' replied Oliver. 'We became lovers soon after we met.'

'You knew the Duchess of Marsden was a married woman?'

A glimmer of embarrassment showed in Oliver's eyes. 'Yes....'

Nigel Baldwin said briskly, 'Mr Seymour, before we go any further it is my duty to remind the jury of certain undisputed facts. You and the Duchess of Marsden were involved in a car crash on Monday 1 August last year.'

The colour drained from Oliver's face. 'I have no recollection of the car crash.'

'Quite so. In fact, you have no memory of the entire week leading up to the car crash, do you?'

'No. My memory is as clear as a bell before that.'

'As a consequence of the car crash, you were left in a coma fighting for your life for a period of three months. You came out of your coma a month after the Duchess of Marsden's death. How long after this were you told she had died of gastroenteritis?'

Oliver's voice trembled. 'After leaving hospital, I spent five months convalescing at the home of my friends Lyle Revel and Hermione Bradbury. At the beginning of April this year they finally told me Diana had died.'

'What was your reaction when you first heard the news about her death?' asked Nigel Baldwin.

'I felt a terrible sense of sadness,' said Oliver. 'It's my belief Diana went to her grave blaming herself for the car crash and the injuries I sustained.'

'In retrospect how did you feel when you remembered you had helped yourself to another man's wife?'

'I knew I had behaved inappropriately,' said Oliver. 'When I returned to my home in Richmond-upon-Thames, I read Diana's old love letters. I – I was overcome with emotion and remorse. It was wrong of me to take her away from her husband, but it seemed the right thing to do at the time.'

'I would like to remind you, My Lord, the love letters referred to by the witness have been entered as exhibits 11

A to D. Mr Seymour, everyone accepted that the Duchess of Marsden had died of gastroenteritis, but you did not. Why is that?'

Oliver drew a deep breath. 'Earlier this year, Channel Seven commissioned me to make a documentary about the James Maybrick murder case. As a result, I learned the symptoms of gastroenteritis and arsenic poisoning can often be mistaken. For some time, one of the members of my club in London had been hinting Diana's death was not necessarily due to natural causes. Admittedly after he'd had too much to drink –'

'What is the name of the member?'

'Jean-Luc de Breteuil. He was deeply bitter and blamed his divorce on the fact his ex-wife Angelique had been having an affair with the Duke of Marsden. As a direct consequence of my growing suspicions, I paid a discreet visit to Diana's doctor because I was concerned her husband might have poisoned her.'

'Do you remember when this was?'

'It was during the week of Royal Ascot – on the morning of Friday 22 June, in fact,' replied Oliver. 'Dr Cheadle turned down an offer to appear on my program *Faces and Places*, but during our conversation I asked him about Diana's death. He admitted there had been no autopsy. Also, I learned that the only medication she had taken in the last year of her life were some Tagamet capsules that had been prescribed for her after the car crash. Apparently, she continued taking these up until the time of her death to treat her reoccurring bouts of gastroenteritis.'

'What did you do next?' asked Nigel Baldwin.

Oliver moistened his lips. 'I visited the St. Francis Xavier Hospital later that morning and thanked Dr Sutherland for all the care his staff had given me while I was in a coma. I also questioned him about Diana's health before she died. Dr Sutherland told me she was prescribed Tagamet capsules after the car crash for her bruised shoulder. He also confirmed there had been no autopsy.'

'Did you make Dr Cheadle and Dr Sutherland aware of your suspicions about the Duchess of Marsden's death?'

'No, it was a frantically busy period for me. Later that day I had to go to Yorkshire and begin filming more episodes for the new series of *Faces and Places*. Following my return to London, I remembered Diana had told me she'd never suffered from a day's illness in her life.'

'How soon afterwards did you summon up the courage to write to the Home Secretary requesting an exhumation?'

'At the beginning of July,' said Oliver grimly. *'I stated it was my belief Gervase was a cold-blooded murderer who had poisoned his wife for her money...'*

'Thank you, Mr Seymour. I have no further questions.'

Mr Justice Swindon turned to the defence. 'Sir Roland, I take it you wish to cross-examine Mr Seymour?'

Sir Roland Anstruther rose to his feet. Oliver Seymour had made a favourable impression on the jury, and the barrister was anxious to prevent the witness from making any more disclosures that might weaken the defence's case even further.

'On the contrary, My Lord, I have no questions for Mr Seymour....'

The prosecution's next witness was Dr Cheadle, an elderly, softly-spoken man with stooping shoulders and white hair.

Nigel Baldwin asked, 'Dr Cheadle, could you please tell the court in what capacity you knew the Duchess of Marsden?'

'Following her marriage to the Duke of Marsden I was her personal physician for the last two years of her life.'

'Presumably you were familiar with her medical history prior to this,' said Nigel Baldwin. 'Had she ever suffered from any major illnesses or undergone any operations?'

'No.'

'What was the general state of her health in the time that you knew her?'

'Diana was a very active woman for her age,' said Dr Cheadle. 'She was fond of boasting she'd never taken so much as a vitamin pill in her life.'

'On Monday 1 August last year she was injured when her Daimler crashed off the side of the road. How soon after this did she consult you in your professional capacity?'

'It was a week later. I was called to Arlington to treat her for an attack of gastroenteritis. It was the first in a series of attacks – as it turned out.'

'Did it occur to you, Dr Cheadle, that she was suffering from the effects of arsenic poisoning?'

Dr Cheadle looked visibly distressed. 'The symptoms of arsenic poisoning are similar to food poisoning and some severe gastrointestinal disorders. But it never crossed my mind that someone was poisoning her.'

Nigel Baldwin asked, 'What medication was the Duchess of Marsden taking at the time of her death?'

'After the car accident, she was examined by Dr Sutherland at the St. Francis Xavier Hospital. Her shoulder was bruised because her car had struck a tree and he prescribed some Tagamet capsules to relieve the pain. On my advice she continued to take Tagamet capsules to treat the effects of her attacks of gastroenteritis. This was the first time I had prescribed any medication for her in the two years I'd known her.'

'What happened on the last day of her life – Friday 30 September?'

'It was an exciting day for Diana,' replied Dr Cheadle. 'Her grandson Sebastian was getting married at Arlington. Diana suffered from a mild attack of gastroenteritis after lunch. But she insisted on attending the wedding that evening. Shortly before the ceremony began, I was called away. An elderly patient of mine in Brimhurst had taken a turn for the worse. Gervase later told me Diana collapsed during the wedding ceremony. The hot weather was thought to be the reason behind her fainting spell. Gervase – along with his son Rupert – carried her upstairs and laid her out on her bed. Apparently, she recovered consciousness and spoke to him.'

'Did the Duke of Marsden tell you what she said?'

'Diana asked him what had happened. He reassured her that she was going to be all right. After that she said a few words in French and appeared to drift off to sleep. I think he said her exact words were *Nu Dans Sa Chambre.*'

'Did he understand what she meant by that?'

Dr Cheadle looked puzzled. 'Gervase wondered if she might have been referring to a poem or a book. He says it never occurred to him that she might have lapsed into unconsciousness. Even so, he took the sensible step of phoning for me. I sent word I would come along to Arlington as soon as I had finished treating my patient. As a precautionary measure Gervase says he stayed by Diana's side while Rupert returned to the wedding. It wasn't until later Gervase realized she had stopped breathing. His immediate response was to phone me again. On arriving at Arlington, I found him in a highly distressed state. Beyond confirming that Diana was dead, there was little else I could do.'

'You had no hesitation in citing gastroenteritis as the cause of death on her death certificate?'

'None at all.'

The next witness for the prosecution was Arthur Cotterill, an elderly man with a weather-beaten face who spoke in a thick country burr.

Nigel Baldwin rose to his feet. 'Please state your name and occupation.'

'Arthur Cotterill – head gardener at Arlington.'

'What were you doing at Arlington on the afternoon of Monday 1 August last year?'

'I was clipping the hedge by the side of the water terrace,' replied Cotterill. 'Around three o'clock Mr Seymour arrives in his Jaguar. A minute or so later the Duchess of Marsden comes outside with her suitcase. She was followed by her husband.'

'Did the Duke of Marsden speak to Mr Seymour?'

'Aye – shouting is more the word.'

'What was the nature of the altercation?' asked Nigel Baldwin.

Cotterill fidgeted with his cloth cap. 'Mr Seymour refused to leave Arlington without the Duchess of Marsden. The Duke told Mr Seymour that he was damned if he was going to divorce his wife or let her go away with him. The Duke took the car keys from the ignition of Mr Seymour's Jaguar and threw them into the water terrace.'

'Did the Duke of Marsden say anything else?'

Cotterill nodded vigorously. 'He said he was teaching Mr Seymour a lesson in wife-snatching etiquette. One he wouldn't forget in a hurry. He added that if Mr Seymour was still there in ten minutes' time he'd have him put down like one of his injured hounds.'

Nigel Baldwin gave the witness a look of amazement. 'You're telling this court the Duke of Marsden threw Mr Seymour's car keys into the water terrace - thereby effectively preventing him from leaving in his Jaguar - and then ordered Mr Seymour to get off his property?'

'Aye.'

'Where was the Duchess of Marsden's Daimler parked?'

'About fifteen yards away in front of the portico.'

'What happened after the Duke of Marsden threw Mr Seymour's car keys into the water terrace?'

'The Duke hurried back inside the house.'

Nigel Baldwin pretended he hadn't heard the witness correctly. 'Hurried back inside the house? He was attempting to bully his rival in love into leaving without his wife, was he not?'

'I was surprised His Grace backed off so easily. Normally he's a man who stands his ground.'

'You were surprised His Grace *backed off so easily.*' Nigel Baldwin repeated the statement for the benefit of the jury. 'After throwing Mr Seymour's car keys into the water terrace did the Duke of Marsden advise his wife and Mr

Seymour to leave Arlington *in her Daimler?'*

'Objection, My Lord!' Sir Roland Anstruther, counsel for the defence, rose to his feet, furious. 'My learned friend is leading the witness.'

Mr Justice Swindon directed his steely gaze at Nigel Baldwin. 'Sir Roland is quite right. You really must adhere to the rules of evidence, Mr Baldwin.'

Unfazed by the rebuke, Nigel Baldwin turned back to the witness. 'Mr Cotterill, what happened next?'

'The Duchess of Marsden and Mr Seymour drove away from Arlington in the Daimler. After that Hemmings the chauffeur comes running up to me.'

'How would you describe his manner?'

'Aye – in a proper state he was. He asked me why I let them go off in the Daimler. Earlier that afternoon, he'd told the Duke of Marsden the brakes lines were leaking brake fluid. Anyone getting behind the wheel of the Daimler could easily have a fatal crash.'

Nigel Baldwin turned to Mr Justice Swindon. 'I have no further questions for the witness, My Lord.'

Sir Roland rose to cross-examine the witness. 'Mr Cotterill, were you present when Mr Hemmings is alleged to have told the Duke of Marsden that the brakes of the Daimler were defective?'

'No, I was not...'

Colin Hemmings, a morose-looking man with dark hair that hung over his forehead like rats' tails, was giving evidence.

Nigel Baldwin, counsel for the prosecution, asked, 'Mr Hemmings, how long were you employed as the Duke of

Marsden's chauffeur?'

Hemmings spoke in a soft, whining Scottish accent. 'Two years.'

'Please describe the events of Monday 1 August last year?'

'On the morning of the car crash, I was told the Duchess of Marsden wanted me to drive her to Market Chadwell. My instructions were to be waiting with the Daimler by the portico at three o'clock that afternoon. I was fifteen minutes early because she didn't like to be kept waiting.'

Nigel Baldwin asked, 'Did you normally drive the Duchess of Marsden around in the Daimler?'

'Yes, it was her car. Whenever she went anywhere with her husband, they always used his Rolls Royce.'

'When was the last time you took the Duchess of Marsden out in the Daimler before the day of the crash?'

Hemmings cast his mind back. 'It would have been two weeks before that.'

'How did you discover the Daimler was leaking brake fluid?'

'I forgot my sunglasses and went back to my room above the garage to get them. That's when I saw a puddle of brake fluid on the floor of the garage. It was obvious the brake lines had been leaking. I hurried back to the portico and discovered the Daimler's brake fluid reservoir was practically empty. At that moment the Duke of Marsden came around the side of the house. I told him what the problem was. He said he'd speak to his wife about going to Market Chadwell another day. He surprised me by insisting *he* would return the Daimler to the garage. *"Make sure you leave the keys in the ignition,"* he added. *"I don't want you or anyone else having an accident."* He then went into the house.'

Nigel Baldwin's voice sharpened. 'Mr Hemmings, did it not strike you as irresponsible – *possibly even dangerous* – for the keys to remain in the ignition given the brakes were potentially lethal?'

'Anyone might have come along and helped themselves to the Daimler,' agreed Hemmings.

'Did you not warn him of this?'

'I didn't want to rub the Duke of Marsden up the wrong way. He can be difficult to please at the best of times.'

'What did you do next, Mr Hemmings?'

'I returned to my room above the garage. It was a warm day and I dozed off in front of the TV. I was woken by the sound of a car passing by my quarters. I looked out of the window and saw the Duchess of Marsden and Oliver Seymour leaving Arlington in the Daimler.'

'Did you try and stop them?'

'It was too late,' replied Hemmings, swallowing hard. 'I ran outside and spoke to the head gardener Arthur Cotterill. I told him he oughtn't to have let them leave because of the brakes being so lethal. When I explained to His Grace what had happened his exact words were, *"It can't be helped."*'

'The Duke of Marsden gave no sign of being worried or agitated in any way?'

Hemmings glared at the accused man in the dock. 'On the contrary, he denied I had told him the brakes of the Daimler were faulty. He knew all right because I had gone to the trouble of telling him an hour or so earlier. He fired me on the spot and told me to leave Arlington immediately.'

There was an ominous rumble, reminiscent of an approaching storm, from the public gallery.

'Did the Duke of Marsden say anything else before you left him?'

Hemmings nodded. 'His Grace ordered me to keep my mouth shut and added that if an accident came about because of my gross negligence then he would damn well make sure the police arrested me. The smug, lying hypocrite. I was so angry at the way he spoke to me I packed my bags and went up to London and caught the next train back to Scotland. It wasn't until recently that I read about the Duchess of Marsden's car crash in the newspapers following her husband's arrest for her murder. In light of all that's happened, I wouldn't be surprised if he was hiding a guilty conscience on the day of the crash – especially now his wife has been found poisoned to death...'

Nigel Baldwin turned to Mr Justice Swindon. 'No further questions, My Lord.'

Sir Roland Anstruther rose for the defence.

'Mr Hemmings, you have painted a vivid picture of yourself as a model employee. But the truth of the matter is that the Duke of Marsden fired you because you were becoming increasingly unreliable and drinking too much, is that not so?'

'He fired me for the reasons I've said.'

'In fact, the real reason you fell asleep in front of the TV in your room is because you'd been drinking too much.'

'That's a damned lie!'

Sir Roland continued, 'It was only *after* the Duchess of Marsden and Oliver Seymour left Arlington in the Daimler that you remembered you had forgotten to tell anyone that the brakes were defective, is that not so?

'It's lies on your part – all lies!'

'On the third of January this year, were you arrested for drink driving and disqualified from driving for a period of twelve months?'

'Yes, but it's got nothing to do with what happened the day the Daimler ran off the road.'

Sir Roland's voice hardened. 'You're still furious at having been fired by the Duke of Marsden, aren't you?'

Hemmings clenched his hands. 'Why shouldn't I be? I've never been fired before in my life!'

'Were there any witnesses present when you allegedly told the Duke of Marsden about the faulty brakes?'

'No, but I told him *before* the crash. I swear to it.'

Sir Roland smiled. 'The Duke of Marsden will testify you told him *afterwards*. You've deliberately lied under oath to exonerate yourself from blame and in order to have your revenge against the employer who quite rightly fired you for gross negligence...'

Hemmings snorted angrily. 'I'm telling the truth and anyone who thinks I'm lying can go to hell...!'

21

Irene Lowestoft's circumstances had changed a lot since Gervase had gone on trial for Diana's murder. She was prone to bouts of depression and loneliness and welcomed the opportunity to unburden her feelings to her guests.

'The tabloids are convinced Gervase poisoned Diana,' said Irene fretfully. 'They shouldn't be allowed to say such terrible things. You couldn't hope to meet a kinder man. Everyone I know – including the servants – speaks so highly of him. Did I tell you Gervase always lets the south lodge keeper take his holidays in June so he can visit his family in Canada? Gervase was such a comfort to me after George died. The money from the sale of our manor house in Market Chadwell wasn't enough to settle George's debts. Gervase kindly offered me a home here at Arlington after Diana died.'

The significance of those words 'after Diana died' was not lost on Hermione. She was aware, along with Lyle, that prior to this Diana had refused to offer her cousin a permanent home with her and Gervase. A lot of changes had taken place at Arlington since Gervase had been arrested for Diana's murder. He had been refused bail and had been remanded in custody at HMP Wandsworth in southwest London pending the outcome of the trial. Rupert was renting a flat in Sloane Square because he had vowed to help his father prove his innocence. Angelique was living with Frederick Steen in Regent's Park in order to be closer to her goddaughter Gabriella and the latter's husband Sebastian. Friends of Angelique and Frederick had been given to understand they were 'unofficially engaged'. According to Rupert, this was a ruse on Angelique's part to downplay the importance of her relationship with Gervase although she remained as determined as ever to marry him after the trial was over.

Lyle was gazing thoughtfully at Irene. 'Who do you think poisoned Diana?' he asked in his most persuasive voice.

'I shouldn't wonder if it was Angelique de Breteuil,' replied Irene with ill-concealed venom. 'Diana had only been dead two weeks when she moved into Arlington. A month later she instigated divorce proceedings against her husband Jean-Luc. Her goal was to become the next Duchess of Marsden and she almost succeeded until Gervase was arrested for Diana's murder!'

'You must find it lonely living here while everyone else is away in London,' said Oliver.

Irene smiled gratefully at him for his understanding. 'Claudia is still here,' she said. 'She comes and goes as she pleases. A lot of the time I'm here by myself apart from the servants. Some friends of mine have invited me to stay with them in Cornwall.'

'Which part of Cornwall?' asked Oliver.

'Somewhere called Fowey.'

'Fowey is a charming little seaside port,' said Oliver. 'I was billeted there during the war as a wireless operator with the Royal Navy.'

'At first I was tempted to accept their invitation,' said Irene, 'but then I decided I couldn't – not while Gervase is on trial for Diana's murder. He ought to be here at Arlington with me instead of caught up in this dreadful nightmare. If anyone should be on trial for Diana's murder, it's Angelique de Breteuil. She's a thoroughly immoral woman –'

Claudia entered the drawing-room. 'I'm sorry to have kept you waiting,' she said. 'Rupert was calling from London. Gervase is holding up under the strain of the trial as well as can be expected.'

'Poor man – poor man...' murmured Irene. 'Along with everyone else, I feel so powerless. If only there was *something* I could do to help him...'

Later that night, as her friends were leaving Arlington, Claudia said, 'I didn't like to say so in front of Irene, but Rupert told me on the phone that the prosecution's case is getting blacker by the day.'

'After listening to Hemmings' testimony in court, I'm convinced Gervase knew the Daimler's brakes were dangerous *before* the car crash,' said Lyle. 'My inner voice is telling me Gervase fell victim to a moment of madness on the day of the car crash. That explains why he threw Oliver's car keys into the water terrace. He wanted Diana and Oliver to leave Arlington in the Daimler because *he was hoping the brakes would fail and they would both be killed.* It must have come as quite a shock when his wish-fulfilment partly came true and the Daimler crashed off the side of the road.'

'If the members of the jury have any sense they'll believe Hemmings' testimony,' said Hermione. 'Did I tell you he was once employed by Lord Milsham?'

'No, you didn't,' said Claudia.

'Hemmings was Lord Milsham's chauffeur for almost five years,' replied Hermione. 'After Lord Milsham went to live abroad in tax exile, I was surprised to hear Hemmings had been taken on by Gervase. Hemmings is a socialist and disapproves of blood sports.' She looked at Lyle and added with a sigh, 'We've wasted our time coming here. We haven't learned anything useful.'

Oliver was gazing admiringly at the ceiling of the dome. 'It's easy to see why Gervase resorted to murder to keep Arlington. *The Siege of Troy* is as beautiful as the mural Pellegrini painted on the ballroom ceiling at Thurlestone Hall. Claudia, I wish you'd let me take you away from here. I can't stand the idea of you living under a murderer's roof.'

'You once almost succeeded,' Claudia reminded him, 'but you became glued to the television watching the St. James's Palace Stakes.'

'*Chief Singer's* win made for a brilliant opening to this year's Royal Ascot week,' said Oliver with a grin.

Claudia's smile faded. 'It wasn't long afterwards that you wrote to the Home Secretary asking for Diana's body to be exhumed,' she said with a catch in her voice. 'The outcome of the autopsy has changed all our lives. My grandmother's money should never have gone to Gervase. It should all have gone to Sebastian and me as Diana's next of kin.'

She broke off, flushing. Her outburst surprised her companions.

'My inner voice is telling me Irene Lowestoft is very

ambitious socially,' said Lyle. 'I wonder if she shot George and poisoned Diana to pave the way to becoming the next Duchess of Marsden?'

'If that was Irene's plan it backfired spectacularly,' said Hermione. 'She obviously didn't know about Gervase's ongoing affair with Angelique.'

'Irene is too self-centred to have murdered anyone,' said Claudia dismissively.

'On the contrary, I would have said most killers are extremely self-obsessed,' murmured Lyle. 'They can only see the world from their own point of view. That's what makes them so dangerous. *They never consider anyone else's feelings apart from their own.*'

Hermione turned to Oliver and said, 'I've never been to Thurlestone Hall. What's it like?'

'I paid a brief visit there during my stay in Yorkshire after I finished filming *Faces and Places,*' said Oliver. 'Irene's father went bankrupt and lost everything including Thurlestone Hall. I can understand now why Irene was so envious of Diana's wealth and social position. But it doesn't alter the fact that all the evidence points to Gervase's guilt.'

Claudia's gaze fell on the vase of flowers gracing the octagonal table. 'What beautiful moth orchids!' she exclaimed. She turned to Oliver and added, 'They remind me of the ones you gave me for Christmas.'

'The scientific name for them is *Phalaenopsis amabilis,*' said Oliver, clearly hoping to impress her.

'Only you would know that,' chided Claudia softly.

Oliver gazed adoringly at her. 'Are you sure you won't reconsider my offer? My house can't possibly compare to Arlington, but you must surely have guessed by now that I'm in love with you.'

'I can't leave Arlington,' said Claudia with a tremor in her voice. 'At least not yet. Not while there's a chance I might uncover a vital piece of evidence that could secure Gervase's conviction.'

'I want to see Gervase convicted of Diana's murder as much as you do,' said Oliver reassuringly. 'I know I'm a lot older than you, but at least offer me some hope and say you'll think about marrying me.'

'There's no point making plans to be together until after the trial is over,' said Claudia. 'I've made a vow to see this through to the bitter end for my grandmother's sake. For the time being, you're going to have to accept my principles clash with yours.'

'I once knew a high-minded fellow,' confided Oliver, 'who refused to pay his parking fines and went to prison. Being in prison drove him up the wall. After he was released, he vowed not to be such a high-principled person ever again. He was an atheist and he told me the only thing you can expect to find in prison is God. The police searched Arlington before they arrested Gervase. You're not going to find any evidence against him after all this time.'

Claudia's eyes glimmered with tears. 'Oliver, please don't make this any harder on us both than it already is.'

'I won't – I promise.' Oliver put his arms around her and held her close. 'It shouldn't be long now before the trial is over. There's nothing I want more than to spend the rest of my life with you...'

Hermione gazed at the stricken couple and felt a sharp pang of empathy for them. Where Diana's death was concerned everyone involved needed closure, but it could only be achieved if justice was served properly.

There was a curious gleam in Lyle's eyes. 'Oliver, how

many people have you invited on to *Faces and Places?*' he asked suddenly.

'At least four hundred.' Oliver looked to Claudia for confirmation of his estimate. 'It wasn't easy in the beginning finding articulate and interesting guests.'

Lyle's voice trembled with suppressed excitement. 'Suppose one of the people you invited on to the show – under his new identity – was Captain Dietrich?'

Oliver stared at him in astonishment. 'The week leading up to the car crash is a complete blank in my mind. But even if you're right, Captain Dietrich would never have accepted my invitation. The risk of appearing on television and being recognized by someone from his past would have deterred him.'

'He would have written back refusing to appear on the show,' insisted Claudia.

'That's when you must have noticed his signature was the same as Captain Dietrich's,' said Lyle triumphantly. 'It's entirely possible you kept the letter Captain Dietrich wrote to you under his new alias.'

Hermione drew her breath in sharply. 'I think we should get a good night's sleep,' she said, 'and search the files at Valiant Productions first thing tomorrow...'

The following morning Hermione and her cohorts arrived early at the offices of Valiant Productions and began a thorough search of the premises. Two hours later their buoyant mood had evaporated and everyone was showing signs of irritability.

'Why don't we have a coffee break?' said Hermione,

attempting to lighten everyone's mood.

'Make my coffee double strength,' said Lyle, reluctant to admit his natural optimism was fading.

'We've wasted our time ransacking my office,' complained Oliver. 'There's no sign of the letter Captain Dietrich supposedly wrote to me!'

'We don't even know for certain that Oliver invited Captain Dietrich on to *Faces or Places*,' pointed out Claudia. 'Or that he wrote back to Oliver under his new alias declining to be interviewed. If we were going to find anything, we would have done so by now.'

'I couldn't agree more,' said Oliver.

Lyle was rummaging through a box file. 'This looks interesting,' he said on a rising note of excitement. 'It's a photo of Captain Dietrich. According to the date on the envelope, Armand Mariette posted the photo to Oliver on the day of the car accident.'

A feeling of revulsion came over Hermione as she gazed over Lyle's shoulder at the black and white photo in his hand. The image showed a head and shoulders shot of Captain Dietrich in Gestapo uniform.

'The photo was taken decades ago,' she said disgustedly. 'It's not going to help us find Captain Dietrich *now*.'

At Lyle's urging, they continued to search Oliver's office for another hour, but they were unable to find any evidence to support the theory that Captain Dietrich had corresponded with Oliver. Before they left Valiant Productions, Lyle looked once again at the photo of Captain Dietrich.

'What are you thinking?' asked Hermione.

'I was reminded of our visit to Cedar Lodge Nursing

Home,' replied Lyle thoughtfully.

'It's a miracle the Mariettes' former valet survived Captain Dietrich's execution squad,' said Hermione with a shiver.

'For someone who's now blind,' remarked Lyle, 'Marcel Depardieu showed remarkable insight into the human spirit when he told us, *"By ignoring the murderers of the past, we pave the way for the murderers of the future."* Hermione, I'd give anything to know where Captain Dietrich is. I can't help feeling he's lurking somewhere in the shadows – laughing at us...'

22

On Monday the prosecution's case continued with Dr Gavin Bond, the expert toxicologist, being called to the witness box. Grey-haired, florid-faced and heavy-jowled, he answered the questions put to him in an authoritative voice but was inclined to be long-winded in speech.

Nigel Baldwin came to the rescue of the jury. 'So what you're saying Dr Bond is that the cause of death was arsenic poisoning?'

'Yes.'

'How easy is it to obtain arsenic?'

'Arsenical substances are widely used in industry and agriculture. They can be found in ordinary household items such as pesticides and herbicides.'

'For the benefit of the jury could you describe the symptoms of arsenic poisoning?' asked Nigel Baldwin.

'The symptoms can include feelings of faintness, nausea, a burning sensation in the stomach, diarrhoea, intense thirst, retching and vomiting. There can also be loss of appetite, weight loss, pains in the joints and extremities, a metallic taste in the mouth or a garlic-like odour on the breath. Often the eyes are red and watery, the hair begins to thin or fall out, dark blotches appear on the skin. There can be numbness of the hands and feet. Sometimes the gait is unsteady. The tongue can also become reddened or covered in a white coating. It's important to stress that only *some* of these symptoms may be evident in someone suffering from arsenic poisoning. This can make detection difficult at the best of times.'

'Correct me if I am wrong, Dr Bond, but arsenic is one of the most common elements of the earth's soil, is it not?'

'Very much so. It's a customary practise when exhuming a casket from the ground to take soil and water samples in the vicinity of the grave. This is to ensure that elements in the earth, such as arsenic, can be identified, so that any minerals seeping into the body are not mistaken for the cause of death. The Duchess of Marsden was laid to rest in the family mausoleum at Arlington. Her casket at no time came into contact with any soil.'

'Thank you, Dr Bond. Would it have been at all possible for arsenic to have been introduced into the body after death – perhaps by the embalming process which would have been undertaken to preserve the body?'

'Since the mid-nineteenth century the inclusion of arsenic in embalming fluids has been outlawed. The Duchess of Marsden's body was *not* embalmed. She was systematically poisoned by someone who wished to bring about her death by unlawful means.'

'Were you able to tell over how long a period she was poisoned before her death?'

'When a person swallows arsenic a large amount accumulates in the hair and nails within a matter of hours,' replied Dr Bond. 'Owing to the hot summer that had passed a considerable degree of decomposition had taken place. It was still possible to obtain excellent hair samples after her body was exhumed. Her hair was not dyed and I had no difficulty establishing arsenic was her murderer's choice of weapon.'

Nigel Baldwin turned to Mr Justice Swindon. 'May it please Your Lordship, I would like to show to the jury exhibit 7. The sample of hair that was taken from the Duchess of Marsden's head.'

Mr Justice Swindon inclined his head. 'You have my permission, Mr Baldwin.'

Sir Roland Anstruther, counsel for the defence, opened his mouth as if to protest, then closed it again. The prosecution was anticipating his theatrical flourishes and upstaging him. A sealed plastic bag containing a clump of thin hair with split ends was produced and passed to the jury who regarded it with an air of fascinated horror.

Having aroused the jury's pity for the dead woman, Nigel Baldwin continued, 'Dr Bond, were you able to establish over how long a period the Duchess of Marsden was poisoned before she died?'

'Beginning at the root there was nearly an inch of arsenic concentrated in the shaft of her hair *suggesting she had been slowly poisoned for nearly two months before she died.*'

'What was the result of tests carried out on the bottle of Tagamet capsules found by the police in the Duchess of Marsden's room after she died?'

Dr Bond's reply drew a buzz of shocked outrage from the public gallery. *'Every single one of the capsules contained arsenic...'*

Detective Inspector McGowan, a thin, nondescript officer with the Gosford C.I.D., was in the witness box giving evidence for the prosecution.

Nigel Baldwin asked, 'Detective Inspector McGowan, what did you do when you received a copy of the forensic pathologist's report stating the Duchess of Marsden had been poisoned?'

Detective Inspector McGowan replied in a dry, crisp voice, 'I immediately went to Arlington and requested an interview with the Duke of Marsden.'

'Were you granted one?'

'No, I was told he was holidaying in Venice. Along with several scene of crime officers, I made my way to the Duchess of Marsden's suite of rooms and conducted a thorough search of the sitting-room, bedroom and bathroom. Apparently, little had changed since the day of her death. Her granddaughter Claudia Rylander had not got around to sorting out her grandmother's belongings. I found a bottle of half-empty Tagamet capsules in a drawer of the Duchess of Marsden's dressing-table. The label bore her name and the details of the chemist that supplied the medicine.'

'The name of the chemist being?'

'The Brimhurst Pharmacy. The toxicology report confirmed the capsules contained arsenic in white powder form. Two clear sets of fingerprints were found on the bottle itself. One set belonged to the Duchess of Marsden and the other belonged to her husband.'

'Did you also search the Duke of Marsden's bedroom?'

'Yes – there is a connecting door between the two suites

of rooms. At the back of one of the drawers in the Duke of Marsden's dressing-table, I found an enamel box. It contained jewellery as well as a quantity of white powder – roughly a teaspoon's worth – and several empty red capsules. The toxicology report confirmed the powder was arsenic. The empty red capsules contained traces of Tagamet. Beneath a pile of socks in a drawer of the Duke of Marsden's tallboy I found a handwritten card from his mistress – a certain Angelique de Breteuil.'

'Could you please examine exhibit 17? Is this the card you found in the drawer?'

'Yes – it's dated two weeks *after* the Duchess of Marsden's car crash.'

'Would you please read aloud the message on the card?'

Detective Inspector McGowan cleared his throat. '"My dear Gervase, I need hardly tell you the roses were lovely. Please don't send any more. Jean-Luc is becoming suspicious. You've been sending me too many lately and I'm finding it hard to maintain the fiction that they are from my mother. Your adoring, Angelique."'

'Did you find anything else?' asked Nigel Baldwin.

'A book on poisons was hidden on top of the Duke of Marsden's wardrobe. Chapter three gives a detailed account of arsenic poisoning. On his return from Venice, he was arrested on a charge of murdering his wife. I asked him if he had tampered with her bottle of Tagamet tablets. He denied the charge. I then remarked it must have been a messy business emptying the capsules and filling them with arsenic. I asked him if the white powder and empty capsules found in his enamel box were left over from the substitution of his wife's bottle of Tagamet capsules. He strenuously denied the suggestion.'

'Did the Duke of Marsden admit to having an affair with Mrs de Breteuil?' said Nigel Baldwin.

'He denied it in the strongest possible terms,' replied Detective Inspector McGowan. 'But my inquiries through the Italian police had already established he and Angelique de Breteuil had stayed in a privately-rented palazzo during their holiday in Venice.'

Sir Roland appeared calm and serene as he began his cross-examination. 'Detective Inspector McGowan, I don't dispute you found certain items of incriminating evidence in the Duke of Marsden's bedroom, but you've really no way of knowing for certain, have you, whether he put those items there himself – or whether they were put there by someone who wished to incriminate him?'

'I've investigated plenty of murder cases in my time, but never one where there was a stronger motive. The Duke of Marsden inherited six hundred million pounds under the terms of his wife's will...'

The prosecution's next witness was Alice Hazlett, a thin, faded woman who was a former servant at Arlington. She was softly spoken and exuded an air of moral rectitude.

'I was disgusted when Mrs de Breteuil moved into Arlington two weeks after the Duchess of Marsden died. The servants were told she was there to refurbish some of the rooms, but none of us believed it.'

'Why do you say that?' asked Nigel Baldwin.

'The breakfast-room at Arlington was refurbished by Mrs de Breteuil in July last year at the Duke of Marsden's request. But the Duchess of Marsden disliked the new oriental design of the wallpaper and had the breakfast-room redecorated following her car crash. After the Duchess of Marsden's death, Mrs de Breteuil reinstated her original oriental design.'

'Did Mrs de Breteuil eat her meals with the servants?'

Alice Hazlett shook her head vigorously. 'She was too grand for the likes of us. One morning four weeks after the funeral, I saw the Duke of Marsden kissing Mrs de Breteuil's hand at the breakfast table. It seemed a despicable way for a widower to behave. On another occasion, I heard Mrs de Breteuil ask him to instruct one of the servants to remove the Duchess of Marsden's portrait from the drawing-room. She didn't like the idea of his dead wife looking down on them during afternoon tea. The portrait was relocated to the High Saloon.'

'Did their behaviour arouse your suspicions in any other way?'

'Earlier this year in June, the Duke of Marsden rented a cottage overlooking Swinley Park for the entire week of Royal Ascot. He was accompanied by Mrs de Breteuil. Arlington was run on a skeleton staff during the family's absence.'

'How can you be sure she went with him?'

'Mrs de Breteuil told me she was accompanying His Grace to Swinley Park and asked me to pack her suitcase before she left. It was obvious she saw herself as the new mistress of Arlington. On her return, she was wearing an expensive diamond engagement ring on the fourth finger of her left hand...'

Frederick Steen was called next to the witness stand. He gave the impression of a man stoically performing a painful duty.

'Mr Steen, was the Duchess of Marsden in the habit of writing to you regularly?' began Nigel Baldwin.

Frederick spoke in a muted voice. 'Yes, she was a wonderful help to me in organising my daughter's wedding to her grandson. Over a two-month period before the wedding Diana wrote to me on a number of occasions.'

'Exhibit 37 G is a letter by the Duchess of Marsden,' continued Nigel Baldwin. 'It's dated Tuesday 27 September last year – some three days before she died. The letter was written at Arlington and addressed to you at your home in London. The postmark on the envelope in which the letter was sent bears the following day's date. Could you explain to the court how it is that you only opened and read the letter within the last fortnight?'

'I must have seen the envelope lying on my desk,' said Frederick regretfully, 'assumed I'd read the letter inside and placed it in a bundle of other letters I'd already opened and read from Diana. Ten days ago, I was cleaning out my writing desk when I came across the letter. I realized at once I hadn't opened it.'

'What was your reaction when you read it?'

Frederick spoke with a tremor. 'Shock...horror...pity... I saw at once it was my duty to take the letter to the police.'

Nigel Baldwin nodded. 'I quite understand, Mr Steen. If it pleases you, My Lord, I shall read the letter out loud to the jury myself.' He cleared his throat and began speaking.

'My dear Frederick,

I've decided to divorce Gervase. You were right when you said he only married me for my money. I feel such a fool for not listening to you sooner.

Yesterday while Gervase was out, I searched his room and found a letter from his mistress Angelique. I also saw some red capsules inside an enamel box on his dressing-table. The capsules had been pulled open and a white powder appeared to have spilled out. This has frightened me a lot because they look exactly like the Tagamet capsules my doctor prescribed after the car crash. Now I'm wondering if Gervase was desparate enough to syphon the brake fluid from my Daimler in an earlier attempt to kill me and Oliver.

Sebastian's and Gabriella's wedding is in three days' time. Gervase wouldn't dare try and kill me with so many people in the house. We've been sharing the same food which means the poison has got to be in the Tagamet capsules. I've stopped taking them and will be bringing them up to London for forensic analysis.

If anything happens to me, I want you to take this letter to the police. Try not to worry about me. I survived worse terrors than this during the Second World War. I'm placing my trust and love in God as I've always done.

Your devoted friend,

Diana'

As Nigel Baldwin finished reading the letter pandemonium broke out in the public gallery.

23

Hermione spent the afternoon cleaning the chapel at Milsham Castle. Despite having no one to help her since one of the cleaners from the village had fallen ill, she went about the task quietly and efficiently. Afterwards she went outside and inspected the glass-covered noticeboard by the chapel's entrance. It contained an out-of-date funeral notice from last year. Mrs Elliott had misspelt Marjorie Pym's name on her battered Corona typewriter, but the wording was still clear.

A Loyal and Faithful Servant Unto the Lord
The funeral of MARGERY PIM who departed this life
on 4 October will be held here at 11 a.m. on
Thursday 13th October 1983.
'Blessed are the meek for they shall inherit the earth.'

The servants at Arlington had been given the morning off so they could attend the service, but Hermione doubted if anyone had mourned the passing of the old maid.

Gervase had arranged for Pym to be interred in the chapel's crypt alongside her late master George Lowestoft. It had come as no surprise to Hermione and Lyle to learn that their impoverished employer, Lord Milsham, had benefited financially from the arrangement.

'Sometimes our misconceptions get in the way of our seeing what we should...'

What exactly had Pym meant by those words? Was it a coincidence she had been standing outside the gun room when George Lowestoft was shot? Had she also known who had poisoned Diana? Or was she simply a bitter old woman who had pretended to know more than she really did? It occurred to Hermione that Pym was an enigma and probably likely to remain one.

That night Irene Lowestoft was in her element entertaining her guests in Arlington's formal red dining-room. Perhaps she was imagining what it would have been like to become the next Duchess of Marsden.

Gabriella and Sebastian had surprised Irene by coming down from London. No mention was made of Gervase's trial and the sensation that had erupted earlier that day when the letter Diana had written to Frederick Steen had been read out in court. Three handwriting experts had subsequently testified that the letter was undoubtedly genuine. If Irene resented Frederick Steen for testifying against Gervase, she was careful to keep her feelings to herself for the sake of her guests.

'Are you going to tell Irene about the special surprise you've got planned for her?' asked Gabriella, gazing adoringly at Sebastian.

'Gabriella and I are taking a holiday in the New Year,' said Sebastian, with an ingratiating smile. 'We insist on you coming along as our guest, Irene.'

Claudia stared at her brother in surprise. 'Where are you going?' she blurted.

'South Africa,' replied Sebastian.

Hermione and Lyle exchanged glances. They both suspected the idea of taking Irene on holiday was Gabriella's rather than Sebastian's.

'We plan to visit Cape Town and Johannesburg,' continued Gabriella. 'The highlight of our trip will be a visit to Victoria Falls and the Rainbow Forest.'

'There's nothing I'd like more than to visit South Africa,' said Irene, gazing fondly at the couple. 'George and I were planning to go there before he died. I'm very grateful to you both for your kind offer. I'll have to check with my doctor closer to the time. He may not approve of me going on account of my bronchitis.'

Hermione was aware that Sebastian was not normally a considerate person. She wondered if this was his way of impressing Gabriella? Or was he genuinely trying to make amends to Irene for embezzling her husband George?

After dinner was over, Irene took her guests to the drawing-room for coffee. Sebastian and Gabriella entertained everyone by showing them a home movie of their honeymoon in Greece and the Cote d'Azur. Marrying Gabriella had clearly transformed Sebastian's life. He was obviously deeply in love with her and relished working in an executive role for her father's pharmaceutical company.

Later that night, after the couple had departed for London, Hermione had no difficulty introducing the subject of servants.

'Bosworth is an excellent butler,' she remarked. 'These days a good servant is worth their weight in gold. You must miss your maid Pym a great deal.'

'I relied on Pym a lot,' confided Irene. 'As you know, I was forced to sell the manor house in Market Chadwell after George died. A live-out housekeeper used to come in during the week and make the most marvellous meals. The rest of the time we only had Pym to take care of our needs. She was devoted to us. We used to take her to church every Sunday.'

'So I remember you telling me,' said Oliver. 'I was grateful to you for lending me your photos of Diana for the documentary I was making about her life.'

'Poor Diana lost so many of her possessions during the war,' said Irene, 'including photos of herself as a young woman. I was only too pleased to lend you what photos I had of her. If George and I had known you were going to call on us, I would have prepared something special for afternoon tea. I always gave Pym Friday afternoons off so we had to make do as best we could.'

Oliver smiled in recollection. 'On my way home, I stopped off in Market Chadwell for a newspaper. I wanted to see if a horse I'd bet on had won its race. I was frightfully chuffed to win two hundred pounds. Someone pointed Pym out to me as she left the chemist. She was wearing a black cloche hat and a maroon coat.'

'One normally doesn't notice what a servant looks like,' said Irene snobbishly. 'But I doubt if anyone who ever saw Pym forgot her face. She was such a stern and disapproving creature. I expect she was collecting my eye drops. It was only three days later that Diana and you were involved in the car crash, wasn't it?'

'Yes...it was a dreadful business,' replied Oliver in a subdued voice.

'The news upset George and me a great deal,' continued Irene. 'We needed a glass of port to calm our nerves. It wasn't a very good port so I gave the bottle to Pym since it was half empty. She kept it by her bedside. To my surprise, she polished it off within a week.'

'Had Pym worked for you for long?'

In response to Hermione's question, Irene replied, 'Oh, yes, she became my personal lady's maid when I turned eighteen. During the Second World War, I became a FANY and drove an ambulance during the Blitz. Pym was frightened of the bombs and refused to accompany me to London. She spent the duration of the war at Thurlestone Hall growing vegetables for the war effort. She only resumed her duties as my lady's maid after the war was over. The reason I kept her on all these years is because she was the one person I could talk to about my childhood home. It's extraordinary how Thurlestone Hall still has a pull on my affections all these years later. Now Pym has gone there's no one else who remembers it like I do...'

Lyle gently stemmed the flow of Irene's reminiscences by saying, 'A blue folder was left on the table in the Great Hall on the night George died. We wondered if you might know what happened to it?'

'I haven't the slightest idea,' said Irene. 'Was it important?'

'Lyle and I think Pym might have taken the blue folder,' said Hermione. 'What sort of person was she?'

'Life had turned Pym sour,' said Irene. 'A couple of years before the war ended, she fell pregnant and was forced to marry one of the young under-gardeners at

Thurlestone Hall. His name was Albert. He was a brave fellow and signed up for the RAF as soon as he was eligible. His plane was shot down over the North Sea. The shock of being widowed was too much for Pym and the baby was stillborn. Although I never met Albert, I don't think Pym ever recovered fully from the trauma of losing him and their baby. She seemed to take a perverse pleasure in the misfortunes of others. She'd keep a secret for ages, then blurt it out at a moment that was most disadvantageous for the individual concerned. The older she got the more peculiar she became. She enjoyed reading Greek tragedies because she said it amused her when fate came crashing down on other people's heads. Perhaps that's why the Trojan War appealed to her so much. Some of her opinions were frankly rather strange. No formaldehyde, she used to say. Naturally, I saw to I that her wishes were respected.'

'It sounds as if she resented others who were happier and better off than she was,' remarked Oliver thoughtfully.

'I expect you're right,' said Irene. 'For all her devotion to me, Pym let me down terribly after Sebastian's and Gabriella's wedding.'

'In what way?' asked Lyle in his most ingratiating manner.

'On the Saturday morning, I returned to the manor house in Market Chadwell. It was set to be auctioned in a fortnight's time. Pym had promised faithfully to help me pack up my belongings. Normally she was as good as her word, but I found her dead in her bed on the Tuesday morning. Her death came as such a blow after all her years of faithful service. I don't know how I would have coped without Gervase's help. He paid for Pym's funeral and made sure she enjoyed the same decencies as Diana. Oddly enough, Pym's death prevented her from going up to London on the Wednesday to meet someone in Trafalgar Square.'

'Who was she planning to meet?' said Lyle.

Irene shook her head in wonder. 'She was awfully mysterious and wouldn't say. I got an even bigger surprise when I looked inside her nightstand. There was the most extraordinary horde of sherry bottles I've ever seen. It seems she drank herself to sleep each night like a fish. Perhaps she was drowning her sorrows.'

Claudia frowned. 'What do you mean by drowning her sorrows?'

'Pym was orphaned at an early age,' replied Irene. 'Barnardo's was her salvation because the training she got there enabled her to embark on a life of domestic service. Nothing remarkable ever happened to her. Although now I come to think of it, a friend of hers from Barnardo's once found herself in trouble. Despite being a Roman Catholic and disapproving of abortion, Pym overcame her misgivings when the pregnancy threatened the girl's life. She gave her friend some money to have a termination.'

Hermione's interest was piqued. 'Did the friend go ahead with the abortion?'

'The back street abortionist the girl went to almost killed her. Pym later gave evidence against the man at his trial. He went to prison for quite a long time, I'm told. He was Italian or French – I can't remember which. Pym's friend died a year or so after the trial. The poor girl was terminally ill although she didn't know she had cancer until a couple of weeks before she died. Naturally, this all happened before the 1967 Abortion Act was passed. Nowadays women can receive proper medical assistance although I can't say I've ever approved of abortion owing to my strong Catholic upbringing. Pym always wished she hadn't given her friend the money for the abortion. The guilt never entirely went away.'

'Irene, I think I may have come across Pym on a visit to my dentist last year,' said Lyle with a curious gleam in his eyes. 'Did she also wear black gloves with her maroon coat and black cloche hat?'

Irene stared at him in surprise. 'Yes, she did as a matter of fact. She'd had the same outfit for years.'

Lyle was silent, recalling his visit to 98 Harley Street. After leaving his dentist, he had stood on the landing and observed Jean-Luc de Breteuil thrusting a wad of notes into the hand of an unknown woman. *'Your demands have got to stop,'* he had told her. *'This is all the money I'm going to give you.'* Was Pym the mystery woman who had been blackmailing Jean-Luc?

'What surprised me after Pym died was the amount of money she had in her bank account,' added Irene. 'For the last year of her life a thousand pounds was deposited into her account every month.'

'Twelve thousand pounds is a lot of money,' exclaimed Hermione. 'Who do you think gave it to her?'

'I assumed it was a mistake on the bank's behalf,' said Irene with a sigh. 'Her handbag also contained five hundred pounds in cash. I've no idea where it came from. Now she's dead I doubt if we'll ever know the truth of the matter.'

Later that night, as they were driving home in Casanova, Lyle said elatedly, 'I wouldn't mind betting Jean-Luc de

Breteuil is the illegal back street abortionist Irene Lowestoft told us about.'

'You mean the one who almost killed Pym's pregnant friend?' murmured Hermione.

Lyle nodded vigorously. 'I'm convinced Pym was the mystery woman I saw visiting Jean-Luc's surgery. I think she recognized him all these years later and turned her hand to blackmail.'

'A thousand pounds is a lot of money,' said Hermione. 'I don't imagine Jean-Luc was happy to part company with it on a monthly basis.'

'It all fits together rather nicely, doesn't it?' said Lyle. 'Jean-Luc must have changed his name and become a qualified dentist after he was released from prison. It's possible he poisoned Diana and Pym to prevent them from exposing his criminal past...'

Hermione came to a decision. 'I think we should phone Uncle Roly as soon as we get home...'

'So do I,' agreed Lyle.

'The prosecution is calling Jean-Luc to the witness stand tomorrow to testify against Gervase,' added Hermione. 'I wonder if he realizes he could be walking into a trap?'

'If our suspicions are correct,' said Lyle on a rising note of excitement, 'this could be the breakthrough the defence needs...'

The following afternoon, Hermione and Lyle watched from the public gallery as Jean-Luc de Breteuil entered the witness box. If Sir Roland Anstruther played his cards astutely during his cross-examination, there was every possibility the tide of public opinion would turn in Gervase's favour.

Jean-Luc de Breteuil was dressed in a grey pin-stripe suit designed by Gieves and Hawkes of Saville Row. He carried himself with considerable dignity and conveyed an impression of impeccable breeding. He licked his lips while waiting for the counsel for the prosecution to begin questioning him.

'Mr de Breteuil, how long were you married to your wife?' asked Nigel Baldwin.

Jean-Luc spoke in a low, restrained voice as if determined to keep a grip on his emotions. 'Angelique and I were married for twenty years.'

'Did you divorce her of your own free will?'

'She asked me for a divorce two weeks after the Duchess of Marsden died. My immediate response was to refuse because I've always loved my wife.'

'Indeed, I imagine you still do, Mr de Breteuil.' Nigel Baldwin's tone implied sympathy.

Jean-Luc's mouth trembled. 'Yes.'

'Why did you give in and consent to a divorce?'

Jean-Luc hesitated. 'It was what my wife wanted.'

Nigel Baldwin said with some acerbity, 'I'm aware of *that*, Mr de Breteuil. But you have just indicated that you did not wish to divorce her. What made you change your mind?'

Looking visibly distressed, Jean-Luc replied, 'I had made a series of unwise bets on some racehorses. My creditors were pressing me to pay them. They were threatening to resort to violence. The Duke of Marsden offered me £250,000 to divorce Angelique. I would never have accepted his offer if there was any other way out of my predicament. Divorce is totally abhorrent to me.'

Nigel Baldwin gave the witness several seconds to gather his composure, then he said briskly, 'To the best of your knowledge, how long had your wife's affair with the Duke of Marsden been going on?'

Jean-Luc's reply was barely audible. 'Eight years.'

'Did you never object to it?'

Jean-Luc shook his head. 'I was frightened Angelique would leave me if I said anything. Rather than risk losing her, I turned a blind eye to what was happening...' His voice trailed off into silence.

'Was that the only reason, Mr de Breteuil?'

'Gervase was also a good friend – possibly my best friend. I was always grateful to Angelique and him for conducting their affair discreetly. As long as they did that, I felt I could cope. I choose to put my wife's happiness before my own.'

'Mr de Breteuil, please describe your relationship with the Duchess of Marsden.'

'I knew Diana first in my professional capacity as a dentist. She had been coming to me for ten years before she married Gervase. We became friends after her marriage.'

'Was it a close friendship?'

'No – I was closer to her husband. She and I never discussed our spouses' adultery. It would have been distasteful to both of us to do so.'

'The Duchess of Marsden visited your surgery last year on Friday 23 September – a week before she died. What happened?'

'She had her customary check-up. Her manner seemed

tense. I put this down to the fact that she had told me Gervase would be picking her up afterwards. I worked as quickly as possible replacing her amalgam filling with another since the old one had dropped out. Gervase arrived half an hour later. Before leaving they had a blazing row in the sitting-room of my surgery.'

'You were present during this argument?' asked Nigel Baldwin.

'No. I remained in my surgery, but the door to the sitting-room was ajar. Diana told Gervase she was going to make him open Arlington to the public because it cost too much money to run privately. Gervase declared he would sooner poison her than let the public pass through Arlington's doors.'

Nigel Baldwin leaned forward, his expression one of well-simulated shock and outrage. *'He actually threatened to poison his wife?'*

Jean-Luc dabbed his brow with a handkerchief. 'His exact words were, *"Sooner than let the public tramp through Arlington I'd rather poison you."*'

'What was the Duchess of Marsden's response?'

'Before they left the surgery, Diana told Gervase she was going to make him sorry for speaking to her like that. A fortnight after her death, I came across Gervase's love letters to my wife. I found them hidden in a hat-box at the back of Angelique's wardrobe. It was wrong of me, but I couldn't resist the temptation to read the letters. I felt I had a right to know what was going on in my marriage.'

'If it pleases you, My Lord, I would like the witness to examine exhibit 25 B,' said Nigel Baldwin. 'Mr de Breteuil, do you recognise this letter?'

'It's one of the letters I found in my wife's hat-box.'

'Could you please read the letter out loud to the jury?'

Jean-Luc cleared his throat and read in a faltering voice, '"My darling Angelique, your friendship has meant so much to me over the years. I want you to take comfort in the thought Diana can't live forever. One day we'll be together, I promise. Your adoring Gervase."'

'Mr de Breteuil, could you tell the court when the letter is dated?'

'It's dated Thursday 28 July last year – a mere four days *before* Diana narrowly avoided death when her Daimler crashed off the road.'

'What interpretation did you put upon the letter when you first read it?'

'I took it to mean that Gervase had arranged Diana's car crash,' replied Jean-Luc. 'I remembered Angelique telling me Diana suffered several attacks of gastroenteritis before she died. It occurred to me that Gervase had poisoned Diana.'

'Did you tell anyone about your suspicions?'

Jean-Luc looked embarrassed. 'I might have mentioned the matter to one or two members of my club after I became imbued with too much alcohol. I was having difficulty handling the strain of my divorce.'

'Did you consider going to the police?' asked Nigel Baldwin.

'There was my social position to consider,' said Jean-Luc, moistening his lips. 'One doesn't accuse a duke of the realm of murder unless one has incontrovertible proof. Gervase was once my friend. I would have been deeply ashamed if the accusation had proved unfounded. I now bitterly regret not confiding in the police as soon as Diana died.'

'Thank you, Mr de Breteuil.' Nigel Baldwin turned to Mr Justice Swindon. 'I have no further questions.'

Sir Roland Anstruther rose for the defence. 'Mr de Breteuil, you must have been deeply shocked when you heard the Duchess of Marsden had been poisoned.'

'I was filled with unimaginable horror,' said Jean-Luc. 'I regarded Diana and Gervase as good friends.'

'Where was your dental assistant on the day the Duchess of Marsden visited your surgery?'

'Away on holiday.'

Sir Roland's eyes narrowed. 'So what you're saying is that there were no witnesses to the alleged argument between the Duchess of Marsden and my client.'

'I can't help what I overheard.'

'You have told the court that the Duchess of Marsden was determined to open Arlington to the public because she was no longer prepared to pay for its upkeep. Yet no one else – apart from you – appears to have known about these elaborate plans. The Duke of Marsden would hardly have threatened to poison his wife if he was *already* doing so, now would he?'

'It was a heated argument lasting almost five minutes. Gervase was incandescent with rage.'

'That's more an accurate description of how you felt, isn't it?' Sir Roland's cynical tone had become derisive. 'The Duke of Marsden had betrayed your friendship by frolicking between the bedsheets with your wife. He had reduced you socially to a laughing stock. Shunned sexually by your wife, forced by financial considerations into giving her a divorce, it's only natural you should want to get your own back on them both.'

'I'm not a vindictive man,' said Jean-Luc coldly.

'Oh, I think you are, Mr de Breteuil,' said Sir Roland. 'When did the police first approach you in connection with the Duchess of Marsden's murder?'

'The day before the exhumation when I handed over her dental records. I can't remember the date.'

Sir Roland stared at him with the utmost incredulity. 'Mr de Breteuil, you have told this court how shortly after the Duchess of Marsden's death – a mere two weeks to be precise – you suspected she was poisoned. The discovery of the Duke of Marsden's love letters in your wife's hat-box inflamed your suspicions. You subsequently bandied your suspicions around your club while you were drunk, didn't you?'

'Yes.'

'When did you hand your wife's love letters over to the police?'

'A month after Gervase's arrest – at the same time I told them about the argument in the sitting-room of my surgery.'

Sir Roland shook his head in bemused disbelief. 'Rather than tell the police about the letters and the alleged argument when they came to you the first time, *you waited a month.* Thirty-one days is a long time. Time enough for anger, humiliation, jealousy and revenge to fester, isn't it? What are you hoping will happen to my client if the jury returns a verdict of guilty?'

'Gervase will go to prison.'

'Thus preventing him from marrying your ex-wife whom you profess to still love.'

Jean-Luc's eyes flashed with anger and he had difficulty restraining himself. 'It would serve him right for murdering

Diana.'

'The springs of justice flow from knowledge, not from malice and revenge,' said Sir Roland. 'You're a proud man, aren't you? Descended no less from the Huguenots?'

'Yes, but I don't see –' Jean-Luc broke off abruptly, gazing furtively around the court, like a rat sensing it was trapped.

'Mr de Breteuil, would you say you have a strong sense of justice?'

'Yes.'

'Do you believe all murderers deserve to be punished?'

'Of course.'

'Should a thief be punished as much as a murderer?'

'The punishment should fit the crime.'

'As in the case of a back street abortionist who nearly kills one of his patients while removing an unwanted foetus?' asked Sir Roland silkily.

A trickle of sweat ran down Jean-Luc's face and he swayed a little on his feet. 'I don't know what you mean...'

'Mr de Breteuil, I would remind you the penalty for perjury is severe.' Sir Roland paused a moment before delivering his knockout blow. 'Does the name Raoul Garnier mean anything to you? The Duchess of Marsden knew *that* was your real name. She also knew you are a convicted back street abortionist. *You poisoned the Duchess of Marsden to prevent the truth about your criminal past from coming out, didn't you?*'

'No –!'

'Before the Duchess of Marsden died, she found the incriminating evidence in the Duke of Marsden's bedroom put there by *you* and assumed her own husband was trying to poison her. That explains why she wrote to Frederick Steen in the mistaken belief that her own husband was trying to kill her, doesn't it?'

Jean-Luc gave a strangled cry. *'Oh - God, I think - I think I'm having a heart attack...'*

There was an excited buzz from the public gallery.

Nigel Baldwin, counsel for the prosecution, rose quickly to his feet. 'My Lord, this witness is in no fit state to continue answering questions. *He clearly needs urgent medical attention...*'

24

After leaving court number one of the Old Bailey, Sir Roland Anstruther spoke to Hermione and Lyle beneath the dome in the Grand Hall.

'You were both right to suspect Jean-Luc de Breteuil is a convicted abortionist,' said Sir Roland. 'After being released from prison, he changed his name, became a qualified dentist and conned his way into British high society. He married Angelique and set up a dental surgery at 20 Harley Street.'

'Everything in his life was perfect until a clinic for sexual diseases opened on the third floor,' remarked Lyle.

'Why was that such a problem?' asked Hermione bewilderedly.

'Jean-Luc's elderly clients began to shun him,' explained Sir Roland, 'because they were worried people would think they were visiting the clinic rather than his surgery. Jean-Luc found a solution to his problems when he heard Solomon Atkinson was about to retire. He bought the lease on Solomon Atkinson's dental surgery at 98 Harley Street along with a list of Solomon Atkinson's clients who included Marjorie Pym. As you both rightly surmised, Pym recognised Jean-Luc from her past and began blackmailing him. It seems he paid her a thousand pounds on a monthly basis.'

'That's why Pym had twelve thousand pounds in her bank account,' said Hermione. 'Irene Lowestoft found an additional five hundred pounds in her handbag after her death. We don't know where the money came from.'

'Perhaps she was blackmailing someone else,' suggested Lyle.

'Such as –?'

'Captain Dietrich.'

'We've no proof of that,' remonstrated Hermione. 'In fact, our best attempts to trace him have failed. He would hardly have paid her such a paltry sum for her silence.'

'Perhaps Captain Dietrich gave the money to Pym as a down payment. Her death could have prevented him from having to pay her larger sums.'

Hermione wondered if Lyle was right. 'Uncle Roly, what's going to happen if Jean-Luc doesn't recover from his heart attack?'

'You mean if he dies?' said Sir Roland. 'The defence will still claim that he murdered Diana to prevent the truth of his criminal past from coming to light.'

'Have you spoken to the authorities about Marjorie Pym?' said Hermione anxiously.

'I think you're both right to suspect she was poisoned because she knew too much,' said Sir Roland. 'You'll be pleased to know I've already applied to the Home Secretary to have her body exhumed...'

Before leaving London, Hermione and Lyle visited Frederick Steen's town house to acquaint Angelique de Breteuil with the latest developments in the trial. It didn't require much acumen on their behalf to realize Angelique was a bundle of nerves. The notoriety of her affair with Gervase had led to the tabloids labelling her a homewrecker. The public had shunned her interior decorating firm and she had been forced to close it down. She had been living under virtual house arrest for several months in a bid to escape the attention of the media. Abandoned by her clients and friends, Angelique was currently marooned on an island of loneliness.

'Jean-Luc has been rushed to hospital with a suspected heart attack,' said Hermione. 'No one knows if he's going to survive.'

'I've long ceased to care what happens to my ex-husband,' said Angelique, struggling to maintain her composure.

Lyle spoke. 'Jean-Luc was panic-stricken – absolutely terrified, in fact – when Sir Roland accused him of being a convicted back street abortionist. We think the accusation precipitated his collapse in the witness stand.'

Angelique's resistance crumbled as her overwrought emotions got the better of her. 'The police came here and questioned me before you arrived,' she said with a shudder of disdain. 'They wanted to know if I could tell them anything about Jean-Luc's former life as Raoul Garnier.'

'Were you able to help them?'

'He kept his sordid past a total secret from me,' said Angelique. 'I would never have married him if I'd known about it.'

'Jean-Luc testified in court that he overheard Gervase threatening to poison Diana during a visit to his surgery,' continued Lyle. 'Hermione and I are wondering if there's any truth in his claim –'

Angelique looked stunned. 'Jean-Luc is making this up to spite me,' she said angrily. 'He hasn't forgiven me for divorcing him. There was no way we could have stayed married. His gambling debts had spiralled out of control. Now we're divorced he's determined to destroy whatever happiness Gervase and I might have together.'

'It's obvious Jean-Luc still loves you,' said Hermione gently.

Angelique's eyes flashed. 'Jean-Luc wouldn't know the meaning of the word love,' she insisted. 'I only wish there was something I could do to help Gervase. Having nothing to do each day is driving me up the wall. Sebastian and Frederick are at work during the week. Gabriella is busy running her art gallery. In a few days' time, I'm being called to the witness stand to testify against Gervase. The prospect terrifies me.'

'Did it ever cross your mind Gervase might have murdered Diana so he could marry you?' said Lyle.

For a moment he thought Angelique was going to burst into tears, but she pulled herself together and said sharply, 'No, of course not. Gervase isn't capable of murder. It's obvious from what you've told me that Jean-Luc poisoned Diana.'

'We're wondering if someone might have bribed Jean-Luc to testify against Gervase,' said Hermione. 'Do you know if Gervase has any enemies?'

Angelique shook her head slowly. 'No one comes to

mind – apart from Jean-Luc. After Diana's car crash, he sent her a box of Belgian chocolates.'

Lyle stared at her. 'Are you saying –?'

'I wouldn't be surprised if Jean-Luc doctored them with arsenic,' said Angelique. 'I didn't want to go to Arlington for Diana's and Gervase's wedding anniversary party, but Jean-Luc insisted we go.'

'You think he had an ulterior motive?'

Angelique drew a deep breath. 'Jean-Luc must have slipped away from the party and gone upstairs to Diana's bedroom. It would have been easy for him to fill her Tagamet capsules with arsenic and return to the party.'

'You're convinced Jean-Luc is the murderer?'

Angelique's eyes narrowed with suppressed anger. 'I'm no longer surprised by anything he says or does. It's now clear the man I was once married to is a vile, despicable monster...'

As Hermione and Lyle were leaving Frederick Steen's town house, they were accosted in the front hall by his daughter Gabriella who was on her way out.

'It's lovely to see you both,' she exclaimed in a breathless rush. 'I had no idea you were here. Daddy and Sebastian are at work.'

'We've been telling Angelique about the latest developments in the trial,' said Lyle.

Gabriella's voice faltered. 'The news about Jean-Luc's suspected heart attack is dreadful, isn't it? The police were here earlier asking lots of questions about his past.'

'The strain of the trial has taken its toll on everyone,'

said Hermione. 'It wasn't possible to talk openly at Arlington in front of the others last night. How are you coping?'

Gabriella's eyes were clouded with pain and confusion. 'I honestly don't know. The last year or so has been incredibly difficult for Sebastian and me. Our wedding day ought to have been the happiest of our lives. But seeing Diana faint in the chapel was awful. Sebastian couldn't believe it when she died and left all her money to Gervase.'

'Did neither of you suspect Diana had been murdered?' asked Lyle gently.

Gabriella shook her head and bit her lip. 'It never occurred to us for a single moment. When we found out Gervase had poisoned Diana, we were horrified. Sebastian is convinced Gervase was embezzling George Lowestoft. By the time Sebastian offered to sort out the poor man's finances, it was too late to save him from bankruptcy. Gervase destroyed all George Lowestoft's business papers after he died so we'll probably never know the full extent of what happened.'

'Do you think Gervase is guilty of Diana's murder?' said Hermione, watching her closely.

'It's such a terrible business,' said Gabriella bewilderedly. 'I really don't know what to think. Diana was convinced Gervase was trying to poison her.'

'It's a miracle the letter she wrote to your father turned up after all this time,' said Lyle. 'Frederick must have been shocked by its contents.'

Gabriella's mouth trembled. 'If Daddy had read the letter sooner, Diana's life might have been saved,' she said sadly. 'Sebastian is so angry with Gervase for poisoning her. It's impossible to talk to him on the subject. My father refuses to discuss the matter out of respect for Angelique's feelings. The stress is getting to me. It – it would help if I had someone I could talk to. Diana was such a lovely person. I really miss her.'

'This looks like your taxi,' said Lyle, as a black cab pulled up before the kerb.

'I've got a meeting at my art gallery with an important client.' Gabriella gazed at them with large, forlorn eyes. 'It would be wonderful to have a proper chat sometime. Why don't you both come to afternoon tea later in the week?'

'We'd love to,' said Hermione.

Gabriella smiled gratefully at them. 'I'll give you a call once I've checked my business diary.'

'I feel sorry for Gabriella,' confided Hermione, as they watched the taxi containing their friend merge into the early evening traffic.

'So do I,' said Lyle. 'Gervase's trial is casting a shadow over her happiness with Sebastian.'

'Sebastian has got a nerve telling Gabriella that George Lowestoft was embezzled by Gervase,' added Hermione indignantly. 'I'll never stop believing Sebastian was responsible.'

'Do you think Gabriella wants to speak to us about anything in particular?' said Lyle.

Hermione shook her head. 'Gabriella strikes me as being frightened and confused by everything that's happened. She simply needs someone to listen while she pours her heart out to them. Sebastian won't let Gabriella or anyone else discuss the subject of his grandmother's murder in his presence. It's not his intention to add to Gabriella's suffering. He's doing it to protect her.'

Lyle was inclined to agree. 'What did you make of our encounter with Angelique?' he asked as they drove away from Regent's Park in Lady Godiva.

'I doubt if Angelique will shed any tears in the event Jean-Luc's suspected heart attack turns out to be fatal,' replied Hermione.

'The tears ex-wives shed over their former husbands are usually of the crocodile variety,' Lyle assured her.

Hermione frowned. 'There's something about Angelique that doesn't add up,' she added slowly.

Lyle's expression was unusually grim. 'Diana didn't trust Angelique either,' he reminded her.

'And with good reason,' said Hermione. 'Angelique coveted Diana's husband and lifestyle. But there's no way she would have poisoned Diana and then implicated Gervase in her murder...'

'It could be a mistake to assume both acts were committed by the same person,' said Lyle gravely.

'If we're right and Diana was poisoned by Angelique,' said Hermione, 'she can't have known that Gervase would end up being arrested for his wife's murder. Or that Jean-Luc would incriminate Gervase by planting the bogus evidence in his bedroom at Arlington...'

25

On the way home, Hermione and Lyle stopped off at the Drunken Admiral in Brimhurst for some much needed liquid refreshment. Poppy Carter was looking thoroughly miserable behind the bar.

'I hardly see Rupert anymore,' she complained. 'Since the trial began, he's been spending all his time in London.'

'He's worried about his father,' said Lyle.

'Gervase and Rupert are a lot more alike than I realized. Sometimes I doubt Rupert and I will ever marry. Something always comes along and gets in the way of our happiness.'

'Diana's death has been tough on us all,' said Hermione sympathetically.

'I'm not sure I'll ever get over the shock of finding out she was poisoned,' said Poppy. 'Rupert was ever so fond of her. He's adamant Gervase is innocent, but the trial has gone from bad to worse. I don't know what to say to Rupert anymore to console him. A rift has come between us and it's not likely to go away.'

'Poppy, you mustn't think like that,' said Hermione, dismayed by her outburst.

Poppy's eyes filled with tears. 'On the night Lyle was knocked unconscious at Milsham Castle, Rupert asked me to marry him. There's no chance of that happening as long as everyone in the village thinks I caused his uncle's horse riding accident. I should have known it was a mistake to hope we could ever be happy together…'

'You just need to give it more time.' said Hermione reassuringly. 'Poppy, the police still haven't caught whoever attacked Lyle. Have you given any more thought to what happened that night?'

'I've told you all I know,' said Poppy. 'Rupert and I were asleep. The sound of the alarm woke us. We have no idea who tried to break into Milsham Castle.'

'Lyle saw a light in the library before he was attacked. Do you remember whether you left it on?'

Poppy shook her head helplessly. 'I honestly can't remember. Rupert and I had a drink in the library before we went to bed.'

'Clear your mind *and think…*'

'I'm almost certain Rupert switched the light off when we left the library. But I went back downstairs later to get my cardigan. I might have left the light on then.'

'Poppy, this is really important.'

'It's so long ago. I just can't remember. I'm sorry.'

'Lyle might have been killed,' said Hermione.

'That's hardly Poppy's fault,' said Lyle reasonably. 'You should ease up on her.'

'It makes me so angry knowing your attacker is still at large,' said Hermione.

'We may never find out who tried to break into Milsham Castle,' said Lyle. 'It's possible we're just going to have to get used to the fact.'

'Lyle is probably right,' said Poppy. 'Do you remember the two men who rented Glastonbury Cottage?'

Lyle's curiosity was piqued. 'Pacek Kowalski and Lawrence Leightonstone?'

Glastonbury Cottage was a rental property owned by Lyle on the outskirts of Compton Sutton. It was situated along a lonely lane and in recent months he had been unable to find a tenant.

Hermione spoke. 'They rented Glastonbury Cottage from us the day after we returned from the Norfolk Broads. Why do you ask?'

'They used to come in here for drinks,' said Poppy.

'Lyle met them,' said Hermione. 'I never did. What did they look like?'

'Hermione refuses to believe me when I tell her how ugly they were,' said Lyle. 'They reminded me of the first and second murderers in *Macbeth*.'

'Lyle isn't exaggerating,' said Poppy. 'You wouldn't want to meet either of them in a dark alley. They were lean, muscular types with faces like death skulls. I've never met two men who sounded more disillusioned with life than they did. Lawrence Leytonstone – the one with the crooked nose and long stringy hair – was no prince charming, I can tell you. I wondered if he was a professional boxer, but he claimed he and his friend were former medics in the British Army. Apparently, they served in the Falklands War. He said the smell of gangrene is something he'd never forget. He was a bit of a flirt and tried to chat me up until his friend told him to back off.'

'When was the last time you saw them?' asked Hermione curiously.

'The day before Lyle was attacked. Pacek Kowalski – the one with the shaved head – came into the Brimhurst Pharmacy. He bought a container of Vaseline for a friend. When I asked him what his friend wanted it for, he said his friend coats his nostrils with Vaseline to combat his hayfever symptoms.'

Hermione and Lyle stared at each other. 'I found a container of Vaseline in the bushes outside the library window,' she recalled. 'It never occurred to me that it was dropped by one of your attackers.'

'There was a price tag from the Brimhurst Pharmacy on it,' Lyle reminded her.

'There, what did I tell you?' said Poppy triumphantly. 'It may have escaped your notice, but ever since those two left Compton Sutton at the end of June the burglary rate has gone down.'

The bar began to fill up with customers and Hermione and Lyle retired to a corner table. Over dinner their conversation turned inevitably to Gervase's court case. Jean-Luc de Breteuil had been released from hospital earlier that afternoon. His suspected heart attack had turned out to be nothing more than a severe panic attack. Was Hermione's uncle Sir Roland Anstruther right to insist Jean-Luc had poisoned Diana because she had discovered his true identity? The couple grew tired of arguing the facts of the case and were relieved when Poppy stopped by their table to clear their plates.

On an impulse, Hermione found herself asking, 'Poppy, have you ever met the Duke of Marsden's former chauffeur Colin Hemmings?'

'I'll say I have,' replied Poppy with a grimace. 'I knew Colin long before that when he was still employed as Lord Milsham's chauffeur.'

'Have the two of you been an item?' asked Hermione shrewdly.

'Aren't you a clever one!' remarked Poppy. 'We only went out together for six weeks. I ended our relationship because he was jealous of my bulldogs Cornelius and Daisy.'

She took away their plates and a short while later served them coffee.

'That's Colin sitting at the far end of the bar,' she said, indicating a man with dark hair that was hanging over his forehead like rats' tails. 'For the last week he's been coming in here and deliberately sulking. It won't do you any good, I warned him. I'm not getting back with you and that's a fact.'

'Hemmings testified for the prosecution,' said Hermione. 'He alleges Gervase knew the brakes of the Daimler were defective *before* Diana and Oliver crashed off the side of the road.'

Poppy looked stricken. 'Rupert never mentioned it to me. I had absolutely no idea.'

'Rupert probably didn't want to upset you,' said Lyle quickly.

Poppy's expression hardened. 'This is the last time Colin comes in here and gets served. He can go somewhere else for a drink in future.'

At that moment Gervase's son Rupert entered the pub from the High Street and came over to Poppy and gave her an enthusiastic hug and kiss. The sight of the couple holding hands and gazing lovingly at each other was too much for

Hemmings. Seething with jealousy, he banged his empty glass down on the bar.

'I'll have another pint,' he declared loudly.

'Haven't you had enough already?' asked Poppy, turning scarlet with embarrassment.

'You never used to be so high and mighty!' muttered Hemmings. 'You used to be content to go out with a commoner like *me*. That's all changed – now you're seeing your fancy man!'

By now the pub had fallen silent and everyone was listening into the conversation.

'Steady on, Hemmings,' said Rupert in a surprisingly controlled voice. 'You don't want to do or say anything you might regret. Now there's a good chap.'

There was a tense silence, then Hemmings turned abruptly and swaggered to the door. His progress was blocked by the arrival of two uniformed police officers. The taller one addressed him.

'Colin Hemmings?'

The greeting was met with a scowl. 'What do you want?'

'I'm Detective Sergeant Avery of the Gosford C.I.D. I'm arresting you on suspicion of killing Mortimer Cosgrove –'

Poppy gasped out loud. Everyone listened in shocked silence as Hemmings was read his rights. He was quick to make his displeasure known.

'You won't pin this on me,' he snarled. 'The van involved in the incident was found wiped clean of fingerprints in Pelham Wood –'

'That's something only the driver of the van would know for certain,' said Sergeant Avery.

'So it was *you* who stole my van that day,' blurted

Poppy.

Hemmings glared at Poppy. 'What have you been *saying*?'

Poppy flushed. 'There's no need to look at me like that. Anything you've done you've brought on yourself.'

Sergeant Avery added, 'There was a clear set of fingerprints on the loudhailer attached to the roof of the vehicle. If you refuse to let us take your fingerprints, Mr Hemmings, we'll lift them from the glass you've been drinking from –'

Hemmings' shoulders sagged in defeat as he was handcuffed and escorted out of the pub by the two police officers. Now that she was no longer suspected of killing Mortimer Cosgrove, Poppy burst into tears of relief. Rupert took her into his arms and hugged her tightly.

Hermione turned to Lyle and spoke to him in an aside. 'It's nice to know your wild card paid off,' she said happily.

Lyle shrugged modestly. 'Once news of the arrest becomes known, Sir Roland shouldn't have any difficulty persuading the jury that Hemmings' testimony was entirely false and malicious.'

Hermione frowned. 'Does that mean you've changed your mind about Gervase's moment of madness?' she asked.

Lyle smiled. 'On the contrary, there's no doubt in my mind that Gervase knew the Daimler's brakes were defective *before* the car crash rather than afterwards.'

Hermione stared at him incredulously. 'And you're going to let him get away with it?'

'I'm much more interested in bringing Diana's killer to justice,' said Lyle. 'The hell Gervase is currently going through is punishment enough.'

Presently, the arrival of some new customers prompted Poppy to dry her tears and go behind the bar and help her uncle serve them. A beaming Rupert came over to Hermione and Lyle and shook hands with them.

'I want to thank you both for helping me prove Poppy's innocence,' he said. 'The last four years have been incredibly difficult for us both. Lyle, what made you suspect Hemmings?'

'Sir Roland asked me to think up a way to discredit Hemmings' testimony against your father,' replied Lyle. 'I have Hermione to thank for telling me Hemmings is a socialist and disapproves of blood sports. Sir Roland took a gamble on my hunch being right and contacted the police.'

'Gervase is no longer in a position to object to you marrying Poppy,' said Hermione smiling.

Rupert's expression fell. 'There's no chance of that happening until he's acquitted of poisoning Diana and the real killer is brought to justice.'

'Why aren't you in London with your father?' said Lyle.

Rupert released a sigh.

'It's been a distinctly worrying day,' he confided. 'Two boys were fishing when they found a submerged vehicle in the lake in Pelham Wood. The police have been asking all sorts of questions.'

Hermione was puzzled.

'What makes the police think you might know something?'

'Pelham Wood forms part of the Arlington estate.'

'Were there any bodies in the vehicle?' asked Lyle.

'No, thank goodness. The police have no idea why it was

abandoned. I've got enough on my mind at present without having to worry about this as well.'

26

'I'm never going to forgive you for this!' Angelique glared at her ex-husband across the drawing-room of their former marital home in Bruton Street. 'The lies you told against Gervase in court today were unforgivable.'

'I told the truth!' insisted Jean-Luc coldly. 'I've done nothing with which to reproach myself.'

He was taken aback by the look of loathing in his ex-wife's eyes. What had happened to the woman who had once smiled adoringly at him and said 'I do' as he slipped her wedding band on to her finger?

'Gervase is not going to be convicted of Diana's murder because of your hate-filled testimony,' hissed Angelique. 'I'm going to make you pay for the lies you've told –'

'Angelique, I think you should leave.'

Jean-Luc felt wretched. It had been a mistake to discharge himself from hospital that afternoon after recovering from his severe panic attack. The police had interviewed him a few hours ago. They seemed to think he might have killed Diana to stop the truth about his past from coming to light. Being confronted by Angelique had capped off a truly awful day for him. He followed her to the entrance hall. She opened the front door, then turned and faced him.

'Who are you really, Jean-Luc?' she demanded.

Jean-Luc swallowed hard and said, 'I don't have to answer these questions.'

'I don't believe for one minute that you overheard Gervase threatening to poison Diana,' said Angelique. 'I think you made that up.'

'Angelique, I'm not feeling well –'

Despite the tremendous anger she was feeling, Angelique was puzzled. 'Why have you lied about your past all these years? Why are you so frightened?'

'As Raoul Garnier I performed a series of operations without the – er – appropriate medical qualifications. I didn't want to testify against Gervase, but I was forced into it. The person who made me do this isn't going to get away with it.'

'What person?' demanded Angelique. '*Tell me their name.*'

Jean-Luc was trembling. 'For your own safety, I can't tell you any more than I have.'

Angelique glared at him. 'You're going to have to come up with a better answer than that in court, Jean-Luc. I'm going to tell the jury you killed Diana because you were terrified she was going to expose your disgusting criminal past.'

'Angelique, *please don't do this to me,*' groaned Jean-

Luc. 'I'm – I'm sorry everything went wrong between us.'

'Not half as sorry as you're going to be,' vowed Angelique. 'You're not going to get away with trying to destroy the love Gervase and I have for each other.'

Jean-Luc felt a dull, throbbing pain in his temples as he watched her leave, then he returned to the drawing-room and glanced at the ormolu clock. He hadn't eaten all day. He was famished. Why was the pizza company taking so long to deliver his pizza?

He poured himself a brandy from the decanter, then sat down and washed a mouthful down his throat. The punishment for perjury was prison and he felt an encroaching madness. He was not going there alone. He was going to take the other person with him. He'd spoken to his blackmailer on the phone a short while ago and had made his feelings clear on the subject.

The brandy dulled the edges of Jean-Luc's torment. He imagined he was meeting Angelique for the first time and falling in love with her all over again. The room swam out of focus, then back into focus again before it steadied itself. He felt a sense of desperate longing for Angelique that was like a physical ache.

The sound of the ringing doorbell drew Jean-Luc back to the present. How long had he been day dreaming? Several minutes? An hour – or was it even longer?

The grandfather clock in the entrance hall chimed half past seven. He saw his ex-wife's handbag on the hall table and a sudden wild hope fluttered inside his ribcage.

Suppose Angelique had come to her senses and discovered she loved him far more than she could ever love Gervase?

The thought brought tears to Jean-Luc's eyes. He would

have done anything to relive his time with her again before everything had gone so terribly wrong between them.

Jean-Luc opened the door. In his drunken state the cool night air disorientated him. Instead of slamming the door shut in his killer's face, he staggered backwards as two bullets from a silenced semi-automatic pistol buried themselves in his chest.

The next morning, Hermione and Lyle were having breakfast at Nettlebed when they were startled to hear on the radio that Jean-Luc de Breteuil had been murdered at his home in London the previous night.

'Were you expecting this to happen?' demanded Hermione.

Lyle stared at her in shock. 'The killer is obviously a lot more ruthless than I realized –'

The couple's plans for the day were temporarily forgotten as they came to terms with the latest development. Hermione was scheduled to play the cello that afternoon with the Gosfordshire Symphony Orchestra at the Royal Opera House in Gosford. The recent improvement in the weather meant Lyle was booked to give lessons on Lord Milsham's tennis court to several paying female residents from Compton Sutton. Although each of them claimed she wished to improve her game, Hermione suspected they were more interested in flirting with Lyle on account of his good looks.

The phone rang.

'That will probably be your uncle,' said Lyle, snatching up the receiver.

After a brief exchange of words, he pressed the hands-free button on the wall phone and the fruity voice of Sir Roland Anstruther came over the speaker in an urgent rush.

'Lyle, have you heard the latest news about Jean-Luc de Breteuil? He's been found shot dead at his home in Bruton Street.'

'Hermione and I just heard the news on the radio,' said Lyle quickly. 'Have the police discovered who killed him?'

'Angelique de Breteuil paid him a visit last night. The police found her handbag on the table in the front hall. She says she forgot to take it with her. Apparently, Jean-Luc was still alive when she left him shortly after seven o'clock. Lyle, have you any idea who did this?'

'My inner voice is telling me Jean-Luc's testimony against Gervase was a put-up job. That would explain why it contained so many discrepancies. I think the real killer coerced him into perjuring himself by threatening to expose his criminal past.'

Sir Roland groaned. 'Why didn't I think of that sooner?'

'After you gave the game away in court,' continued Lyle, 'the killer had only one course of action open to him – or her – and that was to silence Jean-Luc.'

'We don't know that for a fact,' objected Hermione. 'Jean-Luc might have fabricated his testimony against Gervase out of pure spite. I wouldn't put it past Angelique to have poisoned Diana and shot Jean-Luc.'

'Please don't make this case any more complicated than it already is,' protested Sir Roland. 'I've got some good news for you both where Colin Hemmings is concerned. The Gosford C.I.D. have charged him with Mortimer Cosgrove's death.'

'Did the fingerprints on the loudhailer belong to him?'

asked Lyle eagerly.

'The police made a positive match,' confirmed Sir Roland. 'They're extremely grateful for your tip-off. Hemmings was interviewed following his arrest yesterday evening. He confessed to being a former member of the *League Against Cruelty to Animals*. He also admitted to startling Mortimer Cosgrove's horse with the loudhailer attached to Poppy's stolen van. But he insists he never meant for Mortimer Cosgrove to be thrown from his horse and killed. When the case goes to court, Hemmings' defence counsel will probably get the charge of murder reduced to manslaughter. More's the pity....'

Lyle intruded on the barrister's thoughts. 'Have there been any developments regarding the vehicle that was found abandoned in Pelham Wood?'

'The police have now removed the station wagon from the lake,' replied Sir Roland. 'I doubt it will take them long to trace the owner through the registration plates. All the same, it's an odd thing to have happened...'

That afternoon's concert of Italian Baroque music was well-received at the Royal Opera House in Gosford, and an elated Hermione returned home to find a plump woman with a matronly air standing timidly on Nettlebed's front doormat. It was Diana's former personal maid Doris Honeychurch.

'Hermione, I hope you don't mind my calling on you,' she said apologetically. 'Something is troubling me about the Duchess of Marsden's death, and well, I – I suppose I was hoping that speaking to you might set my mind at rest. You were her goddaughter and she always had a high opinion of your capabilities...'

Hermione heard the distant repetitive thwack of a tennis ball coming from Lord Milsham's tennis court where Lyle was giving a lesson to one of his regular female clients. She glanced at her watch and calculated that Lyle would be busy for another hour or more which would give her plenty of time to find out what was bothering her visitor.

'Doris, you've done the right thing in coming to see me.'

'I assume you know I'm now living with my sister in Compton Sutton? After the Duchess of Marsden's death, I couldn't bring myself to go on working at Arlington.'

'Diana would want you to tell me everything you know.'

Over a cup of Darjeeling tea in the living-room, Hermione encouraged Doris to unburden herself.

'Ever since I found out the Duchess of Marsden was poisoned, I've felt so unsettled in myself... Little things keep nagging me, but I've no way of knowing if they're important or not.'

'I'd like to help in any way I can. What exactly is troubling you?'

Doris hesitated, then drew a breath and plunged into her narrative. 'Shortly before the Duchess of Marsden's body was exhumed, I went to her bedroom to say a prayer for her. In fact, it was the day I left Arlington for good. I was surprised to see her lovely Georgian hairbrush and mirror were missing from the dressing-table.'

'Why should anyone take them?' said Hermione.

'I don't know. It seems such an odd thing for someone to do. Something else puzzled me, too.'

'What was it?' prompted Hermione.

'Before the Duchess of Marsden died, Mrs Lowestoft

asked me to leave a book on her bedside table. Naturally I did as she asked. The book was called *The Illustrated Language of Flowers*. The Duchess of Marsden had written her name on the flyleaf, but it was gone. Someone had removed the page.'

'What became of the book?' asked Hermione.

Doris said self-effacingly, 'The last thing I did before I quit my job and left Arlington for good is return the book to the library.'

Hermione stared at her guest in surprise, then she realized the woman opposite her had dealt with the matter in the way any self-respecting maid would have done. She had instinctively tidied up after her employer. The fact that her employer had been dead for several months had made no difference to her.

'Doris, did Diana ever talk to you about the night George Lowestoft was shot?' she asked slowly.

'Mr Lowestoft's death upset the Duchess of Marsden a lot,' said Doris. 'A week before she died – on the morning she had her dress let out an inch for the wedding – she said to me, *"I could have prevented George's death. But I made the mistake of not believing him when he said he was in financial difficulties."* At the time she was reading a book – the one I told you about. *The Illustrated Language of Flowers.* When I asked what she meant, she replied it was a natural response to want to punish someone when they had wronged another person. But in this case, she said, it might provoke Sebastian into committing further financial indiscretions in the future.'

Hermione's eyes widened in surprise. 'What else did Diana say?'

'She added it was time she took her duties as a

grandmother seriously and reinstated Sebastian and Claudia in her will. Her decision, she said, was long overdue. She wrote to her solicitor that very day asking him to draw up a new will.'

'What do you think she meant by Sebastian's financial indiscretions?'

Doris gazed earnestly at Hermione. 'I took it to mean that Sebastian had helped himself to Mr Lowestoft's finances. I don't see how it could be any other way.'

Hermione drew her breath in sharply. She had never told Diana about Sebastian's alleged embezzling activities; it would have been too cruel to enlighten her after George Lowestoft was killed. It was all the more ironic that Diana should have discovered the truth for herself before she died. But who could have told her?

'There's probably nothing in what I'm saying,' added Doris anxiously, 'but what if Sebastian murdered Mr Lowestoft? I'm wondering what I ought to do in the matter. You see, if he's capable of embezzlement he could be capable of just about anything – including poisoning his own grandmother...'

Hermione came to a decision. 'You've done the right thing by telling me, Doris. You can leave it to me to do the sensible thing.' She hesitated and then added, 'According to Gervase, the last words Diana spoke before she died were *Nu Dans Sa Chambre*. Do they mean anything to you?'

Doris nodded vigorously. 'Well, yes, unless I'm mistaken, it's the name of a painting belonging to Mr Frederick Steen. It was painted by a Frenchman called Michel Dupree. He was a friend of the Duchess of Marsden.'

Hermione stared at her. 'Are you absolutely sure?'

'Oh, yes, the Duchess of Marsden was fond of talking about the past as the elderly often are. We used to have long chats about various things. The painting originally belonged to her friends Theodore and Odette Mariette. A week before the wedding, the Duchess of Marsden saw the painting in the drawing-room of Mr Steen's house in London. It seems he bought it off a young married couple after the war ended. I got the impression she would have liked to buy the painting off Mr Steen.'

'Why do you say that?' said Hermione.

'The Duchess of Marsden was extremely fond of Michel Dupree. He died of emphysema during the war. The elderly are often sentimental. I expect she would have liked it as a token of their friendship.'

Hermione drew a deep breath. What the other woman had told her had come as a surprise. It was quite a coincidence considering she and Lyle had once suspected Frederick Steen of being Captain Dietrich. But at least she now had the comfort of knowing what had been going through Diana's mind shortly before she died.

Before Doris Honeychurch left, the two women visited Lord Milsham's chapel, lit a candle and said a prayer for Diana. Afterwards, as they walked back down the driveway, the repetitive thwack of a tennis ball intruded on their thoughts from behind the bank of rhododendrons.

'Doris, you were friends with Marjorie Pym, weren't you?'

'I was probably one of the few friends Marjorie had,' confided Doris. 'The week before she died, she talked a lot about retiring and getting a nice place for herself. Honeysuckle Cottage in Compton Sutton had caught her fancy. Wherever do you think you'd get enough money to buy a place like that, I asked her? That's when Marjorie admitted she'd helped herself to a blue folder from the Great Hall on the night Mr Lowestoft was killed.'

Hermione's pulse quickened. 'Did she tell you what was in it?'

'Marjorie said it contained a secret about one of the guests at Arlington that would provide her with a comfortable income for her retirement.'

'I don't suppose she told you which guest?'

Doris shook her head. 'No, Marjorie's head was often filled with stuff and nonsense. It helped her to cope with the dullness of her life.'

'I wonder what she did with the blue folder?'

'If I'm to believe Marjorie's account of herself, she hid the documents in the blue folder somewhere at Arlington. There's a possibility Marjorie did uncover someone's secret, but I don't think it at all likely. I humoured her by saying it all sounded very promising. Now she's dead we'll probably never know the truth of the matter...'

Half an hour after Doris Honeychurch's departure, Lyle waved goodbye to Felicity Bachman and watched her drive off in her BMW. She was one of his more flirtatious clients and he had smiled his way politely through their game of tennis which had been heavy with sexual innuendo on her part. As he sauntered into the kitchen with an amused grin on his face and helped himself to a cold drink from the fridge, he was accosted by Hermione who gave him a full account of Doris Honeychurch's visit.

'Diana's hairbrush and mirror are missing from her bedroom at Arlington,' she concluded. 'I wouldn't be at all surprised if Pym saw the killer leaving Diana's bedroom on the evening she died. The old biddy must have realized an analysis of the hairs in the brush would prove Diana was poisoned.'

'And you think Pym took the hairbrush in order to blackmail the killer?' said Lyle.

'Blackmail seems to have been quite a hobby of hers,' said Hermione. 'If Pym had left the mirror behind, it would have drawn attention to the fact the hairbrush was missing, so she had to take that, too. There's something else you should know. Pym not only admitted to taking the blue folder from the Great Hall, but she also told Doris Honeychurch that she hid the documents inside the folder *somewhere at Arlington.*'

'Did Pym say where she hid the documents?'

'No, I'm afraid not,' said Hermione. 'Based on what Doris told us, I'm more convinced than ever that Pym was murdered because she knew who poisoned Diana. With any luck, it won't be long now before we find out the result of Pym's autopsy...'

Later that night, Hermione was about to drift off to sleep when Lyle sat up, switched on the bedside lamp and exclaimed softly, 'My God, I can't believe I didn't think of it sooner –'

'What are you talking about?' she asked in a tired voice.

'The submerged vehicle that was found in the lake in Pelham Wood. Who do we know who owns a station wagon?'

Hermione stared at him. 'None of our friends do –'

'Have you forgotten the two tenants who rented Glastonbury Cottage?'

'Pacek Kowalski and Lawrence Leightonstone left here months ago,' protested Hermione. 'Glastonbury Cottage is empty and all their belongings are gone.'

'We don't know for a fact they left there.'

'Are you suggesting someone murdered them and dumped their bodies in the cellar?'

Lyle scrambled out of bed and began getting dressed. 'Last time we visited Glastonbury Cottage there was a peculiar smell coming up from the floorboards.'

'We agreed it was probably dead rats,' Hermione reminded him.

'Suppose we were wrong?'

'Why would anyone want to murder Pacek Kowalski and Lawrence Leightonstone?'

'There could be any number of reasons we don't know about,' said Lyle. 'Go back to sleep. I won't be long.'

'We don't know for certain they're dead,' said Hermione. 'For all we know their station wagon might have been stolen by joyriders and later abandoned in the lake.'

Lyle's expression was unusually grim. 'There's only one way to find out if my inner voice is right...'

On the journey to Glastonbury Cottage, Hermione was unable to suppress her feeling of foreboding. She was aware of the tension emanating from Lyle as he gazed silently over the steering wheel at the road in front of them. Lady Godiva's headlights struggled to push back the darkness.

The hedgerows and lanes assumed a grey, wraith-like quality and gave the appearance of jumping out at them.

As they turned off the main road and shuddered along the pothole-riddled lane that led to Glastonbury Cottage, Hermione wondered if Pacek Kowalski and Lawrence Leightonstone had left Glastonbury Cottage because they were fed up with traversing the rutted track in their station wagon. Or was Poppy Carter right to suspect the pair had moved on in search of new victims after robbing scores of properties in the neighbourhood?

'This place is far more secluded than I remember,' said Hermione with a shiver. 'Couldn't this have waited until morning?'

'It's too late to turn back now,' said Lyle with a bluntness that rankled her.

Glastonbury Cottage had not been aired properly for months and the floorboards creaked beneath the couple's feet. The smell had worsened since their last visit. The pungent odour was at its worst in the kitchen. They threw the windows open and gratefully drew the night air into their lungs.

In the middle of the kitchen, a table and a set of chairs were positioned over a closed wooden trapdoor leading down to the cellar. Hermione's heart beat faster as she helped Lyle drag the table and chairs to one side of the kitchen. She wished she hadn't complained about the smell on their previous visit. If she had kept her opinions to herself, she and Lyle would almost certainly be in bed fast asleep without a care in the world. She told herself, for the umpteenth time, it would have been better if they had waited until the morning and asked the police to investigate the source of the smell.

Hermione switched on the flashlight she had taken from Lady Godiva's glove compartment and directed the beam at the trapdoor.

'Are you ready?' asked Lyle tersely.

Hermione nodded impatiently. Lyle grabbed hold of the metal ring attached to the trapdoor and jerked it open. The stench that rose up from the cellar was a hundred times worse than either of them had imagined.

Hermione screamed. In the wavering beam of the torch, the faces of Pacek Kowalski and Lawrence Leightonstone stared up at them from the bottom of the stairs while hungry rats scuttled around their decomposing bodies.

27

It was well after midnight by the time Hermione and Lyle returned to Nettlebed. They were exhausted from their grisly nocturnal adventure. The amount of stolen goods the police had found in the cellar with Pacek Kowalski and Lawrence Leightonstone indicated the two dead men had been highly experienced thieves. But the motive for their murders remained unknown.

Hermione and Lyle slept late into the morning and were woken by a phone call from a police officer who explained that the Gosford C.I.D. had taken over the inquiry from the Compton Sutton village police force because it did not have sufficient resources to tackle such a large investigation. They were asked to present themselves at Gosford Police Headquarters later that day in connection with the murders. The couple agreed and spent the rest of the morning making an inventory of the defective lightbulbs that needed replacing up at the main house. The necessary, if highly tedious task, was followed by a light lunch.

On their arrival at Gosford Police Headquarters that

afternoon, Hermione and Lyle were introduced to Detective Inspector McGowan who struck them as a sensible, down-to-earth officer who did not suffer fools gladly. After being questioned once again about the events of the previous night, they were invited to sign witness statements. Their visit was much more cut and dried than either of them had anticipated.

As they were driving home in Lady Godiva, Lyle remarked, 'Thanks to Detective Inspector McGowan, we now know a number of lock picking tools were found on the dead men's bodies.'

Hermione frowned. 'It sounds as if Pacek Kowalski and Lawrence Leightonstone had returned from doing a job just before they were murdered. I'll bet you anything you like they were responsible for the attempted break-in at Milsham Castle.'

'We'll probably never know for certain,' said Lyle.

'Are you forgetting the container of Vaseline that I found outside the library?' said Hermione, staring at him in surprise. 'Unless I'm mistaken, the police will find the fingerprints on it belong to the two murdered men...'

Later that night, Hermione and Lyle were watching television when Nettlebed's front doorbell rang. The couple ushered their visitors into the living-room.

'We're sorry it's taken us so long to get here,' said Claudia breathlessly.

'The message you left on my answer service said there's been a major development in the case,' said Oliver. 'What on earth has been going on?'

Hermione and Lyle were touched by how anxious and concerned their friends sounded on their behalf.

'There was a report on the news earlier tonight,' said Claudia. 'It stated two unidentified men had been found murdered at Glastonbury Cottage.'

'Lyle and I made the gruesome discovery last night,' said Hermione with a grimace.

Oliver stared at them in astonishment. 'Thank goodness you're both all right. Who were these men? And what reason could anyone have for murdering them?'

'Pacek Kowalski and Lawrence Leightonstone were former tenants of ours,' replied Hermione.

'Pacek Kowalski?' repeated Oliver. 'What sort of name is that?'

'Pacek Kowalski was of Polish descent,' explained Lyle. 'He was born and raised in England. The two men were medics in the Falklands War. On their return to England, they left the army and drifted into a life of drugs and crime. The number of lock picking tools the police found on their bodies was extraordinary.'

'They robbed scores of properties in Gosfordshire with a view to financing their cocaine habit during the time they lived at Glastonbury Cottage,' added Hermione. 'There was a huge stash of stolen goods in the cellar which the pair hadn't got around to selling before they died. They must have been dead in the cellar for anywhere up to six months. The police haven't released their names to the public yet.'

'You can rely on us not to tell anyone,' said Claudia quickly.

'The police suspect Pacek Kowalski and Lawrence Leightonstone were snorting cocaine in the kitchen prior to being shot and dumped in the cellar,' said Lyle.

'How on earth can they be sure of something like that?' said Oliver with a puzzled look in his eyes.

'The killer's clean-up operation was slipshod,' said Lyle. 'The police found microscopic traces of blood and brains – along with some cocaine powder – on and around the kitchen table.'

'Oh, my God, how revolting,' said Claudia with a shudder. 'Have the police arrested anyone yet?'

Lyle shook his head. 'No, it's early days as far as the investigation is concerned. The lease on Glastonbury Cottage expired at the end of June this year. We naturally assumed Pacek Kowalski and Lawrence Leightonstone had left of their own free will.'

'Who in their right mind would want to kill a pair of burglars?' demanded Oliver. 'It doesn't make sense.'

Hermione spoke. 'Lyle and I wouldn't be surprised if the pair were murdered on the same night he was attacked at Milsham Castle.'

'What do you mean – attacked?' said Oliver, staring at them bewilderedly.

'Hermione and I were woken by Lord Milsham's alarm going off,' explained Lyle. 'I hurried up to the main house to investigate. I was standing outside the library when someone walloped me over the back of the head. Hermione later found me unconscious and rang for an ambulance. It seems Pacek Kowalski and Lawrence Leightonstone were startled into flight before they could steal anything.'

Oliver stared at him in shock. 'I can't believe you didn't tell me!'

'I asked Hermione and Lyle not to say anything,' said Claudia with an apologetic grimace. 'You'd already been through so much – surviving the car crash and the shock of hearing about Diana's death. We didn't want to upset you any further.'

Lyle saw the hurt in his friend's eyes and said, 'If it's any consolation, Oliver, I soon regained consciousness. The doctors kept me in hospital for a couple of days as a precautionary measure. It wasn't long before I was back to my normal self. Throughout my ordeal, Hermione fussed over me like a mother hen. Never underestimate the importance of having a good woman in your life. I need Hermione as much as you need Claudia.'

'I don't want to be left in the dark like this again,' said Oliver, his voice thick with emotion.

'Stop worrying, Oliver. We promise not to keep any more secrets from you. Hermione found the keys to Glastonbury Cottage pushed through our front door letter flap a day or two after I was attacked. The killer obviously wanted us to think the two men had left the area.'

'Have the police identified the owner of the station wagon that was found in Pelham Wood?' asked Claudia suddenly.

'The police have confirmed it belonged to Pacek Kowalski,' replied Lyle. 'They think the killer disposed of the two men's bodies in the cellar and then submerged the vehicle in the lake. As far as the police are concerned, the motive for their murders is unclear.'

Hermione spoke. 'Lyle has hidden a copy of Captain Dietrich's draft report in Lord Milsham's library. We think Captain Dietrich may have hired Pacek Kowalski and Lawrence Leightonstone to retrieve the draft report. Their failure to do so evidently precipitated his decision to kill them.'

'I ought to have guessed Captain Dietrich was somehow involved in this business,' said Oliver with a note of exasperation in his voice.

'It obviously doesn't pay to get on the wrong side of Captain Dietrich,' said Hermione. 'Anyone who gets too close to him suffers awful consequences. After the car crash, your life was left hanging in the balance. George Lowestoft asked a lot of questions about the car crash, then shortly afterwards he was found shot dead in mysterious circumstances –'

'Murdered most likely,' interjected Oliver.

'I'm convinced Irene Lowestoft's maid was also murdered,' said Hermione, 'because she knew too much. In fact, I think Pym stole Diana's hairbrush and mirror from her bedroom at Arlington in order to blackmail the killer.'

Oliver looked puzzled. 'In what way would the hairbrush and mirror have incriminated the killer?'

'An analysis of the hairs in the brush would have shown Diana was poisoned with arsenic,' said Lyle.

'Is this the same maid Irene Lowestoft was talking about the other night?' asked Oliver.

'Her full name was Marjorie Pym,' explained Hermione. 'She died some months ago in her sleep at Irene Lowestoft's manor house in Market Chadwell.'

'I saw an out-of-date notice for Pym's funeral when I was staying here last Christmas,' recalled Oliver suddenly. 'It was pinned to the noticeboard outside Lord Milsham's chapel. It stated she was a loyal and faithful servant unto the Lord.'

'Perhaps someone ought to have told her blackmail is a fool's game,' added Hermione with a shiver.

Lyle and Oliver remained in the living-room discussing the case while the two women went to the kitchen to prepare some hot soup for supper.

'It will be an enormous relief when this wretched business is cleared up,' said Oliver. 'Once Gervase's trial is over, I intend to marry Claudia. The letter Diana wrote to Frederick Steen, in which she accuses Gervase of tampering with her medication, shouts aloud his guilt, wouldn't you say?'

There was a dreamy, contemplative look in Lyle's eyes. 'Diana might have been wrong to assume Gervase was trying to kill her,' he said. 'Following the car crash, any one at Arlington might have added arsenic to the Tagamet capsules that were prescribed for Diana. The evidence in Gervase's bedroom might have been planted there. I've never investigated a case where there are so many clues and red-herrings.'

Oliver leaned back in his armchair and gazed affectionately at his friend. 'Someone should give you a jigsaw puzzle.'

Lyle grinned unexpectedly. 'Why do you say that?' he asked, suspecting he knew what his friend's reply would be.

'Hermione was saying you solve murders more quickly when you're doing a jigsaw puzzle. It calms your nerves and helps you to listen to your inner voice!'

'It happens to be true, Oliver.'

'My head is spinning,' complained Oliver. 'There are too many questions in this case that remain unanswered. It might help if I made some notes.'

Lyle supplied Oliver with a notepad and a pen. The latter spent several minutes jotting down his ideas. He then handed the list to Lyle who read it in silence.

Questions Needing Urgent Answers

1) Who - apart from Gervase - could have been desparate enough to syphon the brake fluid from the Daimler, shoot George Lowestoft, poison Diana and kill Jean-Luc de Breteuil?
2) Did the same person also kill Pacek Kowalski and Lawrence Leightonstone and dispose of their bodies in the cellar of Glastonbury Cottage?
3) Did Marjorie Pym steal Diana's hairbrush and mirror in order to blackmail the killer?
4) Is the killer Captain Dietrich?
5) Where is he now and under what name is he living? (I am prepared to surrender all my worldly goods to find out)

Lyle nodded approvingly. 'You've drawn up an admirable list of questions,' he said.

'Can you think of any important questions I've left off the list?' asked Oliver anxiously.

Lyle was silent for several moments and then he smiled. 'I can think of a couple of questions,' he said. 'Was the same weapon used to shoot George Lowestoft, Jean-Luc de Breteuil, Pacek Kowalski and Lawrence Leightonstone? And more importantly *where is it now*?'

28

Lyle was having a shower the next morning when he heard his name being called followed by the sound of footsteps thudding on the stairs. Hermione burst into their bedroom as he came out of the en suite with a towel wrapped around his waist.

'I've discovered Captain Dietrich's identity,' she cried. 'The proof has been here at Milsham Castle all along.'

Lyle stared at her in astonishment. 'What are you talking about?'

'He was a guest here two years ago. Take a look at his signature in the visitors' book and you'll see *it's the same as Captain Dietrich's.*'

Lyle's pulse quickened as he read the entry in the visitors' book.

> Dear Lord Milsham,
>
> It has been an enormous privilege being invited to Milsham Castle to play croquet in your delightful company.

All good wishes,
Frederick Steen

Lyle was elated. *'Frederick Steen's signature is the same as Captain Dietrich's!'* he exclaimed.

'We've finally got our man,' said Hermione happily. 'Frederick Steen must have been suspicious when I invited him to dinner at Milsham Castle. His reply was written and signed by Gabriella. Her entry on the next page of the visitors' book is identical to the handwriting on the letter that Frederick Steen sent to us.'

Lyle turned the page and gazed at Gabriella's signature. 'You're absolutely right,' he said in an awe-struck voice. 'Frederick Steen must wear green contact lenses to disguise the fact his eyes are blue.'

'Diana wrote to him several times before the wedding,' recalled Hermione. 'He must suffer from arthritis and get Gabriella to write his letters for him. That would explain why Diana never suspected he was Captain Dietrich.'

'It never occurred to me to check Milsham Castle's visitors' book,' said Lyle admiringly. 'What made you think of it?'

Hermione laughed aloud with joy. 'I was up at the main house, sorting through the mail, when I saw the visitors' book. It suddenly occurred to me that Captain Dietrich might have been a guest of Lord Milsham's – and, hey presto, I was right!'

'Frederick Steen must have remembered his real signature was in the visitors' book,' said Lyle.

'The discovery must have given him a nasty jolt,' agreed Hermione. 'His plan to break into Milsham Castle and retrieve it – with the help of Pacek Kowalski and Lawrence Leightonstone – was foiled when the dodgy alarm went off. After the hue and cry that arose, Frederick Steen was probably too frightened to attempt another break-in.'

'I can't believe we were so easily deceived by the letter Gabriella wrote on her father's behalf,' said Lyle wonderingly.

Hermione frowned. 'In view of what we now know about Frederick Steen, I don't think Diana tried to stop Sebastian's and Gabriella's wedding because she was feeling unwell.'

'No, I don't, either,' said Lyle.

'A week before the wedding, Diana saw a painting called *Nu Dans Sa Chambre* at Frederick Steen's home in London,' continued Hermione. 'He claimed he had bought it after the war from a young married couple. Diana must have realized Frederick Steen had looted it from the Mariettes' chateau on the night he murdered them as Captain Dietrich. The last words she spoke to Gervase – after collapsing in the chapel and being carried to her bedroom – were "*Nu Dans Sa Chambre.*" After all the cruelty and suffering Captain Dietrich has inflicted on others, I'm going to enjoy seeing him convicted of his war crimes.'

'Contrary to what I told you,' said Lyle cheerfully, 'the copy I made of Captain Dietrich's draft report was never hidden in Lord Milsham's library. It's been here at Nettlebed all along.'

Hermione stared at him in surprise. *'Where?'*

'There's a framed picture on the staircase landing –'

'Are you referring to the sketch of Arlington?' she asked.

'The copy of the draft report is hidden in the back of the

frame,' said Lyle.

'I might have guessed!' said Hermione with a spurt of annoyance. 'Do you know how fed up I've become straightening the picture each time I walk past?'

Lyle smiled unashamedly. 'I knew you'd sleep a lot better next to me if you weren't worried about being burgled.'

Over breakfast in the kitchen, Hermione said, 'We're only going to get one shot to bring Captain Dietrich to justice *and we've got to get it right.'*

Lyle nodded in agreement. 'Do you remember how Irene Lowestoft told us she has friends living somewhere in Cornwall?'

Hermione frowned in an effort of recollection. 'The name of the seaside village has slipped my mind.'

'Apparently they invited her to visit them,' added Lyle.

'For some reason I can't help thinking of my first cello teacher Maureen Bennett.' Hermione clicked her fingers in sudden recollection. 'The name is Fowey. It rhymes with Joey – the name of Maureen's eldest brother.'

'Would you mind phoning Irene Lowestoft and asking her for the name of her friends?' asked Lyle.

A look of disbelief sprang up in Hermione's eyes. 'You're saying you want me to find out *the name of the friends who invited her to stay with them in Fowey*?'

'Precisely.'

Hermione was stunned. 'Are you serious?'

'Perfectly.'

'Is that all?'

Lyle nodded complacently. 'Yes.'

'In what way is this going to help us bring Captain Dietrich to justice?' asked Hermione bewilderedly.

'Be patient and you'll find out soon enough,' said Lyle gravely. 'I'm going up to London. There's an important fact I need to corroborate. The entire case hangs on it...'

Hermione phoned Irene Lowestoft at Arlington as soon as Lyle had left for London. She had no trouble in obtaining the information he had asked her to get. But she was completely baffled as to why he wanted to know the name of Irene's friends in Cornwall.

There was no time for Hermione to brood on the matter. She drove to Brimhurst Studios where she spent the day with the Gosfordshire Symphony Orchestra recording the soundtrack for a three-part World War Two documentary called *Operation Overlord.* The company was blessed to have Bulgarian-born Biserka Petrova as their conductor. Despite the harrowing subject matter of the documentary, the day passed in a blur of artistic creativity and technical virtuosity.

On Hermione's return to Nettlebed, she carried out several domestic chores around Milsham Castle without giving much thought to what she was doing. The idea that the nightmare she and Lyle had endured for so long might soon be over filled her with a mixture of hope and trepidation. Waiting for Lyle to arrive home played havoc on her nerves and she wished he had taken her more fully into his confidence. Within the last eighteen months, a total of six people had died in violent circumstances.

The phone rang sharply and a shaft of fear shot through

Hermione. It was Gabriella Steen calling from London to invite Hermione and Lyle to afternoon tea at her father's town house the following afternoon. Angelique de Breteuil was expected to spend most of the day testifying in court, and Gabriella would have the entire town house to herself. Hermione accepted the invitation and hung up with a trembling hand.

Suppose Frederick Steen knew they were on to him and was using Gabriella as a pawn to lure them into a trap? If so, they were going to have to be on their guard...

Shortly before six o'clock, Hermione heard a crunch of gravel as Lady Godiva pulled up in the driveway. A wave of relief washed over her. Until then, she hadn't realized how tense she was feeling. She was putting the kettle on the green Aga in order to make the tea when Lyle sauntered into the kitchen.

'Are you all right?' she asked.

'Everything is going according to plan,' said Lyle reassuringly. 'Did you speak to Irene Lowestoft?'

'The name of her friends are Lord and Lady Tremayne,' she told him.

'Was she expecting their letter?'

'I really wouldn't know,' said Hermione. 'How did you know they wrote to her? They might just as easily have phoned her.'

'It would have been impossible for Lord and Lady Tremayne to have phoned Irene if she was telling us the truth,' said Lyle, smiling unexpectedly. 'It's obvious they wrote inviting her to stay with them – in fact, it really couldn't have been any other way...'

Hermione stared at him. 'Are there going to be any more killings?' she asked anxiously.

'Not if I can help it...' Lyle gazed at the unfinished jigsaw puzzle that was lying on the breakfast table. The black and white pieces showed Daphne du Maurier rowing a small boat from Fowey towards Ferryside. He slotted the last remaining pieces into the jigsaw puzzle and then added softly, 'It won't be long now before my plans to expose Captain Dietrich are finalised...'

Later that night, Hermione and Lyle were sitting up in bed watching the classic Alfred Hitchcock movie *Rebecca* when the phone rang. Lyle took up the receiver as the end credits were rolling.

The voice of his friend came across the line. 'Lyle, I know it's late – but there's something I want you to know,' said Oliver excitedly. 'Claudia and I have just sold the television rights of *Faces and Places* to CBS. There's going to be an American version of the show. I'm going to be wealthy beyond my wildest dreams.'

'That's wonderful news,' said Lyle warmly. 'A lot has been happening since we last spoke to each other.'

Oliver released a sigh. 'I'll be glad when this business is over and Gervase is convicted of poisoning Diana. I wouldn't be surprised if he attacked you the night the alarm went off at Milsham Castle. You might easily have died of hypothermia if Hermione hadn't found you lying unconscious outside the library.'

'Oliver, the end is in sight.'

'What are you saying?'

'I need your help to set a trap for the killer,' said Lyle. 'Whatever you do *you mustn't breathe a word of what I'm about to tell you to anyone.*'

'You can rely on me not to tell anyone apart from Claudia –'

'No, Oliver. I don't want you to even tell her. There's going to be a gathering of the suspects at Arlington tomorrow night. I want your permission to give a private screening of the documentary you made about Diana's life.'

'What's this all about?'

Lyle smiled. 'Listen carefully, my friend, *and I'll tell you everything* –'

29

'After six long years the war was over. It was time for Diana and the French Resistance to lay down their weapons and rebuild their lives. As a young girl, Diana enjoyed the novels of Daphne du Maurier, pictured here in 1931 rowing from Fowey to Ferryside. It was Diana's dream after reading *Rebecca* to be mistress of a home every bit as grand as Manderley. In 1981 Diana's wish came true when she married the Duke of Marsden and became chatelaine of Arlington, one of England's most famous country estates.'

A series of fast-moving still images accompanied Oliver's narration of the television documentary – a black and white photo showing Daphne du Maurier rowing towards Ferryside, a colour poster of the movie *Rebecca* featuring its stars Laurence Olivier and Joan Fontaine, a long shot of Diana arranging a vase of flowers in the library, then walking elegantly out of the room. The music score rose to a crescendo and the credits rolled against a background shot of Arlington's water terrace.

The lights came up in the High Saloon at Arlington, causing everyone to blink and stir in their seats.

'Paul Smith's camera work was excellent,' said Sebastian with a note of awe in his voice. 'I'm glad I hired him.'

There were several appreciative comments of this kind, then Rupert stood up and said, 'I'd like to thank you all for joining me in watching this tribute to Diana's life. As you know, my father is currently in custody and can't be with us tonight. The reason I've invited you all here on Gervase's behalf is to unravel the mystery of Diana's death with the help of –'

The door opened and Bosworth the butler appeared announcing, 'Mr Steen.'

Frederick Steen entered the room. Everyone apart from the tycoon was wearing evening dress because they had dined earlier in the formal red dining-room.

'Frederick, I'm delighted to see you.' Rupert shook hands with him. 'My father has asked me to tell you that he holds no ill feelings towards you for testifying against him in court.'

'I'm grateful to Gervase for his understanding, Rupert.'

'Please – won't you take a seat?'

Rupert gestured to the chair by the side of the fireplace and Frederick Steen sat down.

Rupert went on, 'Lyle Revel's flair for solving murders is well known to the police and at my father's request I'm now going to invite him to share his discoveries with us.'

Looking tall and resplendent in his tuxedo, Lyle stood up and gazed at the circle of suspects before him. 'Diana's car crash has played a pivotal part in this case,' he said in a calm, unhurried voice. 'Just before it happened, Oliver confided to Diana that he had discovered the whereabouts of a wanted male fugitive. I was obliged to ask myself if the fugitive had tampered with the Daimler's brakes *or if someone else had.*

'The next act in the drama was the mysterious shooting of George Lowestoft, a man who asked too many questions about Diana's car crash and ended up dead. Did George Lowestoft discover who was responsible for draining the brake fluid from the Daimler? Claudia was secretly in love with Oliver and might have decided to put an end to his affair with her grandmother – unaware that he would also be in the Daimler with Diana when the brakes failed. Diana's husband Gervase not only desired her money, but he was also in love with his mistress and wished to marry Angelique.'

'George was my father's best friend,' protested Rupert. 'I refuse to believe Gervase could have murdered George or anyone else.'

'Not even to save Arlington?' taunted Lyle. 'Are you forgetting the dead man was shot with Gervase's Walther PPK? On the other hand, Rupert, you knew that unless your stepmother Diana died and left her considerable fortune to Gervase, there would be nothing left for you to inherit after your father's lifetime – except a title and a pile of debts. What you wanted more than anything was to marry Poppy Carter, the impoverished daughter of the local chemist. On the night of Diana's and Gervase's wedding anniversary, you smuggled Poppy into your bedroom. Rupert, are you able to state you were with Poppy when George Lowestoft was shot?'

Rupert frowned angrily. 'No, of course not! I was one of the first people to find the body.'

'I had already left Arlington by then,' said Poppy with a tremor in her voice.

'Presumably by the servants' passage so as not to be seen?' queried Lyle with an ironic smile. 'On the night of the car crash, one of the servants from Arlington came to you with a prescription for Diana's Tagamet capsules. It would have been easy for you to fill the capsules with arsenic before handing them over to the waiting servant.'

'I was far too fond of Diana to do any such thing.'

Poppy's eyes brimmed with tears and Rupert squeezed her hand in a comforting gesture.

Lyle's voice hardened. 'Any one of you *might* have orchestrated Diana's car crash and shot George Lowestoft to prevent the truth from coming out. The most likely suspect was Sebastian since George Lowestoft was being embezzled by him.'

'That's an outrageous lie!' flared Sebastian. 'I never did anything of the sort!'

Lyle said grimly, 'I was forced to ask myself, *was the shot Sebastian and I heard the actual one that killed George Lowestoft?* Or had Sebastian shot him *before* that with a silencer attached to the pistol? It would have been easy for Sebastian to light a firecracker with a long fuse in the servants' passage to simulate the sound of the pistol shot which went off a couple of minutes later. By which time Sebastian had joined everyone in the Great Hall. To all extents and purposes Sebastian had a perfect alibi.'

'Any one at Arlington might have shot George and lit the fuse in the servants' passage to give themselves an alibi,' said Sebastian coldly. 'You're not going to fix this on me.'

'Yes, any one of you could have murdered him that way,' agreed Lyle, his gaze flitting over the assembled company, 'including Gabriella whose love for Sebastian is so strong she wouldn't hesitate to kill anyone who threatened his safety.'

Gabriella gazed defiantly at him and said nothing. She looked young and beautiful – and suddenly very cruel...

Sebastian's voice was tight with anger. 'Leave Gabriella out of this –'

Lyle ignored him and went on inexorably, 'Irene Lowestoft had an even stronger motive for murder because it has always been her secret ambition to marry Gervase for his title *after her own husband and Diana were out of the way.* What you didn't know, Irene, is that Gervase had a secret mistress in Angelique and that he wished to marry her. In the end, your marital plans came to nothing.'

Irene's eyes were clouded with pain. 'Do you really believe I could have killed my own husband?' she demanded. 'George was my life.'

Lyle turned to Angelique. 'As Gervase's mistress, you must have been furious when you heard Diana had cheated death in the car crash. It would have been easy for you to add arsenic to the Belgian chocolates that Jean-Luc and you sent to Diana after her accident. On the night of Diana's and Gervase's wedding anniversary, you had ample opportunity to go to her bedroom while everyone was celebrating in the Long Gallery. It would hardly have taken you any time at all to substitute her Tagamet capsules for poisoned ones, then return to the party.'

Angelique glared at Rupert. 'Are you going to let Lyle insult me like this?' she asked indignantly. 'Your father will be far from pleased when he finds out.'

'You also went to your former marital home in Bruton Street on the night Jean-Luc was murdered,' said Lyle.

'What was the purpose of your visit?'

'I wanted to give Jean-Luc a piece of my mind,' replied Angelique with a flash of anger. 'I told him he would never win me back by telling such despicable lies about Gervase. He insisted he was forced to testify against Gervase because he was being blackmailed over his criminal past. He added that the person who made him do it wasn't going to get away with it.'

'Did Jean-Luc tell you the person's name?'

Angelique shook her head. 'Jean-Luc refused to confide in me. I must have left him about ten past seven. Whoever killed Jean-Luc came to the house after that.' She added in a brittle voice, 'I don't know who sabotaged the Daimler's brakes, shot George or poisoned Diana, *but it wasn't me.*'

'No one tampered with the brakes,' said Lyle simply. 'Hemmings the chauffeur testified in court that he found a *puddle* of brake fluid on the floor of Arlington's garage where the Daimler was parked. *This indicates the brake fluid leaked out of the rusted holes in the brake lines.'*

'Meaning George never saw anyone interfering with the brakes?' asked Rupert bewilderedly.

'Precisely,' said Lyle. 'The car crash was a genuine accident. On the night George Lowestoft died, Diana refused to help him out of his financial difficulties. He had cried wolf so many times in the past that it never occurred to her that he was in trouble this time. He left the High Saloon intoxicated with alcohol and in an acute state of mental anxiety. He was unable to see a way out of his problems. The reason why the police never found a traditional suicide note is because *George Lowestoft didn't write one*. He chose to communicate the reason for his suicide through floriography which is mostly forgotten by today's generation.'

'Floriography?' repeated Poppy, looking perplexed. 'I've never heard of it.'

'Otherwise known as the language of flowers,' said Hermione, taking her place by Lyle's side. 'During the rigid moral climate of the Victorian era individuals sent flowers and floral arrangements in coded messages to each other in order to express feelings that could not be spoken aloud. For instance, rosemary is for remembrance and red poppies are for consolation. Bosworth, before Mr Lowestoft went to the gun room he left a bouquet on his wife's pillow. What flowers were in the bouquet?'

'I saw Mr Lowestoft take the flowers from the vases in the corridor,' said Bosworth promptly. 'The bouquet featured meadow saffron, dog roses, purple hyacinths, francisca latifolia, butterfly weeds, sweet scabious, globe amaranths, red roses, gum cistus and a single pansy with a broken flower.'

'Earlier today,' said Hermione, 'Lyle and I knew for certain that George Lowestoft had committed suicide after we located a book here in Arlington's library called *The Illustrated Language of Flowers.* It was originally published by George and Routledge and Sons in 1856 and edited by Mrs L. Burke. Since then it has been reprinted many times.' She picked up a recent edition of the book and opened it. 'The book gives the meaning of every flower found in the bouquet George Lowestoft left on his wife's pillow a few minutes before midnight.'

'You can only begin to imagine Irene's reaction,' said Lyle, 'when she saw the bouquet after his death. Meadow saffron means –'

'*My best days are past,*' supplied Hermione.

'Dog roses –'

'I love you and it causes me both pleasure and pain –'

'Purple hyacinths –

'I am sorry –'

'Francisca latifolia –'

'Beware of a false friend –'

'Butterfly weeds –'

'Let me go –'

'Sweet scabious –'

'Widowhood –'

'Globe amaranths –'

'Immortality and unfading love –'

'Gum cistus –'

'I shall die tomorrow –'

'Red roses –'

'I love you –'

'A pansy with a broken flower –'

'Adieu, but remember me...'

Hermione put the book down and Lyle resumed speaking.

'Bosworth, do you recall what Mr Lowestoft did after he left the bouquet on Mrs Lowestoft's pillow?'

'Indeed, I do, sir,' said Bosworth. 'He put a framed photograph of Sebastian Rylander, along with a sprig of ivy and dogsbane, on the table in Mrs Lowestoft's room. He also opened the curtains, then went downstairs to the gun room.'

'What can you see when the curtains are open at night?' asked Lyle.

'Nothing but pitch darkness, sir.'

'And what about during the day?'

'A black mulberry tree,' replied Bosworth.

'Three unlikely clues,' said Lyle, nodding quietly to himself. 'The black mulberry tree, the photo of Sebastian and the sprig of ivy and dogsbane. The curtains were open so that in the morning Irene Lowestoft would see the mulberry tree whose meaning is –'

'I shall not survive you,' said Hermione.

'The sprig of ivy and dogsbane next to the photo of Sebastian told her, quite literally –'

'Your friend is deceitful...'

'George Lowestoft left the bouquet in his wife's room,' remarked Lyle, 'then shortly after midnight he went to the gun room and deliberately shot himself to avoid the scandal of bankruptcy. In his despair, he was convinced he had failed Irene and there was no way out of his predicament.'

'George had such a distinguished career,' said Irene in a broken voice. 'I didn't want his naval reputation sullied by a verdict of suicide.'

'The truth came to Diana a week before her death,' said Hermione gently. 'She was reading *The Illustrated Language of Flowers* when she looked up and was heard to say she could have prevented George's death. Determined to prevent her grandson from embezzling anyone else after she died, Diana wrote to her solicitor that very same day asking him to reinstate Sebastian and Claudia in her will, but she died before she was able to go up to London and sign the document.'

Tears rolled down Irene's cheeks. 'If George had wanted revenge, he would have left behind a handwritten letter implicating Sebastian. Since he was prepared to forgive Sebastian, I decided I would, too. George's life was ruined, but I saw no reason to ruin the life of love and happiness that Sebastian was set to enjoy with Gabriella. One of the maids put *The Illustrated Language of Flowers* in Diana's room at my request. I wanted Diana to know that her decision to cut off Sebastian's allowance and disinherit him had led to the tragedy. Also, I hoped she might reconsider my position and offer me a permanent home here at Arlington.'

She pressed her knuckles to her mouth and sobbed. It took her almost a minute to regain control of her emotions.

'What the hell is everyone looking at me like that for?' demanded Sebastian, furious at having his duplicity exposed. 'I never embezzled George.'

'Contrary to what many people think, I happen to know my father loved Diana very much,' said Rupert quietly. 'The reason he didn't tell her that Sebastian had embezzled George is because he didn't want to upset her. It never occurred to him that Diana would find out before she died...'

Gabriella looked at Lyle and said with superb confidence, 'I'm a rich heiress in my own right and after my father's lifetime I'll be an immensely wealthy woman. Sebastian had no reason to embezzle George or anyone else. If anyone was embezzling George, it was Gervase who's trying to lie his way out of it by blaming Sebastian.'

Lyle drew a deep breath. 'Gervase has been accused of many things including stealing Diana's hairbrush and mirror in a desperate bid to prevent the police from discovering she was poisoned. Such a tactic could only have been expected to *delay* rather than prevent the exhumation.

Once I understood the real reason *why* the killer removed the hairbrush and mirror from Diana's dressing-table all the other facts in the case fell neatly into place...'

30

'This case reaches far back into the past and involves a wanted Nazi war criminal called Captain Helmut Dietrich,' continued Lyle. 'On 5 February 1944, Captain Dietrich led a Gestapo raid on a French chateau outside L'Evette owned by Theodore and Odette Mariette. Not only did he kill the couple for colluding with the French Resistance, he also boasted of the fact in a handwritten draft report that was intended for his commandant. By a fortuitous chain of events, the draft report was left in a blue folder on the table in the Great Hall here at Arlington. By the end of the night, George Lowestoft had committed suicide and the blue folder had been taken by Mrs Lowestoft's maid Marjorie Pym.

'Before I reveal the name under which Captain Dietrich is currently masquerading, I will take you all on a journey. After Germany was defeated in the Second World War, Captain Dietrich used a fake passport and fled to South America. He claimed to be a Polish Jew who had spent the war in a German concentration camp. He told everyone that his entire family had been wiped out by the Germans.

So convincing was the new identity he invented for himself that no one thought to question its veracity. He became a chemist and in due course married a wealthy English pharmaceutical heiress who introduced him into British high society. Her death four years into the marriage left him an immensely wealthy man in a position of unassailable power and respectability.

'On the afternoon of Diana's and Gervase's wedding anniversary, Captain Dietrich sent them a bouquet of lilies with a handwritten card attached to it. Later that night, Marjorie Pym stopped by the table in the Great Hall to admire the lilies. She also took the opportunity to look through the contents of the blue folder. One can only imagine her surprise when she saw Captain Dietrich's handwriting on the draft report was the same as the handwriting on the card attached to the bouquet.

'Pym bided her time and made her plans. She was determined to blackmail Captain Dietrich and retire from her life of domestic servitude. The wedding of Sebastian and Gabriella provided Pym with the perfect opportunity to confront Captain Dietrich. She lured him to the library on the pretext that his solicitor was phoning him. On being confronted with Pym's blackmail demands, Captain Dietrich gave her five hundred pounds in cash as a down payment. She instructed him to pay her fifty thousand pounds on the first Wednesday of each month until further notice. Judging by the expression I saw on her face as she left the library, she was extremely pleased with the outcome of the meeting.'

'Pym was no fool and hid the contents of the blue folder somewhere at Arlington,' said Hermione. 'The hiding place remained a mystery until Lyle and I had a long talk with Bosworth today. He remembered seeing Pym come out of the old nursery. Given Pym's fondness for Greek mythology, we immediately thought of the Trojan horse that helped win the siege of Troy. In the old nursery there is a rocking horse. Concealed under its saddle was the original card that was attached to the bouquet of lilies and a copy of Captain Dietrich's draft report confessing to the murders of Theodore and Odette Mariette. We also found a letter from the couple's son, Armand, translating the draft report from German into English, along with a letter written by Pym. The letter describes her encounter with Captain Dietrich in the library at Arlington and reveals his current identity.'

'But just *who* is Captain Dietrich?' said Rupert.

Lyle smiled grimly. 'Have patience, my friend. We are about to find out. What you are about to see is a short film that I produced with Buzz Malone at Creative Television.'

Hermione doused the lights and switched on a 16-mm projector. An image of an elderly, emaciated man flickered onto the screen. It was the Mariettes' former valet Marcel Depardieu. He was sitting on the terrace at Cedar Lodge Nursing Home in Canterbury apparently looking through a pile of different photos on the table in front of him. Owing to his first-rate acting it was impossible to tell he was blind. The camera angle prevented the audience from seeing that all the photos in his hand featured an image of the same person.

'My name is Marcel Depardieu,' he said. 'Theodore and Odette Mariette were my employers. I'll never forget how Captain Dietrich murdered them. He had the coldest ice-blue eyes of any man I've ever seen. He took me and the other servants to a quarry in a nearby forest. His plan was to execute us all, but it failed because a splinter group of the

French Resistance ambushed his men –' He broke off suddenly and pointed at one of the photos in front of him. 'My God, I don't believe it. *This is Captain Dietrich!*'

He held the photo out to the camera so everyone could see the head shot of Frederick Steen's smiling face. The photo had been taken at Gabriella's and Sebastian's wedding. The silence in the High Saloon was extraordinary.

The same photo appeared against a white background and then moved to the left of the screen as a photo of Captain Dietrich in full Gestapo uniform appeared on the right. After several moments, the two photos moved to the centre of the screen where their images were superimposed over each other.

'Oh, my God!' exclaimed Angelique. *'It's the same set of eyes in both pictures.'*

A startled cry came from Gabriella as two handwriting samples appeared on the screen.

Lyle's voice rang out, loud and clear. 'The image you see before you is the signature on Captain Dietrich's draft report confessing to the Mariettes' murders. The second image shows Frederick Steen's signature on the card congratulating Diana and Gervase on their wedding anniversary. *The similarity of the two signatures is inescapable.'*

The lights came back on. Everyone, including Gabriella and Sebastian, turned and stared at Frederick Steen who was sitting in the chair by the fireplace. His face was ashen-grey.

'My God, Frederick, it was *you,*' said Rupert. 'You poisoned Diana. Was it because you were frightened my stepmother might recognise you and expose your Nazi past after all these years?'

Frederick Steen glared at Lyle. 'How do you account for the fact Captain Dietrich has blue eyes?' he demanded. 'Mine are green.'

Lyle whipped a passport out of his dinner jacket pocket. 'You're currently wearing green eye contact lenses. The photo in your passport shows your eyes are really blue. If you're wondering how I got my hands on your passport, Hermione distracted Gabriella during afternoon tea at your town house this afternoon while I searched your bedroom.'

The colour had drained from Gabriella's face and she was fighting back tears. 'Daddy, what's going on?' she asked in a stricken voice.

Frederick Steen addressed his daughter in a carefully controlled voice. 'Gabriella, I want you to leave. My chauffeur is waiting downstairs.' He cut off her murmured protest. 'Do as I tell you.'

Bosworth the butler held the door open for Gabriella and she left the High Saloon.

Frederick Steen looked at Lyle and said sharply, 'I haven't the slightest idea who poisoned Diana.'

'You had a strong motive for poisoning Diana and Marjorie Pym,' said Lyle. 'Diana died on Friday 30 September. The following day Irene Lowestoft left Arlington and returned to Market Chadwell in the neighbouring county of Aldershire. The manor house was being auctioned off in a fortnight's time and she needed to pack up her belongings. She was accompanied by her maid. Marjorie Pym was found dead in her bed on the morning of Tuesday 4 October. Ordinarily, two elderly women from the same household dying a few days apart would have aroused the suspicions of the authorities. But in this case they died in different counties. Pym's death prevented her from going up to London the following day and meeting you in Trafalgar Square. You must have been delighted to be released from her blackmail demands.'

'Are you saying Frederick poisoned Pym, too?' demanded Rupert.

'As a consequence of my growing concerns,' said Lyle, 'Sir Roland Anstruther applied to the Home Secretary requesting an exhumation. The autopsy results became known earlier today. The poisoning of Marjorie Sharpe – as Mrs Lowestoft's maid was known before her marriage – forms the crux of this case. *She was murdered by her husband Albert Pym...'*

Lyle heard Bosworth's sharp intake of breath and smiled faintly to himself.

'Albert Pym was killed during the war,' protested Irene.

'That's what he wants everyone to think,' said Lyle. 'Could you tell everyone how Pym met her husband?'

'Pym refused to come to London with me after the war broke out,' said Irene. 'The bombings frightened her too much. Most of the gardeners had been called up for active service. Pym stayed at Thurlestone Hall growing vegetables for the war effort. Sometime later I heard one of the under-gardeners had got her pregnant and had been obliged to marry her. A young fellow by the name of Albert Pym. Soon afterwards he joined the RAF and became a fighter pilot. His plane was shot down over the North Sea. The shock of his death was too much for Pym and her baby was stillborn.'

'Albert Pym is alive and here in this room,' said Lyle, looking at Bosworth. 'There were a number of cases during the war when pilots were rescued from the sea by a passing convoy. Albert Pym feigned amnesia throughout his stay in hospital. He had been forced into marriage with a woman he didn't love and he had no wish to return to her.'

'Pym was a dreadfully plain creature even then,' said Irene. 'She received the traditional telegram saying her husband was lost at sea, presumed dead. I thought – we both thought – she had been widowed.'

'Bosworth, could you please turn on the lamp?'

In response to Lyle's request, Bosworth leaned over the table lamp and switched it on. The sudden upward glare of light altered the lines of the butler's kindly face and his expression seemed oddly malignant as he stared back at Lyle.

'Irene, could you please look closely at Bosworth and tell me if he is really Albert Pym?'

Irene Lowestoft gazed helplessly at Bosworth. 'I couldn't say. You see I never met him. Pym told me about him after the war when she resumed her position as my lady's maid.'

'That's what I thought you would say,' confided Lyle. 'Since you are unable to confirm Bosworth is Albert Pym, I will resort to another method of proving his true identity to everyone.' He reached into his pocket. 'Yesterday I went up to London to the record office and obtained a copy of Albert Pym's marriage certificate from 1943. His signature on it matches the one on the Christmas card he gave to Hermione and me last year which is signed with the words *"from one musketeer to another with much love and gratitude, Oliver..."*'

31

Oliver Seymour was sitting on the sofa in the pool of light cast by the lamp. He stared at the marriage certificate and Christmas card Lyle held out to him, then slowly looked up into his friend's face.

Smiling charmingly, Oliver said, 'You're surely not suggesting I'm Albert Pym, are you, Lyle?'

'Your real name is Albert Pym and your handwriting condemns you,' said Lyle. 'After the war was over you reinvented yourself as Oliver Seymour and eventually formed your own television production company. You've dreamed of being wealthy all your life. When you met Diana, you saw your chance to seduce a rich woman who was unhappy in her marriage. Your plan was to convince Diana to divorce Gervase and marry you. A problem arose while you were having afternoon tea with George and Irene Lowestoft at their home in Market Chadwell. You were shocked to learn that your real wife Marjorie Pym – whom you hadn't seen in decades – was still alive. Irene talked to you enough about her servant shortage for you to know that she and George, along with Pym, always went to church on Sunday mornings, *thus leaving the house unattended.*

'By a curious coincidence that same afternoon, you saw Pym leaving the chemist in Market Chadwell. After this there was no doubt in your mind that your wife was very much alive and needed to be removed to pave the way for your marriage to Diana. Pym was a strict Roman Catholic and there was no way she would have agreed to divorce you.

'Two days later, while everyone was at church, you added arsenic to the horde of sherry bottles Pym kept in her nightstand. The following day, you rang Diana at Arlington and told her in the grand romantic manner you were coming to Arlington to take her away from Gervase. Your plans went wrong when the Daimler crashed off the side of the road and you ended up in a coma fighting for your life.'

Claudia was staring bewilderedly at Lyle. 'The only medication Diana was taking at the time of her death was the Tagamet capsules Dr Sutherland prescribed *after the car crash. There's no way Oliver could have doctored them with arsenic.*'

'Diana died of gastroenteritis,' said Lyle.

Hermione stared at him in surprise. 'Are you saying she died of *natural causes*?'

Lyle saw the look of astonishment on everyone's faces and continued, 'Yes, that's exactly what I'm saying. Marjorie Pym, on the other hand, died of arsenic poisoning. On the day of the car accident, Irene Lowestoft gave her maid an innocent bottle of port. The bottle was half empty and Pym drank the port within a week. Pym then helped herself to the sherry laced with arsenic. She had no reason to suspect anything was wrong with her nightcap because the symptoms of arsenic poisoning are the same as gastroenteritis. A month after Diana's death, Oliver finally came out of his coma – having missed out on the opportunity to marry her and get his hands on her fortune.

Lyle turned to Oliver. 'Long after your recovery from the car crash, your missed opportunity gnawed away at you. Gervase had inherited Diana's fortune, but you still saw a chance of getting your hands on it. If Gervase was convicted of Diana's murder, then under English law he would not be permitted to keep Diana's money *which would be divided legally between her next of kin Sebastian and Claudia.* You were determined to frame Gervase for Diana's murder and marry Claudia for her inheritance. *You swapped Pym's body over with Diana's body, then wrote to the Home Secretary accusing Gervase of having poisoned his wife.*

'Arsenic accumulates in a victim's hair. When the toxicologist Dr Bond claimed there were *more than split ends in Diana's hair,* Hermione and I assumed he was being facetious. There was no reason why Dr Bond should have found split ends in Diana's hair *because Poppy's cousin Bridget always cut her hair at six-week intervals.* Dr Bond also insisted that Diana's hair had *not* been dyed which contradicted Irene's claim that Diana had highlights. Hermione spoke to Bridget this morning and she confirmed Diana regularly had highlights put in her hair. Given Diana's *thick,* lustrous hair was her crowning glory, why did the prosecuting counsel hold up a clump of *thin* hair with split ends in court? The only conclusion that could be drawn from these discrepancies is that *the body that was exhumed from the mausoleum was not Diana's.'*

Oliver gave a light-hearted laugh of disbelief. It was surprising how attractive and debonair he looked in the soft lamplight.

'It's an ingenious theory, old sport, but the dental evidence doesn't support it.'

'On the contrary,' said Lyle, smiling, 'Jean-Luc de Breteuil was your cohort in crime. The dental charts he gave the police before the exhumation were labelled as Diana's, but they were in reality your wife Marjorie Pym's. Jean-Luc obtained Pym's dental charts when Solomon Atkinson – his predecessor at 98 Harley Street – sold the surgery and his list of patients to him.

'In the past Pym had had a grey amalgam filling. Jean-Luc testified that when Diana visited his dental surgery the week before she died, *he worked quickly to replace her amalgam filling with another because the old one had dropped out.* But Diana was opposed to amalgam fillings. The reason everyone admired Diana's smile is because she favoured white porcelain fillings. Indeed, on the night of her wedding anniversary, she advised me to have a porcelain filling so as not to spoil the whiteness of my own smile.'

'Am I to believe Jean-Luc swapped over the dental charts purely out of friendship for me?' asked Oliver.

'No, you had a more powerful means of persuasion. You threatened to reveal Jean-Luc's criminal past if he didn't do exactly as you told him. On your instructions he also invented the story of a marital argument between Gervase and Diana in the sitting-room of his dental surgery. You first met Jean-Luc in prison many years ago while serving a two-month sentence for refusing to pay your car parking fines. There's no point denying it, Oliver. At my request, Sir Roland Anstruther has been checking up on you. Years later you ran across Jean-Luc at your club in London. He can't have been happy to meet up with someone from his past. Presumably he asked you to keep quiet about his time in prison and you promised him you would.'

Oliver smiled again. 'I don't see how I'm supposed to have performed this miraculous switching of the bodies.'

'Earlier this year, you laid your plans carefully during Royal Ascot week. While the family was away, you visited Claudia at Arlington and asked her to go away with you. This gave you the opportunity you needed to plant the incriminating evidence in Gervase's bedroom. You also substituted Diana's perfectly innocent bottle of Tagamet capsules with poisoned ones. It occurred to you that the police might analyse the hairs in Diana's brush before going to the trouble of exhuming her body. Since the toxicology test would show that the hairs did *not* contain arsenic, you removed the brush and the mirror from Diana's dressing-table and disposed of them.'

Oliver said in a bemused voice, 'I did all this while I spent the day making love to Claudia in her bedroom?'

Claudia was gazing at Oliver with an expression of growing horror. 'I left you alone – once to have a shower and twice when I went to the kitchen to prepare some food.'

'The date of your visit to Arlington was Tuesday 19 June,' said Lyle.

'How can you possibly know that?' asked Oliver.

'Because Claudia later joked that the reason you didn't succeed in taking her away from Arlington is because you were glued to the TV watching *Chief Singer* win the St. James's Palace Stakes,' replied Lyle. 'Later that week, on the morning of Friday 22 June, you visited Dr Cheadle and Dr Sutherland. They both confirmed, as you already knew, that there had been no autopsy carried out on Diana's body. You played to perfection the part of a man keeping his suspicions to himself.

'Later that afternoon, Claudia phoned Nettlebed on your behalf to say you had learned the whereabouts of the Mariettes' former valet. I wouldn't be surprised if you'd already known for some time. You were apparently unable to go to Canterbury and interview Marcel Depardieu yourself because you were on your way to Yorkshire to film a new series of *Faces and Places*. When Hermione and I agreed to go to Canterbury on your behalf, we had no idea we were being got out of the way. The Elliotts were away on holiday and you expected Milsham Castle would be deserted that night. What you didn't know is that Rupert and Poppy were staying up at the main house. You had already made copies of the keys to Lord Milsham's chapel and crypt by helping yourself to the bunch of keys hanging on the hook by Nettlebed's back door.

'From the first moment I met Pacek Kowalski and Lawrence Leightonstone the actor in me instinctively cast them in my mind's eye as the first and second murderers in *Macbeth*. The two men were used to the smell of death because they were former British medics who had served in the Falklands War. They had since become drug addicts. I wouldn't be surprised if you sweetened your financial bribe by offering them a fresh supply of cocaine in return for helping you to swap over the caskets.

'Later that night, accompanied by your two accomplices, you gained admittance to Lord Milsham's crypt. There you performed the gruesome task of opening Pym's casket and looking inside. As you had hoped, her body had decomposed sufficiently for the facial features not to be recognisable. The three of you transferred her casket to the back of Pacek Kowalski's station wagon, then drove to Arlington.

'Months earlier, on your first visit to Arlington, Claudia had told you that the keys to the mausoleum were kept in the south lodge. The widowed lodge keeper was away in Canada visiting his family just as he did every June. It must have been child's play for two experienced lock pickers like Pacek Kowalski and Lawrence Leightonstone to gain admittance to the south lodge and get the large cumbersome keys to the mausoleum. You then removed Diana's casket from the mausoleum and put Pym's casket in its place. All you had to do before you left is swap the nameplates over on the casket lids. Gervase had paid for both funerals. Both women had enjoyed the same decencies as each other – including being buried in matching caskets.

'After returning the keys of the mausoleum to the south lodge, the three of you drove back to Milsham Castle and put Diana's casket in the crypt. The sound of Lord Milsham's dodgy burglar alarm going off must have sent panic waves through you. Hermione and I had returned to Nettlebed sooner than expected. I went to silence the alarm and was knocked unconscious by you or one of your accomplices.

'You then drove with Pacek Kowalski and Lawrence Leightonstone to Glastonbury Cottage where you presumably congratulated them on a job well done. I shouldn't be at all surprised if you rewarded them with cash and cocaine around the kitchen table. At some point you pulled out a gun and shot them dead. After disposing of their bodies and possessions in the cellar, you got rid of Pacek Kowalski's station wagon by submerging it in the lake in Pelham Wood. Sometime later you dropped the keys to Glastonbury Cottage through Nettlebed's front door letter flap so Hermione and I would think the two men had left the neighbourhood for good.'

A hurt look had sprung up in Oliver's eyes. 'You seriously think I was involved in the attack on you?'

Lyle nodded. 'I only ever told you that I was standing outside Lord Milsham's library when I was hit over the head. Unless you were there that night you couldn't have known whether I was standing *in the hallway outside the library or whether I was outside in the grounds.* You gave yourself away last night by saying, *'You might easily have died of hypothermia if Hermione hadn't found you lying unconscious outside the library.'* It's impossible to die of hypothermia *inside a warm house* which just goes to show you were there in the grounds that night. I was equally convinced you had never been billeted in Cornwall during the Second World War.'

'How can you be so sure?' asked Oliver in a puzzled voice.

'*Rebecca* was one of Diana's favourite books. I was reminded that its author Daphne du Maurier lived in Cornwall as I was piecing together a jigsaw puzzle showing her rowing her boat from Fowey to Ferryside. The 'w' and 'e' in Fowey are silent. Fowey rhymes with joy – not Joey as Irene and you mistakenly thought. When Irene announced friends of hers from Fowey had invited her to stay with them, you immediately slipped up by saying that during the Second World War you were billeted at Fowey. The only conclusion that could be drawn from your mispronunciation of Fowey is that you had *never* resided there in your alleged role as wireless operator for the Royal Navy. People invariably invent falsehoods about themselves when they are trying to cover up their past. I was given to wonder about you a great deal after that.'

'You also mispronounced Fowey when you narrated Diana's documentary,' said Hermione suddenly.

Lyle smiled grimly and said, 'My suspicions were heightened further, Oliver, when you said the mural on Arlington's dome is every bit as splendid as the one on the ceiling of the ballroom at Thurlestone Hall. During the war Thurlestone Hall was bombed by the Germans and reduced to a shell.'

'On the night George died, he confided as much to my father while they were having a drink together before dinner,' said Rupert.

'Only the servants' cottages were left untouched,' said Irene quietly. 'Pym was lucky to survive.'

'Oliver, my inner voice told me you must have seen the mural at Thurlestone Hall *before* it was bombed. It was the custom of the gardeners to decorate the ballroom in swathes of flowers prior to a party. I suggest it was then as one of the under-gardeners that you saw the mural. Your continued interest in horticultural matters is evident all these years later in the beautiful rose and topiary garden you keep at your home in Richmond-upon-Thames. You were also able to tell Claudia that the scientific name of moth orchards is *Phalaenopsis amabilis.*

'Throughout this case your cunning has been extraordinary. Your plan to get Gervase convicted of Diana's murder floundered when Sir Roland Anstruther revealed in court that Jean-Luc de Breteuil was Raoul Garnier. With social ruin and professional disgrace staring him in the face, as well as the threat of a long prison sentence for perjury, Jean-Luc was determined to take you down with him. But before he could you killed him.'

'Confound it all, Lyle, the man was a convicted back

street abortionist,' said Oliver disgustedly.

'Your actions are no less reprehensible for exploiting the fact,' said Lyle. 'After you came out of your coma, you pretended not to remember how you had located Captain Dietrich. Am I right in thinking you removed the letter Frederick Steen wrote to you – declining to appear on *Faces and Places* – from the files at Valiant Productions before we searched for it?'

'You seem to think you're right about everything else,' murmured Oliver.

'I've no doubt you used the letter to blackmail Frederick Steen into testifying against Gervase. Diana's letter to Frederick Steen was a brilliant forgery. You removed the flyleaf bearing Diana's signature from a recent edition of *The Illustrated Language of Flowers* and typed the incriminating letter above it.'

'Have you forgotten the envelope bore the postal date of Wednesday 28 September?' asked Oliver.

'Diana wrote to Frederick Steen several times in connection with the wedding,' said Lyle. 'He lied on your instructions when he said the letter came in that particular envelope. I knew you had forged Diana's letter to Frederick Steen because the same two spelling mistakes also appeared in the list of questions you wrote for me at Nettlebed. You misspelt the word siphoned with a 'y' instead of an 'i'. The word desperate was spelt incorrectly with two 'a's when it only has one.'

'You'll never prove I'm the murderer,' said Oliver defiantly. 'Or that I had any dealings with Pacek Kowalski and Lawrence Leightonstone.'

'Last night while Hermione and I were watching *Rebecca* on television I was reminded that the film's director Alfred Hitchcock was born in Leytonstone. The spelling of the London suburb is altogether different from the way Lawrence Leightonstone spelt his surname. His Christian name was spelt with the letter 'w' – unlike the film's star Laurence Olivier who spells his Christian name with the letter 'u'. After the bodies of Pacek Kowalski and Lawrence Leightonstone were discovered in the cellar, you denied having ever heard of them. But you were able to spell both their names correctly in your list of questions. It was only the following day *that their names were published for the first time in the newspapers.*'

'A lucky fluke?' suggested Oliver.

Lyle shook his head. 'Pacek Kowalski is a Polish name that translates into English as *Paul Smith.* As the credits rolled on Diana's television documentary, *his name was listed as the camera man.*'

Oliver shrugged. 'Life is full of the most extraordinary coincidences.'

'Prior to the break-in at Milsham Castle, Pacek Kowalski bought a container of Vaseline for a friend from the Brimhurst Pharmacy. It was assumed the friend was Lawrence Leightonstone. But the friend was, in fact, *you.* When I was knocked unconscious, the container of Vaseline must have fallen out of my assailant's pocket. The police found a clear set of Pacek Kowalski's fingerprints on the container *along with yours...*'

Oliver smiled wistfully and said, 'You really have dropped me in it, haven't you, Lyle? Next you'll be suggesting the name of Valiant Productions was inspired by the HMS Valiant which rescued me at sea after my plane was shot down.' There was something incredibly disarming about Oliver's boyish smile.

'There's really no need,' said Lyle smoothly, 'since you've been kind enough to tell me.'

In response to a nod from the Chief Constable of Gosfordshire, Detective Inspector McGowan stepped forward and said, 'Mr Seymour and Mr Steen, would you come with me? You're both under arrest for murder.'

'Claudia, I'm truly sorry,' said Oliver ruefully. 'I did all the things Lyle says because I wanted Gervase to be convicted of Diana's murder. I would have married you whatever happened. But I knew it would be so much nicer if we were stinking rich.'

'Do the words love and decency mean *nothing* to you?' demanded Claudia, her eyes burning with unshed tears. 'My grandmother died of natural causes. *How could you frame an innocent man for her murder and put the rest of us through hell?*'

'I'm truly sorry, Claudia.' Oliver's quiet utterance sounded surprisingly sincere. 'I really am.'

Claudia struggled to keep a grip on her emotions. 'I'll never understand how I fell in love with you.'

Oliver turned to his friend. 'Lyle, I want you to know I was really angry with Pacek Kowalski for knocking you unconscious. The Vaseline must have fallen out of my pocket when I knelt down by your body to see if you were still alive. I pretended you were dead to prevent Pacek Kowalski from eliminating you altogether. I deliberately shot Lawrence Leightonstone first over the kitchen table because I wanted to savour the look of fear in Pacek Kowalski's eyes before I killed him...'

Two uniformed police officers opened the double doors of the High Saloon. Frederick Steen and Oliver were read their rights, and then they walked out onto the landing overlooking the Great Hall.

Suddenly Oliver whipped a Beretta out of his jacket pocket. It was the same pistol with which he had shot Jean-Luc de Breteuil, Pacek Kowalski and Lawrence Leightonstone. He grabbed Frederick Steen and pointed the muzzle against his head.

'Keep back – all of you,' ordered Oliver, 'or I'll use this thing.'

Everyone froze. They were too frightened to say or do anything.

'What are you playing at?' demanded Frederick.

'You're my ticket out of here,' said Oliver. 'The authorities want the kudos of trying and convicting you in a court of law for your war crimes. If anyone tries to stop me from leaving, I'll make sure you get a bullet in the head.'

Frederick's breath came in panicky gasps. 'My God, I'm an old man with a weak heart. What happens if I do as you say?'

'I'll let you go as soon as we're safely away from here,' replied Oliver.

Sebastian addressed the police officers. 'Don't try and stop them. We can't risk anyone getting hurt.'

Oliver instructed Frederick, 'Keep two paces ahead of me or I'll shoot.'

The Beretta in his hand was pressed against the small of Frederick Steen's back. The two men hurried off down the east corridor. Oliver glanced over his shoulder to make sure they weren't being followed.

'Where are you taking me?' snapped Frederick.

'The grounds of Arlington are swarming with police,' replied Oliver. 'I've got a helicopter waiting on standby. We need to get onto the roof where I can signal to my pilot to come and pick us up.'

The two men turned a bend in the corridor and began climbing a flight of stairs.

'I've got a private plane at an aerodrome five miles from here,' said Frederick urgently. 'If you help me to escape, I'll pay you a million pounds. We can be out of the country in an hour and a half.'

A few minutes later, the two men emerged upon the circular balcony overlooking the Great Hall. A fierce storm howled against the eight large windows of the gallery. Above them, on the ceiling of the dome, Pellegrini's masterpiece *The Siege of Troy* had never looked more ravishingly beautiful.

'Help me open one of the windows,' ordered Frederick.

'I don't think so.'

The terseness in Oliver's voice was not lost on the older man who turned around and looked at the Beretta pointed at him.

Frederick's body was shaken by a tremor. 'What do you think you're doing?' he asked, glancing around him and sensing escape was futile.

'There is no helicopter,' said Oliver. 'That was a ruse on my part to get you up here.'

Below in the Great Hall, Sebastian saw them and cried out to a police officer, 'They haven't escaped – they're on the circular balcony above us.'

Frederick was breathing hard. His face was beaded with sweat and he looked a dreadful colour. He clutched his chest and staggered towards Oliver.

'Oliver, I asked you a question. What the hell is going

on?'

'For once in my shallow, despicable life I've decided to do something honourable,' said Oliver, his hand tightening around the Beretta. 'This may surprise you, but I was fond of Diana. She meant something to me.'

Oliver's head jerked slightly as the blackness of the night was seared by lightning. There were several loud rolls of thunder. It seemed as if the Heavens were trying to bring the impregnable dome crashing down around them. He relaxed and smiled at the absurdity of the idea.

Frederick Steen clutched his heart and swayed like a drunken man. 'What are you talking about?'

'Diana told me about that morning by the side of the quarry,' said Oliver coldly. 'You gave her and the Mariettes' servants a choice of being shot by your men or lining up at the edge of the quarry and pushing one another to their deaths at two-minute intervals. I'm now giving you a similar choice.'

'We didn't have enough ammunition to execute them all by firing squad,' snarled Frederick. 'Stop play-acting. Five million pounds – I'll give you five million pounds if you help me to escape.'

'Either jump to your death or I'll shoot you,' said Oliver resolutely. 'We don't have a snowball's chance in hell of getting away from here. The police have the house surrounded.'

'Don't fool around with me,' spluttered Frederick, almost doubling up in pain. 'My heart pills – I left them...'

Suddenly he abandoned all pretence of illness and lunged at Oliver with a swiftness that startled everyone watching below in the Great Hall. The two men staggered back against the balcony rail as Frederick tried to claw the

Beretta off Oliver. In the fierce struggle that ensued the pistol slipped from Oliver's hand and plummeted over the edge of the balcony.

The Beretta landed far below with a sharp clatter on the marble floor near Gabriella's feet, then skittled out of sight. The news of her father's past had come as a terrible shock to her. But loving him as much as she did, she had been unable to leave Arlington without him.

There was a look of fury on Frederick's face that turned to outrage as his toupee slid off his head and fluttered over the edge of the balcony. His hands fastened around Oliver's throat and began squeezing the life out of him.

Gabriella cried out frantically, *'Daddy...'*

As everyone below in the Great Hall watched in horror, Frederick and Oliver lost their balance and pitched over the balcony rail. The pair seemed to take forever to plunge to their deaths. Then, as their bodies hit the marble floor, Gabriella screamed as the storm played a violent encore into the night.

32

'I doubt I'll ever forget seeing Frederick and Oliver fall to their deaths.' Hermione's eyes were bright and she spoke with a tremor in her voice. 'It makes me so angry knowing they both eluded justice.'

Lyle said in a subdued voice, 'I blame myself for what happened.'

'The tragedy could have been avoided if the police had handcuffed them before they left the High Saloon,' added Hermione.

Lyle was silent for several moments. 'Gabriella is inconsolable at her father's death.'

'I was wrong about Sebastian,' said Hermione gently. 'He really loves her. That ought to count for something. Claudia has had such a bad run of luck when it comes to men. Oliver met his match in you.'

Lyle shared her sadness. 'The notice Mrs Elliott typed for Pym's funeral resulted in Oliver giving himself away when he drew up his list of questions. For someone who claimed never to have known the dead maid *he spelt*

Marjorie Pym's name correctly. The irony is that *both her Christian and surname were misspelt* on the funeral notice he admitted to having seen outside the chapel at Milsham Castle.'

'You've done a brilliant job ferreting out the truth,' said Hermione. 'Thanks to you the case against Gervase was dismissed and he walked away from the Old Bailey a free man. Everyone is extremely grateful to you.'

'Unlike Diana, Pym exhibited all the classic symptoms of arsenic poisoning prior to her death,' said Lyle. 'Her eyes were red and watery, there was a white coating on her tongue, her complexion was dark and blotched. She also suffered from an unsteady gait. The same couldn't be said of Diana who had an enviable rose-leaf complexion and clear green eyes. No one was more capable than her of making an elegant entrance into a room. Diana had her dress let out an inch a week before the wedding *because she had put on weight.*'

'During the trial it was revealed Diana's body wasn't embalmed,' said Hermione. 'But how did you know Pym's body also hadn't been embalmed?'

'A lot of people object to being embalmed for personal reasons or on religious grounds,' said Lyle. 'Before Pym died, she insisted on no formaldehyde which is one of the active ingredients of the embalming process. Irene told us she saw to it that her wishes were respected. It's a sobering thought, but if Oliver hadn't swapped the bodies over in order to incriminate Gervase, then no one would ever have found out that Pym was poisoned.'

'You mustn't blame yourself for Oliver's death,' said Hermione. 'I know it's not easy for you since he was our friend.'

Lyle released a sigh. 'Armand Mariette and Marcel Depardieu were hoping Frederick Steen would be convicted of his war crimes.'

'At least you prevented Claudia from marrying a murderer,' said Hermione with a shudder. 'Sometimes a small measure of justice is better than none at all.'

Letter from Claudia Rylander to her friends at Nettlebed:

Dear Hermione and Lyle,

The nightmarish events of the past now seem like a distant memory. I can't tell you what a relief it is to write these words and mean them.

I still to this day can't get over how Lyle was right about everything. The body exhumed from Lord Milsham's crypt had porcelain fillings which meant it was Diana's. Solomon Atkinson's evidence clinched the matter just as Lyle said it would. As Pym's dentist, Solomon Atkinson only ever gave her amalgam fillings.

It's comforting to know that Diana died of natural causes. Her body is now back in the mausoleum at Arlington where she belongs. For me she was the most wonderful grandmother. I'm glad for Pym's sake, poor woman, that she's been returned to her resting place in Lord Milsham's crypt.

I haven't told anyone before now, but after Gervase was cleared of poisoning Diana he offered to settle a sum of money on Sebastian and me. I refused because I'd rather any man I met and fell in love with loves me for myself rather than my money.

The horse riding school I've opened at Arlington has been a great success. I'm engaged to the head groom and I've never been happier. Lysander is very much his own man and doesn't let me get away with any airs or graces. After everything I've been through, I don't take our happiness for granted. The past has lost its hold on me. I'm living very much in the present and enjoying life again. I seldom think about Oliver. When I do it's not with tears, but with anger at the hell he put everyone through.

Married life suits Rupert and Poppy. They're both incredibly happy especially now that they've produced an heir and a spare. It's too bad you were unable to attend the wedding of Poppy's bulldogs, Daisy and Cornelius, which took place in the Temple of Four Seasons in the grounds of Arlington. It was awfully sweet and lots of fun.

Sebastian's and Gabriella's love for each other has kept them both strong. I was wrong to imagine it would burn itself out. Sebastian has given his share of Diana's money from Gervase to Irene who continues to live at Arlington. Her greatest dread has always been to live alone and I'm pleased for her sake that Gervase has spared her that fate. Gervase says his relationship with Angelique has kept him sane.

When I think of Diana, I know I can cry because she died, but I choose to smile because she lived. The greatest legacy Diana left us all is her love. After her body was returned to the mausoleum, I was reminded of this one night when everyone toasted her memory with champagne beneath her portrait in the High Saloon.

Thank you both for everything you've done to help my family. I wish you all the happiness in the world.

Lots of love,

Claudia xx

P.S. I hope you like your gift.

Lyle finished reading Claudia's letter as the summer sun filtered through Nettlebed's living-room window and warmed his back, then he asked, 'What gift is Claudia referring to?'

'She sent us a floral tribute,' said Hermione.

'What sort of floral tribute?' asked Lyle suspiciously.

'Marigolds, woodbine and blackthorn.'

'And what's the meaning of that, I wonder?'

Hermione smiled and replied, 'According to *The Illustrated Language of Flowers* the bouquet is her premature way of saying *I prophesize you will marry soon.'*

'Marriage is for having babies,' murmured Lyle with a twinkle in his eyes.

'I couldn't agree with you more,' said Hermione. 'I've got my career as a cellist and you've got your acting career. I'm not sure either of us is ready yet to see crime-solving carbon copies of ourselves running around in nappies.'

Epilogue

Gervase and Rupert were out riding.

The pair's thoughts were on the present rather than the tragic events of years ago. Rupert's and Poppy's sons were now at school and the line of succession was assured.

The winter air was cold and damp. Beneath the horses' hooves the emerald green grass was covered with hoar frost. The two men cantered their horses for a while then came to the crest of a hill. A cooked breakfast and a warm fire awaited them, but they were content for several minutes to gaze in the distance at Arlington. Despite being obscured by mist it was still beautiful.

There was no need for Rupert to ask his father what he was thinking. The understanding between them both was almost telepathic.

"'What you leave behind is not what is engraved in stone monuments,'" quoted Gervase softly, "'but what is woven into the lives of others...'"

THE END

Jared Cade's VIP Readers Club Newsletter

If you have enjoyed this book, sign up for free to receive Jared Cade's newsletter and an exclusive copy of the short story 'The Lonsdale Inheritance' featuring the dynamic sleuthing team of Lyle Revel and Hermione Bradbury. In addition to shining a spotlight on their exciting world and the crimes they investigate, each newsletter will share details of new books, promotional offers and events, as well as insights on Jared Cade's non-fiction writings on Agatha Christie. The link below will take you to substack.com where you can sign up for his newsletter. Your details will not be shared with any third parties and you can unsubscribe any time.

https:/jaredcade.substack.com

Also by Jared Cade

Murder on London Underground

A Lyle Revel and Hermione Bradbury mystery - # 2

Peter Hamilton, London Underground's managing director, is horrified when his ex-wife is pushed under a train.

Following the murder of a second commuter, he receives a phone call from an organisation calling itself Vortex that is dedicated to preventing the privatization of the network. 'You were the intended victim at Baker Street... Next time you won't be so lucky...'

In desperation, Hamilton turns for help to Lyle Revel and Hermione Bradbury, a glamorous couple with a talent for solving murders.

But as the death toll rises, the terrorists release a runaway train on the network...

'A chilling thriller and a great read' - Louise Burfitt-Dons, author of the PI Karen Andersen series

Printed in Dunstable, United Kingdom

63570761R00178